Mike Uden

About the Author

Mike Uden was fortunate enough to leave school in an era when a university education wasn't obligatory. Fortunate, that is, because he didn't have one. He was also lucky in both his choice of job – runner in a film production company – and its location, in London's Soho Square. *'What I didn't learn in the studio, I learnt in the street,'* he says. *'And the streets of Soho were very different back then.'* He soon became a rostrum cameraman and filmed many of the sequences in The Beatle's seminal animated feature *Yellow Submarine.'*

By the time he was he was in his early thirties he was running his own company, doing film special effects, and it was only when the world went digital that he reluctantly left his business behind and joined one of London's top post production houses: Rushes. He soon carved out a bit of a reputation as the 'go to' man if you wanted to create the impossible. *'Making babies talk, putting famous people in places they weren't. If it couldn't be done,'* he jokes, *'I was probably the man who couldn't do it!'*

'But by the time I hit my mid-fifties, my post production future was very much behind me,' he adds, *killed by the long hours, it was simply time to move on.'*

Mike always had a passion for English – both reading it and writing it – so he retrained as a TEFL teacher. *'One of the best decisions of my life,'* he says.

Dead Man Talking is his third book, following *The Sacrifice* (featuring the same mother daughter detective team as this book) and the romantic comedy, *Chemical Attraction.*

Dedication

This book is dedicated to all the crazy characters I worked with in Soho over all those years. Especially those in the production and postproduction industries, and *extra* especially those who worked at Rushes Post Productions. How can you not like working in a business that is located in Soho and has annual dos in Cannes, Las Vegas and Amsterdam!

Mike Uden

DEAD MAN TALKING

AUSTIN MACAULEY
PUBLISHERS LTD.

A CIP catalogue record for this title is available from the British Library.

ISBN 9781785543609 (Paperback)
ISBN 9781785543616 (Hardback)
ISBN 9781785543623 (E-Book)

www.austinmacauley.com

First Published (2016)
Austin Macauley Publishers Ltd.
25 Canada Square
Canary Wharf
London
E14 5LQ

Acknowledgments

This book, together with most of what I write, say or do, would not have been possible without the input, help and general 'being there' from Jan, the kids and the grandchildren.

CHAPTER ONE

We still suffered. Claustrophobia for me and taphephobia for Anna. That's the fear of being buried alive. Just the smell of earth is enough. Or darkness. Or silence, or anything. And all because of a missing persons case. In the end, the only thing missing was our sanity.

So why take another one? Why not stick to nice, safe adultery and divorce? After all, it's what I do: The Andrews Detection Agency. Leafy, suburban London: out of town, infidelity.

It all started with a phone call.

'Hello, is that Pamela Andrews?'

'Yes, speaking.'

'My name's Stephanie Hutchinson and … and, I was wondering if you could help me? You see, my husband. He's gone missing, and …'

Then she started to break up. And I don't mean the line.

It was a Friday night around 7-ish. I'd just locked up my little office-above-the-shops, descended the stairs and was on my way home. I said I'd call her back, and I probably would. So I didn't actually say yes, and I didn't actually say no. The point is, problems-wise, I'd had enough for one week; for one life. Anyway, yes is a very dangerous word. But walking home, I started to think. Why not? Why not hunt the missing rather than stalk the cheating? After all, I needed a challenge, a change. I needed a 'yes' in my life. I'd give it some thought and ring her back.

Monday morning, something to get up for. A yes, not a no. The road to Brighton, not Bromley. I showered, dressed, did something with my hair, applied some lippo, gave a final check in the hall mirror, and left. But Kentish Way was clogged, the A20 solid and the M25, when I finally got there, motionless. My initial enthusiasm was waning.

In front of me was a nodding dog. He lolled his plastic tongue, posing the obvious question. Did I really need all this? Not just the jams, the Missing Persons. A lot had changed since that last one. A lot had needed to. Anna no longer worked with me. She'd gone back into TV researching. As for me, I'd said I'd never touch one again. And here I was, touching one.

So back to that nodding dog question. Did I need it? Well, it had got me out of bed that morning. And the alternative was what? The Andrews *Decep*tion Agency. So yes, I needed it. Anyway, this one didn't sound so bad. At least I wouldn't be treading the footsteps of some molesting, low life scum. Mind you, that's not quite how that last one turned out. He was the one treading footsteps. *My* footsteps. Either way, that was then and this was now. Something to get up for.

The traffic did clear a little. I glided past Gatwick, sailed into Sussex and, by the time I'd made Brighton, felt I'd definitely made the right decision.

It's a different kind of place, Brighton. Somehow, driving along the sea front, on a changeable day, I always get the impression the sea needs Brighton more than Brighton needs the sea. Dandified Regency confidence facing off dark, uncertain seas.

Turning right, away from the front, I found a street of stark whites and pastel pinks. Wonderful, in a stately, organised way. Even more wonderful, a parking meter.

I parked up, got out and checked the meter. Jesus, no wonder there were spaces! Mayfair-on-Sea. I plugged in a card and emptied my account. After a short walk, past glossed railings and polished porticos, I found her address. Regency elegance, oozing wealth.

Up the steps, I rang the bell and waited. A second ring. I stood back and looked around. Should I phone her? Further down the street, a woman was parking a convertible BMW in a resident's bay. She zapped it, picked up two bags and walked in my direction.

Being on steps, above the railings, I was only able see the top half of her body. Dark hair, classy looks. She was wearing a sensible mac, under which, possibly, was office attire. At a guess, a sitting down rather than standing up job.

Getting closer, her bags were heavy. Closer still. Through a strobe of railings, I could see they were Waitrose. Keys in mouth, she saw me and, unable to speak, raised her eyebrows and gave me a ventriloquist's 'Shorry.' I walked down the steps and took one of the bags. She took the keys from her mouth.

'Stupid, of me, trying to fit too much in,' she said, extending her arm. 'Hi, I'm Stephanie, by the way.'

'Pamela,' I said. She had a solid hand shake.

I offered to take one of the bags, she said thanks, and we went back up the steps. She put the key in the latch, turned and pushed. As it opened, it gave a very slight, newly painted, crack. Dulux, I'd say. We bundled into a hushed hallway of high-ceilings, tiled floors, beeswax – and money. We stopped at the first door. Keys again.

She opened up, we pushed through into a modern interior. We put down our bags and took off our coats. She apologised for the mess. There was no mess. She hung up my coat. I followed her to the kitchen and she unloaded her shopping, or the perishable stuff, at least: asparagus, pre-washed salads, kiwis. Decent wine too, but no spirits. Good sign.

New kitchens tend to look similar, but cheap ones clunk and dear ones glide. This one positively sashayed. I almost wanted to open and close drawers for the sheer lust of it.

'Coffee?' she asked.

'Thank you,' I said. 'That would be great.'

She set about scooping, plunging and pouring, during which time I noted many a gadget, though all discreetly hidden. We also start the semblance of a conversation. She was the manager at a local employment agency. Paul, her missing partner, works, or perhaps worked, for a bank.

Walking to the lounge, we shared pleasantries. I was offered a mid-grey sofa; Stephanie took a large, floral armchair. A pretty Chagall hung on one wall, a gilt mirror on another, and a vase of lilies sat on the sideboard. First impressions: the décor definitely wasn't male. Looking more closely, surfaces were dust-free, and the carpet still bore the imprint of a vacuum. Somehow, I couldn't imagine her with a duster and a Hoover so at a guess, the work of a woman-that-does.

Nursing our coffees, I conveyed my sympathies. I'd never had to deal with the consequences of a missing adult before. Being brutally objective about it, I'd say losing a partner isn't quite like losing a child. With a partner you partly, or wholly, blame them: *If only he'd ...* With a child you blame yourself: *If only I'd ...* I know this, I'd been there. So yes, it would be painful, but not quite *as* painful. Men can be replaced. Children can't.

Talking of which, there were two wedding photos on the mantelpiece, but no apparent offspring. So, yes, there'd still be that emptiness – that chasm – but not insurmountable.

She painted a picture of their life together, which seemed fairly normal. They'd met at a friend's party, dated, formed a relationship, moved in together and, after about a year, married and bought a place of their own. At the time of his disappearance, they'd known each other for two-and-half years.

'So presumably you'd only just moved in?' I asked.

'Yes, we were hardly out of packing cases.'

'Do you think it could've had anything to do with it?'

'Stress, you mean?'

'Yes, solicitors, estate agents, commuting.'

'I don't think so. At least, if it was, he never showed it.'

'So there's nothing that comes to mind?'

'That could've …?' She looked away, shook her head, 'No, nothing at all.'

I still hadn't broached the obvious, but I was getting closer. You see, there was one aspect of this case, known to all, of which we still hadn't spoken. A large very elephant in a posh little room. The elephant's name? Pakistan. That's where it had happened – whatever *'it'* was.

Disappearing in Pakistan, to us Westerners, isn't a whole load different to disappearing in Afghanistan – which isn't a whole load different to disappearing in Somalia or Syria. Like I said, the big, ugly elephant, not yet introduced. But I would get there, it would simply take time.

'And how long had he worked there?'

'The bank, you mean? About a year. Headhunted. He's not a banker in the money sense – he's a marketing man, but in banking.'

She put down her coffee and sat back.

'He wasn't head honcho in his old job, and he's ambitious. They wanted someone from the London Market, based over here.'

She then sighed and said: 'They do have a bit of a problem, image-wise … in terms of banking, at least. They're expanding into Europe. Well, why shouldn't they? Barclays are over there, so why shouldn't they be over here? And Paul knows banking. Marketing-wise, I mean.'

I was getting the picture. Young man, but not top dog. Along comes an overseas brand that needs work. If you can push *them* into a bigger league, they can push *you* into a bigger league. And in the meantime, pay big bucks of course.

'And you're going over there to meet them?

'Yes.'

'And you want me to come too.'

'If you could, it would be, well …'

She looked down, didn't finish the sentence. She was possibly going to use the word 'wonderful.' But that wasn't in her vocabulary at the moment. She clearly did need my help.

I could see her logic. I'm an ex-cop with a track record on finding missing people. Actually, that's not entirely true. I wouldn't call it a record. But I did work on one very high profile case. And I was successful. Finding a girl that the police simply couldn't.

And from Stephanie's perspective, if you've given up on the police, mainly because the police have given up on you, who better to accompany you?

But we still hadn't really broached the subject. You see, the Pakistan International Bank had a bit of form when it came to hostages. In 2008, a senior bank official had been kidnapped, a ransom demanded and a ransom duly paid. But there were differences. That was in Islamabad and this

6

was Karachi. And Karachi isn't quite Islamabad. Karachi is an international seaport, a financial centre. Islamabad, by contrast, sits right between disputed Indian Kashmir and tribal Afghanistan. But for all that, it was still in Pakistan.

The British police had shown interest, obviously. As had the Embassy. It had briefly made the TV news. But these things never stay top of the news for long. Missing children do, but not missing men.

Which brings us to one other aspect of this case that clearly separated it from the earlier PIB incident. Back then, two days after going missing, the hostage, a Pakistani national, appeared on video, with his masked captors. Paul, by comparison, had been missing for three months, yet nothing.

But missing persons-wise, it's worth considering a few facts. Over 100,000 adults disappear in or from the UK every year. The vast majority are male and the reasons why are many: family problems, work problems, drink and drugs problems. The common word is problems. Terrorism and kidnapping don't even figure in those statistics.

So had this disappearance not been in Pakistan, it wouldn't have even made the news. Which was why, reasonably, the British police were losing interest. And why, just as reasonably, Stephanie had called me in. All other avenues had failed.

'I'm afraid,' I said, 'If I do come with you, I'm going to be of limited help. All I can do is ask a few questions, check a few places, assuming I'm allowed to, and come home.'

'I realise that,' she said, looking at her fingers. 'But I haven't got anyone else, have I.'

She dropped her head further and put her hand to her face. She was close to tears.

I got up, moved over to her chair and sat on its arm. I touched her shoulder.

After a few silent seconds, she composed herself a little, took her hand from her face and looked up, though not directly at me: 'The police won't make anyone available.'

'Have you spoken to anyone,' I asked. 'Over there, I mean?'

'Yes', she said. 'I've had a video conference with Mr Farooki. He's Paul's boss. But he couldn't really help.'

She sniffed back a tear. 'It's not as if Paul had even made contact with him – when he arrived, I mean.'

'He was last seen at the airport, wasn't he?'

'Yes, CCTV.'

I paused for a bit and thought.

'Have you spoken to our Embassy – over there, I mean?'

'Yes … I Skyped them, but somehow it's not the same, is it? Talking to a screen, I mean. I need to …'

She sighed deeply and looked at nothing. I knew exactly what she meant. That limbo feeling. That need to *do* something, *anything* – go there, see for herself.

Losing someone close, with no proof and nothing tangible, is a terrible, terrible thing.

'Don't worry, Stephanie,' I said, squeezing her arm. 'We'll go, we'll go.'

You know, I hadn't yet signed anything, but I was already fulfilling the first half of my brief. Pamela Andrews. Not just a detective, a *woman* detective.

CHAPTER TWO

I thought long and hard about how to approach this trip. There was a balance to be struck. Would it be me finding out, or Stephanie moving on? Neither could really be achieved. But whatever it was Stephanie needed it, maybe even I needed it.

I suppose I could have done the whole private eye thing: follow the CCTV cameras from Oxford Circus, where Paul was filmed bumping his overnight hand luggage down the escalator. Then I could take the Heathrow Express, from Paddington to Terminal 3, where the images had picked up again, from check-in to departure. And if I'd suggested it, she'd probably have gone along with it. But I didn't. In my mind, I felt simply befriending and talking would be more useful.

But if I'm being completely truthful, there was another reason I wouldn't be taking that route to Heathrow. Less worthy but just as real. The Underground. Since that terrible Su A case, I hadn't been near it. Therefore, I'd be cabbing it from Bromley whilst she'd be coming up from Brighton. So the only person I was really kidding was me. Oh well, we'd still be taking the same flight that Paul took, standing at the same spot at Karachi Airport where he'd stood, and staying in the same hotel he'd stayed in – albeit on previous visits.

We met at the PIA desk, half shook hands, half hugged, then busied ourselves with check-ins and passports and passes, chatting all the time.

At 35, Stephanie was nearer Anna's age than mine, but we still had loads in common. We came from similar parts of the world, me Bromley and she Sevenoaks. Her brother, Tom, worked in TV, like Anna – *and*, as it happened, even went to the same school as one of Anna's exes.

As we went from queue to queue, seat to seat, and finally gate to plane, we found we had tastes in common too – both liking pasta (though not the plane's macaroni!) and a spot of pinot. And when we settled down to books, she'd bought along a David Nichols that I'd read, and I'd bought along an Anne Tyler that she had.

Paul, too, was local, coming from a housing estate in St Mary Cray. But by the time they'd met he was already well out of it, living in a Hoxton loft apartment and working in the City. Small beginnings to big bucks in just five years. Money, clearly, had been his motivation for taking the job. Well, it wouldn't have been the Air Miles, would it?

Time passed, lights dimmed and we closed our eyes. I just couldn't sleep, though Stephanie, I think, did. At one stage, head snuggled onto mine, I could hear her breathing – even smell her shampoo.

You know, in a way, I needed her just as much as she needed me. Another step forward. My first flight since that terrible case. It might seem strange, that flying hundreds of miles above the Earth's surface could have echoes of being trapped hundreds of feet below it. But it's the being enclosed, I suppose – plus the lights out, of course. So in some ways she was going to be my shoulder to lean on too.

This was going to be more than just a trip. It was going to be a journey.

CHAPTER THREE

Crease-faced and bleary-eyed, we climbed from our seats, stretched for our baggage, stood in line and queued. And once we were out we queued again. And again. Each queue almost joining the next. Finally, with passports reluctantly stamped, we were through.

Bang! Senses assaulted! Dust, heat, light, people. Even though we had little luggage, we found ourselves tipping everyone and everything.

Finally, having bribed our way to a taxi, which was ancient, but at least had four wheels and a driver, we fell inside, exhaled, and were off. Very fast.

A world of bright whites, inky shadows and dirty beiges slid by. Painted buses, wobbly three-wheelers, rickety bikes. As for the populace, men were covered and women, by-and-large, were absent.

We reached the safety of The Luxi, a multinational that could, thankfully, have been pretty much anywhere. At this point, anywhere was good: mowed grass, marble reception, air conditioning, even women.

We booked in and were shown to adjacent rooms, corporate, clean and comfortable. I showered, rested for a bit – soft bed, cool sheets – and flicked through their bedside brochure. Image-wise, they were hedging their bets. On the one hand it said: look, we're international! Couples round pools, joggers in gyms and cocktails in cabinets. But on the other hand we have pictures of mosques and people in traditional clothing.

Having rested, though not nearly enough, I got up, showered and dressed. Standing in front of the mirror, adding earrings, I couldn't make up my mind. You see, like the hotel, I had to get it right. We had two definites lined up: the Deputy High Commissioner, where the police would also be present, and the bank.

As for me, hard and predatory was obviously out, but so was soft and mumsy. Suit, blouse and light make up, I suppose. Femininity, modesty, authority – in reverse order.

Passable, I left the room and knocked lightly on Stephanie's door.

She opened it immediately, we shared compliments, then we locked up and left.

A car was waiting outside, this time a Merc, and we got in, told him where we wanted, though he knew anyway, and made our way towards the Clifton district.

Either my eyes were adjusting or we were going through a nicer area. Probably both. It all became pleasanter and pleasanter, and by the time we'd glided through imposing gates, skirted manicured lawns and crunched our way up a long graceful drive it felt as if we were in a different country.

We came to a halt right outside the large front doors of an old colonial residence where we were immediately met by a young woman in a trouser suit and headscarf. Clearly she was of Pakistani origin, but her cut-glass greeting suggested her background probably wasn't. She led us to a hallway of heavy furniture, oak panelling and Victorian oil paintings. It could so easily have been Surrey.

'Good morning,' said a second woman, immediately joining us. 'I'm Veronica – Martin's wife.'

Mid-forties, tall, sensibly blonde and every bit a high commissioner's wife. I found myself wondering whether single ambassadors even exist. Other halves, in this game, must be a must.

We went into a room that continued the theme: mahogany furnishings, leather-bound books, even an unlit fireplace.

'My husband, Martin,' she said.

If I was expecting ambassadorial typecasting, I was disappointed. Rather portly: diplomatic lunches, I'd guess, and very balding. His only stereotyping came from his solid handshake and calm air.

Veronica stayed for the first few minutes and then, when he offered us seats, left us. Whether this wife-to-husband handover was normal, or whether it was because we were women, I couldn't say. But it did seem right.

Just as she left, and before we even had time to be seated, the final participant arrived. 'Ah, may I introduce Superintendent Sharma,' said Martin Hague.

Uniform perfect, moustache waxed, Bilal Sharma was exactly as you'd imagine. And with introductions done, we strolled across the room and took chairs around Martin Hague's very diplomatic desk.

Once seated, I found myself wondering exactly where the Superintendent would fit in Pakistani police hierarchy. I came to the conclusion that the titles weren't quite the same as in the UK, but near enough. Could we have expected someone more senior? Hard to say. There again, really big cheeses can be clueless when it comes to details, so it was fine for me.

Once we'd got over the pleasantries, I slowly eased Stephanie into the conversation.

There were a number of very good reasons for this. Firstly, she knew the story backwards, having lived it far longer than I. Then there was the therapy thing. She simply needed to talk. And finally, when it comes to questioning, two heads are better than one. Seeing answers is as important as hearing them and, generally, I'd be the watcher.

And what did I see? Martin Hague was sympathetic and open, Bilal Sharma less so. For instance, the superintendent's: 'Tell me, Mrs Hutchinson, how are things progressing with the British police?' may have sounded innocuous to Stephanie, but to me he was having a snipe at what was happening (or not happening) back home.

He did make some good points though, saying that absolutely nothing in the case pointed towards terrorism: 'It's not just the absence of a ransom,' he said 'it's the absence of force, of seizure. If Paul had been snatched anywhere near the airport someone would have seen it.'

Martin Hague, by comparison, merely filled in with the occasional doing-everything-we-can type reassurance, giving the superintendent opportunity to have further little digs, an example of which was: 'We've given this more attention than we would've done for a local man, Mrs Hutchinson.' I'd liked to have added: *Yes, Mr Sharma, but that's because local men disappear all the bloody time.* But I didn't, of course.

The Commissioner made the point that Pakistan wasn't even in the top ten when it came to hostage taking, a dubious honour falling exclusively to South American countries, yet kidnapping seemed to be everyone's immediate assumption. It was a fair point, but his later assertion that: 'Only one CCTV image of Paul Hutchinson was picked up at Karachi, against four at Heathrow, and five on the Underground,' was disingenuous in the extreme. *Yes, Mr Superintendent, but the* last *was in Karachi, wasn't it?*

Martin Hague then came up with: 'You know, Stephanie, many, many people go missing every year – and the vast majority turn up safely,' which was reassuring and, well, diplomatic, I suppose.

Sharma then said: 'Yes, I really do feel the problem could lie closer to home, Mrs Hutchinson,' which I felt was a tiny bit tactless. After all, that could refer to some kind of domestic issue.

Yet when he repeated this angle a minute or so later, I realised there was no ambiguity in it at all. It was indeed a reference to Paul and Stephanie's relationship. Now where would a policeman in Pakistan get information about someone's home life in Brighton? The British police? Maybe. But far more likely, the answer lay with his employers. Either way, it did beg another question.

Was Stephanie keeping something from me?

CHAPTER FOUR

Through the windows of our cab, driving back, the same dusty documentary, accompanied by the same noisy soundtrack of car horns and bike bells and hubbub, played out.

I found myself wondering. Now if I were a businessman, regularly staying in a place like this, what would I do? Stay holed up in a hotel room? Unlikely. Seek the company of others? More likely. But what if there weren't many others of his ilk? There didn't seem to be too many hip bars and eateries. And the locals didn't exactly exude cool.

Now it seems to me, and I do have knowledge of these things, that when men can't find friends, they find lovers. And with Paul coming here every other week, what of his marriage – *their* marriage? Should I begin to open up that subject? I could. It is, after all, what I *do*. With Stephanie sitting beside me, it would be easy.

I turned my head and checked, but her eyes were closed. It could wait.

When we pulled up at our hotel, I woke Stephanie as gently as I could, paid the driver and we both got out. Then we walked a few sweltering steps to the hotel lobby, where we were instantly freeze-dried by the air conditioning.

'I'll see you in an hour,' I said, as we walked towards reception to pick up our keys. 'I just need to check a couple of things.'

'Okay,' said Stephanie, looking at her watch. 'I think it'll only take about twenty minutes to the bank by cab.'

'Fine,' I said, 'see you later.'

Once I was sure she'd gone I turned back to the receptionist.'

'I wonder if I could possibly have a word with the manager.'

'Of course,' she said, picking up the phone.

A few minutes later a tall, impassive looking man appeared and introduced himself as Mr Ashkani. I asked him if we could talk somewhere a little more private and he lead me to one of those discreet little table and chair clusters that are always dotted around large international hotel lobbies.

'Do take a seat,' he said, 'How can I help you?'

'Well, firstly, it's not any kind of complaint,' I said, sitting down. 'Your hotel seems excellent.'

'Thank you,' he said, 'I'm glad you like it.'

I paused, then said: 'Mr Ashkani, I've come over here with a Mrs Hutchinson. She's just gone to her room for a rest.'

'Yes,' he said, 'I can imagine. You're both over from London, aren't you?'

'Yes,' I replied, immediately impressed that he knew where his customers came from. 'You see, I'm an enquiry agent and I'm helping her.'

'Enquiry agent?' he said, looking a little uneasy.

'Yes. You see, her husband, Paul, used this hotel a lot. On business, I mean. He's gone missing. You may even have heard of the case.'

Silent recognition. He had.

'And we're here to talk to the police, which we've done, and his employers – the Pakistani International Bank – which is our next meeting. But I was wondering if I could ask you a question or two as well.'

'Yes, go ahead.'

'Well, you may not have the immediate answer to this, you might have to email me, but what I'd like to know is whether his visits here were ... well, typical?'

'Typical?'

'Yes, for a businessman, I mean.'

'I don't follow. How would I ...?'

'No, I realise you wouldn't know everything about his visits. But did anything out of the ordinary ever happen?'

'No, not to my knowledge.'

'So he, well, occupied a room by himself?'

'By himself?'

'Yes, or did he sometimes have, you know ... guests?'

'Businessmen have guests all the time, Mrs Andrews ...'

'I'm talking about overnight guests. To his room, Mr Ashkani.' His face changed. You see, although we could have been anywhere in the world, we weren't. We were in Pakistan. And recently, hotels like his had suffered police raids, cracking down on call girl rackets. Generally, the hotels got away scot-free, but the girls didn't. Either way, it wouldn't do a manager's career prospects a whole load of good.

'Look,' he said, whitening a little, 'we, er ...'

'Mr Ashkani,' I said, holding my hand up, 'I obviously don't expect you to be able to tell me of every coming and going, but you could perhaps tell me if you have any records of guests he may have had.'

'Oh, er, I suppose we ...'

'And please remember I have his wife here with me. She's upstairs. It would be good if ...'

The inference was obvious. In this country, perhaps more than any, there were things a wife didn't need to know about.

After a couple more pleasantries, we swapped business cards, though I hardly needed his, and I made for my room.

With the next meeting now only an hour away, I should, perhaps, have woken myself up with a shower. But I didn't. With jetlag advancing, I kicked off my shoes, unzipped my dress, lay down on the bed and closed my eyes.

'Pamela,' said a distant voice, infiltrating a strange, dusty landscape. 'Pamela, are you in there?'

Stephanie!

Disorientated, I turned over and half opened my eyes. Glowing numbers, bedside clock. 16:34.

I almost fell off the bed, rushed to the door, grappled the lock, flung it open and apologised to Stephanie profusely. I then flew back in, suggesting she goes down to the reception and phones ahead. I then ran into the bathroom, splashed on some water, patted my face dry, pulled on my dress, slapped on some makeup and detangled my hair. Not really good enough but it'll just have to do.

Stepping into my shoes, I gave myself one last look, grabbed my bag, rushed out of my room, hit the lift, jumped in, gently descended, burst back out and found a seated Stephanie looking at her watch. We flew through reception, found a waiting taxi and fell into it.

Finally, we lurched through rush hour traffic getting to the financial district over an hour later than we should have. A brief dash across the blazing pavement and into the bank.

The Pakistan International Bank was much like any other corporate HQ, if a little tired around the edges. I'd also kind of wondered if it would double up as a clearing bank with roped off customers and glassed-in clerks, but it wasn't – simply a large expanse of marble, at the back of which was a semi-circular reception desk and a row of three female faces in corporate navy. Above them was a row of clocks telling us Tokyo time, New York time and London time. I could have done without the reminder!

We asked to see Mr Farooki, then signed in, and were told to take a seat at yet another little cluster of corporate tables and chairs.

Mr Asif Farooki, CEO, looked more Arabic, maybe Mediterranean, than Pakistani: silver hair and self-assured, the kind of man who demands respect and probably gets it.

'Good to meet you, Mrs Hutchinson,' he said, in an accent more English than mine. After a studied pause he cleared his throat and added: 'And I'm most dreadfully sorry about Paul, of course. It must be such a terrible worry to you.'

He then held, rather than shook her hand, and, turning to me, added: 'And it's so good of you to accompany Stephanie, Mrs Anderson, especially given your expertise in this area.'

Then he suggested we go to his office and, whilst we walked, he engaged us both in one of those softly spoken, knitted-browed conversations that politicians employ when they're after your vote.

I suppose I was a little surprised that Stephanie and Mr Farooki hadn't previously met. I thought company directors normally socialised, wives included. There again, there was the distance thing. Or maybe it was just cultural.

He took us past the reception and, via a code-entry door, into a corridor of white partitions and closed doors.

When we got to his office, he tapped in yet another code, pushed the door open, stood back and ushered us in.

For all the fact that the place was built of simple plasterboard and 70's studding, Farooki's office was as leather-bound and fusty as Martin Hague's had been. The only thing missing was a pair of antlers! Now apart from when I was in the Met, and they have to follow certain government guidelines, I'd never been in a really big cheese's office before. But I would imagine that in most places this stuffy old clutter would have been cleared out years ago.

He asked us what we'd like to drink and we both chose coffee. Yet again, he said how sorry he was, especially as Paul was, technically, on company business at the time. Yes, I thought, I suppose he was. An interesting point. This was neither the time nor the place for such things, but if compensation was ever an issue, those spoken words, with me as a witness, might be worth the journey alone.

I took the opportunity to make a few notes on this, asking him if he could tell me a little more about the precise nature of his business on that day.

Apparently, Paul's task was a tricky one. The bank's existing clients are mainly Islamic and PIB could never, in a thousand years, hope to penetrate the main European banking sector. But with Muslim populations growing, that still left a large, relatively untapped market to aim at – across Europe and beyond.

Marketing-wise, a compromise needed to be struck. Most Muslims, despite what some might think, have pretty Western aspirations. And Western aspirations require Western marketing.

The first ad Paul was working on, timed to fit in with the summer, was all about foreign exchange and travel insurance. He'd hired an agency that had pitched a campaign around a happy family beach scene, though slightly more modestly attired, which were targeted at radio, TV and websites with large Asian content.

'I do know he was struggling a bit,' said Mr Farooki. 'The research was pulling him two ways. Clash of cultures, I suppose.'

'But surely you're not suggesting ... You know, stress ...'

At that point, our coffees came in: china cups and saucers, silver tray, separate milk, sugar and tea – even some dinky little biscuity things. While we all took turns to pour and stir, Farooki said: 'I obviously hope not. I mean I'd like to think we weren't pushing him too hard.'

'He did sometimes get stressed,' added Stephanie. 'But I wouldn't say he was any worse than normal. Anyway, even if that's what caused it ... well, people don't just disappear, do they?'

'Quite so,' replied Farooki, 'Logically, I can't think of any reason why someone could leave no trace.'

'Kidnap?' suggested Stephanie.

This answer, blunter than even I would have expected, clearly surprised him.

'Well,' he said, turning more to me, 'I don't have as much experience of these things as you, Ms Anderson, but I would have thought you'd get more trace with a kidnap than some kind of mental breakdown. Otherwise, what would be the point of kidnapping?'

He had a point.

'But you don't think it's work-related either?' I said.

'I honestly couldn't say,' he said. 'But if it *was*, it wouldn't have been to do with this end. After all, initial ideas apart, we hadn't really seen anything. That's why he was coming over – to present the first version to us.'

'Well, no,' I conceded, 'but if things were going badly over there, he'd be feeling stressed about coming over here, wouldn't he?'

'Indeed,' he said. 'But that's exactly why I'd start by checking what was going on over there.'

'Maybe,' I said, appealing to Stephanie as much as Farooki, 'But again, *over there* isn't where he was last seen, is it?'

'I can't explain that,' he said, holding up his hands, 'But if you're looking for the *reason* rather than the *place*, which you do seem to be, I'm simply saying I'd be looking closer to home, that's all.'

Those words again. The High Commission, the police, the hotel manager, and now his boss. Closer to home.

'Mr Farooki?' I said.

'Yes.'

'You said he'd been on company business before he flew over. But he hadn't been at his office, had he?'

'No, I don't believe so.'

'Do you know exactly where he'd been? – in London, I mean.'

'Yes,' he replied. 'Somewhere in Soho.

CHAPTER FIVE

I'd come into this thinking it wasn't anything like as bad as the Su A affair, my previous missing persons case. A missing man cannot be compared to a missing girl, and I still stood by that. But on the flight home, sitting next to a silent Stephanie, it occurred to me that one aspect of it was possibly worse.

She'd been hoping, we'd all been hoping, that it wasn't a kidnap. And it was looking that way, which was good. But normally, when someone walks out of your life, they leave something: a note, a text, phone call, *something.*

Take my ex. I'd heard more after he'd left: custody threats, emotional blackmail etc., than when we'd been together. And there must be many a woman who'd give their right arm to be able to repeat Stephanie's first words to me: *'My husband's just disappeared.'*

Yet deep down, I don't really believe that. Silence isn't golden. It is grim – the very worst thing. Stephanie had absolutely nothing. Not even a cash withdrawal or a credit card bill to cling to.

I'd been thinking about what to do next on this case and, as we descended into the clouds above Heathrow, seat belts on, trays tucked away, now seemed as good a time as any.

'How about I do a bit more on this?' I said.

'More what?' replied Stephanie, putting down her magazine.

'I'm up in Town on Friday anyway, meeting Anna. I could call in at that place where Paul was working. You know, in Soho …'

The plane banked, levelled out and lifted again. As we re-emerged from the clouds, I added: 'She only works around the corner.'

'Oh, you really don't have to …'

'Well, by my reckoning I still owe you a day,' I said, putting my hand on hers, 'Anyway, I *want* to – if you don't mind.'

When we'd agreed on five day's wages, the assumption was that I'd accompany her during the four days of travelling and interviewing, and then spend a day recovering – job done. But the job wasn't done. Not in my book, anyway. I still wanted answers.

'Well Okay,' she sighed, 'If you wouldn't mind.'

So we struck a deal. One more day, gratis, then we'd take it from there.

After a couple more bumpy circles, the plane's body creaking and groaning, we dropped below the clouds again and, gently descending across sodden fields, hit the tarmac and roared to a dawdling stop.

You know, no matter how experienced a traveller you are, and I'm not, I wouldn't mind betting that everyone, deep down, breathes just a tiny sigh at this point in the journey.

With the people around us standing, stretching, and reaching for overhead lockers, Stephanie suddenly said, to no one in particular: *'She'll need some help with the baggaging.'*

'Sorry?' I said.

'I've just remembered. That's what Paul said: *'Okay, but she'll need some help with the baggaging.'*

'When was this?'

'Thursday night, before he left; I was putting some flowers in a vase. He'd brought them at the station, then stopped off for a takeaway. He gave them to me when he got home. I was sorting them out and his phone rang. I couldn't catch exactly what he said because he turned away. But I think that's what he said.'

''She'll need some help with the baggaging?'' I said.

'Yes. He said it was a work call, so I didn't really question it. And we started on the wine after that.' She smiled, perhaps for the first time since we'd met: 'They say you drink to forget. Well, I forgot.'

'So what do you think it meant?'

'Logically, something to do with his trip. There again, he was travelling by himself.'

'Maybe you misheard him. Perhaps he said *"I'll* need some help with the baggage?"*

'I don't think so, but even if I did, it still doesn't make sense. He only had hand luggage and a laptop.'

Filing off the plane, we kind of left it at that. For Stephanie, the key word was probably 'baggaging'. For me, because of my background, it was 'she'. And during our walking and queuing, something else struck me about the little story she'd just told me.

I waited till we got to the carousel before mentioning it. I knew I'd have time there: if there's one thing I can guarantee, it's that my cases will be last, or not at all.

'Stephanie,' I said, as an unclaimed suitcase, held together by string, passed us for the umpteenth time. 'How often did Paul go away on business?

'Almost every week, pretty much.'

'So it was no big deal?'

'In what sense?'

'Well, what with the meal, the flowers and stuff, I was wondering …'

I could almost see her thoughts. The same as mine.

'So he didn't normally buy you flowers.'

Again, she didn't answer. She didn't need to. I took it no further, partly because our bags finally appeared and partly because the obvious never needs stating. Paul had known something. But what?

I'd learnt more since setting foot back in England than I had during our entire trip. Mind you, I was just about to learn a whole load more.

As soon as I hauled my case onto the trolley I noticed it. The combination lock had been tampered with. Not broken, not forced, just altered. With combinations, most people simply memorise the number that unlocks it. I go further. I memorise the digits I reset the barrel to. Looking at the numbers in front of me, they were different. Of course, the barrel *could* get brushed in transit, but if that happened the numbers would all tend to move in the same direction. These weren't. They were totally different to how I'd left them.

'Might be worth checking your case,' I said, nodding to it.

She stooped down and checked it.

'My padlock,' she said. 'It's gone.'

I can't say I was surprised.

We put our cases back on the trolley and wheeled through customs

We were then stopped by the first uniform in the customs hall: 'Where have you arrived from, dear?' asked a large, superior oaf.

'The baggage lounge, *dear,*' I replied.

He gave me an unpleasant look and said: 'We need to take a look inside.'

'I though you already had.' I replied, hauling the cases off the trolley and, with no help from him, plonking them down in front of him.

'Open them?' he said.

'Open them, *please.*' I said.

Deadpan, he added a 'Please.'

I did as he requested and he duly rummaged. Then, astonishingly, we were joined by a dog handler plus his better half – a liver and white spaniel.

He sniffed around a bit (the dog, not the handler) wagged his tail, but didn't sit down.

'Perhaps we should do an IPS,' said Mr Deadpan.

'What's an IPS?' asked Stephanie.

'I think,' I said, 'they're referring to a strip search.' I then paused before adding: 'But they can't, Stephanie.'

I then looked at him: 'Can you, *sir*?'

After a brief silence, eyeballing each other, with me just daring him to contradict, he re rummaged our already over rummaged clothes.

'Handling women's underwear,' I said, 'must be great.'

'Okay,' he said, disregarding my observation and closing the cases. 'You can move on now.'

'I do love a man in uniform,' I said to Steph as we turned and left.

Through customs and into the hubbub of Arrivals, I began to get this strange feeling.

You know, some years back, I saw this experiment. It was filmed in a shopping mall in America. They got hidden people to stare at passers-by. This was to see if we have some kind of inbuilt ESP. Well, about half of us have, it seems. The female half. Time and again, a woman would stop, turn and look back to see if there was someone watching her from behind. Men, tellingly, didn't.

And that's exactly what I was feeling. Wheeling our bags, I suddenly had this uncomfortable sensation. So I stopped and turned. A man, twenty yards back, stopped in his tracks, bowed his head, turned and walked swiftly away. I didn't get much of a look at him and apart from being of medium build with baseball cap and dark glasses, I couldn't tell you anything.

As we waited for a cab, we didn't talk much. I suppose we normally would have, what with the customs and everything. But we were too shattered. I did do some thinking though.

Was all this connected? The word Stephanie had heard was 'baggage' – or *'baggag*ing,' at least. What had we had all the trouble with? And Paul, remember, had disappeared at an airport. It could also tie in with the whole *'closer to home'* thing.

But another issue was troubling me. Our baggage had been forced open, so why search it again? And why, softening up apart, threaten us with a strip search? Then there was the man following us.

Was the government involved in this?

CHAPTER SIX

'But his wife had never visited your hotel,' I said to Mr Ashkani. 'Never even been to Pakistan before our visit.'

'No,' Mrs Anderson,' he replied. 'But our records show differently.'

Still a little jet-lagged and confused, on my next working day I'd opened the blinds of my little office, fired up my computer, switched on the kettle, brewed up a teabag and checked my unread emails. First up had been a message from The Luxi.

Dear Mrs Anderson,

As requested, we've checked our records and can confirm that Mr Paul Hutchinson was a single guest for all his visits over the past three months. The only exception was his last visit, when his wife accompanied him.

Yours sincerely

Mr M Ashkani, Hotel Manager

'Why?' I asked.

'Why what, Mrs Anderson?'

'Why are your records entirely different to what actually happened?'

'They're not *entirely* different, Mrs Anderson. As I said, Mr Hutchinson ...'

'Yes, I know all that, but his wife had never even visited Pakistan. Why would your records show differently?'

'Well, we have certain obligations, Mrs Anderson.'

'Obligations?'

'Yes. You see, sometimes we are required to have different information on our room lists. For the authorities, you understand.'

'So the passport says one thing and your room lists say another?'

'Yes. Of course, we do inform Immigration of the right name. But sometimes, like I say, room lists differ.'

'And that's because of "obligations?"'

'Yes, *moral* obligations'

'Okay, I think I get it. You're not supposed to let an unmarried man and woman share the same hotel room, right?'

'Yes, I mean no.'

'So you checked someone else in as Mrs Hutchinson even though it didn't say that on her passport?'

'Well ...'

'That's illegal.'

'Maybe, but we have no choice, we are an international hotel, we need to be flexible.'

'Okay, Mr Ashkani, here's what you're going to do. You're going to send me an email with a scanned copy of Mr Hutchinson's "wife's" passport on it.'

'But ...'

31

'No buts, Mr Ashkani. That's what you're going to do.'

After I'd put the phone down, I'd thought for a bit, busied myself on bits and pieces, and about an hour later it pinged up: Poppy Foster, 24 years old, British, blonde, and a student.

Suddenly, it seemed, we had the 'she' that 'needed help' with her 'baggage.' Within an hour, I was on the train to London.

In the two years that had passed since the Su A affair, I had hardly travelled up there at all. The reason was simple: trains. Normal trains, I could just about deal with, but the London Underground was an absolute no-no. So I should have seen it coming. Or, perhaps *not* seen it coming, given I had my eyes tightly closed.

You see, on my line up from Shortlands there's a long dark tunnel, punching a hole right through Crystal Palace hill. God only knows how I'd forgotten about it.

I dropped my head into my Metro and shut my eyes. About two minutes later, shaking, perspiring and gripping my paper, we arrived at the sanctuary of Sydenham, and daylight. Then it got easier. Leafy Dulwich became built up Brixton, became Battersea, became the Thames, became Victoria, and no more tunnels.

My first port of call would be lunch with Anna, who I hadn't seen for almost three weeks. My second, after lunch, would be just around the corner in Great Marlborough Street and the company where Paul Hutchinson had last made an appearance: Effigy Postproductions.

Luckily the weather was fine, so no need for Undergrounds. Instead, a long but enjoyable walk, past Buckingham Palace with its snapshooting sightseers, on to St James's Park with its hustling ducks, then crossing the Mall, onwards and upwards, though perhaps morally downwards, to the wicked West End.

I love Soho. In small doses, that is. Like a tarty old aunt – heavy on the lip gloss, liberal with the Listerine, but always welcoming. As a young WPC, based at West End Central, I'd walked that beat a thousand times. In truth, much of it has now been gentrified: clip joints turned cafés, iffy clubs turned offices, and that's probably for the best. After all, I'd arranged to meet Anna at a pavement café that, in the old days, wouldn't even have existed.

I spotted Anna immediately. Table in the sun, head in magazine, hair pulled back and shades on head. This was the Anna I'd got so used to when we'd first worked together. Not, sadly, the Anna at the end of that terrible job. Or the Anna I'd seen so much of lately. The rehabilitation process, since that case, had been slow.

We shared a kiss, exchanged compliments: mine truthful, hers just kind, sat down and talked. Her friends, her work, her life, or the bits she lets me into. Not much about me, but that's fine. I'm a Mum, she's a daughter.

Finally, after an over hovery waiter had visited us for the third time, we chose salads and she asked me how things were going. She already knew about my trip to Karachi because, on landing, she'd been the first person I'd texted. And in setting up this lunch I'd told her about my experiences too: cabs and heat and hotel lobbies. But I hadn't really gone into much detail.

It was a fascinating case, of course, so she listened intently. And when I got to the real crunch, she could totally see my dilemma.

'You've got to tell her, Mum.'

'Oh I will, obviously,' I said. 'But I wouldn't mind finding out more first. All I know is he had a girl in his room, it doesn't mean it's connected to his disappearance. Why wreck a marriage, or even, if he doesn't reappear, a memory of a marriage?'

She thought for a while. Then some friends walked by and she got to her feet and they all chatted for a while. I suppose that's the downside of pavement cafés. Or perhaps, if you're as 'media' and as 'Soho' as they all were, the upside. Anyway, she introduced me to them and I stood up and we shook hands. It made me feel old. I doubted they would have bothered with handshakes if I were their age. There again, most things make me feel old nowadays.

Finally we sat down again, she gave me a bit of gossip about one of the girls I'd just met and we got back down to business.

'Tell you what, Mum, I've had a thought.'

'What's that?'

'Well, this meeting. It's the last one, right?'

'Yes.'

'And it's at Effigy Post, round the corner, right?'

'Yes.'

'Well, why don't we do it together? I know the business, you know the background.'

'Good idea,' I said, and we clinked glasses.

CHAPTER SEVEN

We walked through a sunny Berwick Street, full of bawling barrow boys and picky punters, into the non-market bit: fabrics by the roll, rhinestones by the box, then on to Great Marlborough, where we soon found Effigy Postproductions.

Light and airy, another large reception, but this time artier: rugs on walls rather than floors. We sat ourselves down in a sort of hang-out area, where we were soon met by Rose Denton, their MD.

Tall, greying and fortyish, she was probably a steadying influence in an otherwise very young workforce. We'd only got as far as handshakes when we were joined by a good looking, smart-to-casual, thirty-something called Nick Summers.

'Nick's our Head of Production,' said Rose, as he held out his hand.

Firm grip, pleasant smile, I immediately took to him.

Rose left us, Nick led us on, taking us down corridors marked Grading and Graphics and Animation. He was very well mannered: polite, not smarmy, and filled us in on the work they do: movies, TV programmes, pop videos. 'Anything with a budget,' he laughed, 'but mainly commercials.'

We got to a door marked VFX 1. This was the room, so he told us, that Paul Hutchinson had had his final meeting. He pushed the door open.

In the dark, silhouetted against a backlit wall, sat a single figure. Given all this room seemed to contain was this man, his desk and his monitor, it was pretty spacious.

'Hi, Sam,' said Nick, 'your visitors are here.'

'Hi,' replied Sam, neither getting up, nor extending a hand, just gliding his chair towards us. Even from this single, laconic syllable, his nationality was obvious: Australian. Mind you, the Hot Tuna T-shirt and surfer shorts were a bit of a giveaway too. Pushing forty, mutton-dressed-as-lamb came to mind.

Apart from the seat he'd punted towards us in, there was but one other chair, still at his empty desk. Then, as my eyes adjusted, I noticed a large leather sofa to the back of the suite. I got the picture. We were expected to sit away from Sam's holy-of-holies desk and, if we were lucky, he'd wheel himself nearer to us. Luckier still, he might even speak.

The relationship between Nick and Sam was interesting. As Head of Production, I would have guessed Nick was Sam's immediate boss, but maybe only in name because, having shown us to the sofa, he could hardly squeeze in next to us yet he didn't look happy about sitting next to Sam at his desk either. So he just stood there, awkwardly.

Anna had already given me a run-down of what normally went on in places like this, and there was a strict pecking order. Sam, in this domain, was kingpin. But after that it got complex. The commercial's director would be overall boss, but would bow to Sam's technical knowledge. Then came the advertising Creatives, whose original idea it was. Finally came the client, in this case Paul Hutchinson, who was indirectly paying for it all.

Most of the time, Sam, being the post production whiz kid, would work alone. But when the Director visited, he would sit next to Sam. The client, plus other assorted suits, would sit on the sofa, as far away from the screen as possible. Then there were the Creatives, who, having a foot in both camps, were sometimes on the sofa with the client, sometimes next to Sam.

When things went well, they went very well, but if they didn't, it could be a war. The bigger the budget, the bloodier the battles.

And that, with Paul disappearing after one such meeting, was precisely what we wanted to get to the bottom of.

Clearly this Sam didn't do small talk, so I got straight to the point.

'So tell me about that day,' I said, looking up at him, 'What happened?'

'Run of the mill,' he shrugged, 'nothing special.'

'There was a meeting, wasn't there?'

I got no answer, so I took it as a yes.

'And Paul was in it?'

A slight nod, a slighter curl of the lip.

'So, who else?'

'Me,' he said, 'the Director and the Creatives.'

'Was there a difference of opinion?'

Again, no answer.

'Look,' I said. 'I've already got some background on this, so you probably wouldn't be telling me anything I didn't already know.'

Still no answer, but his eyes said it: *'So why are you asking, lady?'*

'Okay, let's do it the other way,' I sighed. 'I'm going to tell you what I think happened and if you don't answer, I'll take it as a yes.'

I briefly looked at Nick, feeling a little sorry for him. Working with someone like this can't be easy.

'So Paul Hutchinson,' I said, fixing on Sam, 'was making this ad for his bank, right? Happy families on the beach. But he had a disagreement with the director about it. Am I right?'

'Yes,' he said. 'But that wasn't the main problem. We simply used a different take, with the woman more covered up.'

'So what was?'

'The problem? Branding. The director wanted less, Hutchinson wanted more.'

'That's fairly standard, isn't it?' said Anna, chipping in for the first time.

'Yes, but it got personal.'

'In what way?'

'Hutchinson told the Director to sod off. *And* sacked the agency, there and then, on the spot.' Sam then shrugged and added: 'Apart from that, everything was hunky-dory.'

Anna and I exchanged looks, raising our eyebrows. Serious stuff. As a reason for Paul's sudden disappearance, I might even put it in poll position, disappearance-wise.

But what happened next knocked it straight off the top spot.

A girl walked in. Young, blonde, attractive: she was wearing faded jeans, a T-shirt and a pretty smile. Instantly, her face seemed familiar. Then her words confirmed it:

'Hi,' she said, holding out her hand. 'I'm Poppy Foster, Sam's assistant.'

CHAPTER EIGHT

The girl who was in Paul's hotel room, I scrawled on my notepad, as I nudged Anna and watched her eyes widen.

Poppy stayed no more than a few seconds, standing at the door, asking Sam something about graded rushes, whatever they are.

Poppy's arrival, for all sorts of reasons, was clearly going to bring the meeting to an end, but I was desperate to get one more question in. I could hardly ask Sam directly about his assistant's relationship with a client, vanished or not. So I edged my final question, directed at Nick Summers, about as near as I dared:

'Were any of the staff here friendly with Paul?'

'Not to my knowledge,' he said. 'We tend to work with the Creatives more than the accounts people.'

'So none of you socialised with him?'

Sam gave a kind of dismissive snort to this, there was obviously antipathy there, but Nick simply gave a polite 'No.'

We kind of left it at that. I didn't want Anna jumping in, taking the questioning too far. Slowly, slowly, as they say. Anyway, we needed to compare notes.

Back out in the sunshine, Golden Square, aptly named that day, was just around the corner. A park bench beckoned. We made for the sunlit side, checked a bench for pigeon poo, sat down and breathed in. It was a beautiful day and a lovely square.

I have these opinions about seating and talking. Having spent a lifetime at opposite sides of an interview table, I would have, wouldn't I? That's why, for instance, when we found ourselves seated below our last interviewee, in a semi-darkened room, I wasn't overly happy. But park bench conversations are different again. They are for life's opposites: strangers or lovers. Side-by-side, looking outwards, words float away in parallels. No hits and no misses. Across a table, eye-to-eye, thoughts cross and ideas collide.

'So, what do you think?' I said, settling down.

A little way away, on one of the other benches, was a group of drunks, their previously backslapping conversation suddenly erupting into a row, echoing across the square.

'You mean the Poppy thing?'

'Yes.'

'Well, clearly Sam didn't like Paul much, did he?'

'No,' I said.

'So I was wondering if Sam and Poppy had been ... you know.'

'Yes,' I said, 'me too.'

'I mean, he's your client, telling you what to do. You don't like him at the best of times, but then you find out he's shagging your girlfriend.'

I'm not sure I'd have used Anna's terminology, but I certainly followed her thinking.

I said nothing, just looked up. Opposite us, an early luncher was settling into an already occupied bench. You know, people's behaviour interests me. Well, I suppose it would.

Most people go for the middle of the bench. When someone else turns up, they shuffle sideways: one each end. And that's it. Benches designed for four, yet seat only two – max. Even when a park gets busy, few would sit between two. And when, due to pressure of spaces, someone does join them, one of the originals soon leaves – and the middle one shuffles sideways. Back to square one. What does that tell you about sets of threes? They don't work.

'We're going to have to speak to that girl, you know?

'*We*, Mum?'

I smiled at her. Gave her that look. God knows, over the years, she'd given me enough.

We spent the next twenty minutes going over everything. Suspicion-wise, apart from Poppy Foster and Sam, I had my doubts about a number of people. Asif Farooki, Paul's boss, Bilal Sharma the police Superintendent, even Mr Ashkani, the Hotel Manager. After all, if he was prepared to spin a load of bullshit about who was staying at his hotel, why not more bullshit about how and why they disappeared? I'm not necessarily saying he, or any of them, had done anything. It was more that they knew something. More than they were letting on, anyway.

So a nice lunch, a useful meeting, and pleasant, bench-bound, debriefing. What more could I ask?

Well, there was that one last thing, the thing I'd already touched on. Anna was nearer Poppy's age, *and* in the same business. Post production people, like Poppy, need production people, like Anna. So there'd be all kinds of reasons why an ex-film student, just starting out in TV, would be prepared to have a bit of light lunch with someone with a few years under her belt.

More girly, less interrogative, and far more likely to end in a result. In the meantime, I could see if I could set up something with the two other parties: the ad agency and Paul's London office.

Yes, I know I said today would be the last day. And I do realise I'd now completed my contractual obligations. But I hate unfinished business. Especially unfinished interesting business. And this whole thing was certainly turning out to be that.

CHAPTER NINE

Ambling along Brewer Street, about a minute after leaving Anna, a voice came from behind me:

'Pamela, isn't it?'

I turned. A man: tall, slim, middle-aged, was tentatively holding out his hand.

'You probably don't remember me,' he said.

He was right, I didn't. Longish face, silver hair, kindish eyes. If I'd had to liken him to an anything, it would've been an affable old horse.

'Two rows back. Next to Baxter.'

Two rows back? Next to Baxter? Some kind of code?

'St Anne's Catholic …'

'Simmonds!' I exclaimed, rolling back the years. 'Bernard bloody Simmonds!'

'Pamela bloody Blower,' he replied, clasping my hand.

Now I need to explain something here. Once, I was a Blower. Now, I'm an Andrews. OK, divorcées often revert back. I didn't. I can kind of rationalise that. After all, Andrews was already my professional name. Headed paper, door signs, local adds – I wouldn't want to reprint my compliments slips, would I? But if I'm truthful, that's not the main reason. When I was a lass, the world was still an innocent place – or at least, a more innocent place. As was the word blower. Yes, I did sometimes get ribbed in the playground. But only because it sounded like blow off. *'Pam-ela Blow-off, Farty-pants Blow-off.'* Since then, many words have changed, many things have changed. Amongst the words and things the '60s brought us: funky, groovy, fab – was blowjob. I hadn't wanted my daughter to have to deal with that. Or my grandchildren, if I ever have any. So Andrews it remained: the only thing my ex left me of any value. Anna apart, of course.

'How on earth did you recognise me?' I asked before the penny dropped. Stupid question. Of course he'd recognise me. A couple of years back I'd been all over the news. His old classmate in newer, or perhaps older, form.

'Well, I ...' he faltered.

'Of course,' I said. 'The television ... Oh, er, how are you, Bernard?'

Another silly question. Compared to what? You say that to people you haven't seen for a few months, not forty-five years.

'Oh, I'm a ... well, muddling along, I suppose.'

There was then an awkward silence. I realised he was holding my hand. Our half-completed handshake must have ... We de-clasped.

'Have you ... I mean, do you keep in contact? You know, with any of our old classmates?' I asked.

'No, I ... can't say I've heard from any of them ... not for years. How about you?'

'No ... there was Janet ... Janet Dimbleby. Do you remember her?'

'Um, yes, a bit quiet. Used to sit at the back.'

'Yes, that's her. I used to get a Christmas card from her but she married an Australian.'

'Right, well. So she lives in Australia now?'

'Yes.'

We then spent five minutes confirming that we had absolutely no other news about any of our old classmates, or anything else in common, before our conversation sort of petered out.

'I'll, er, well, I'll see you, then,' I said, completing a hat trick of daft statements. Of course I won't. Our paths hadn't crossed in over four decades. Why would they cross again?

'Yes … goodbye,' he said.

'Goodbye,' I replied, turning back into the 21st century.

I walked away with a lightness in my step, I couldn't say why. But it only lasted for a few minutes.

You see, I got that sensation again. Someone watching. Was Bernard Simmonds stalking me?

I stopped, turned and observed. A man, certainly not Bernard, was kneeling down doing his shoelaces up. I couldn't tell you what he looked like because his head was down and yet again he was wearing a baseball cap. Similar build to the man at Heathrow though.

I took a side street that ran straight into Leicester Square, from there I doubled back. If he's still behind me, he's tailing me.

Piccadilly Circus. Busiest place on Earth. I ducked into a shop, strode past a rack of tasteless tee shirts, whipping one off as I passed, and continued to the changing rooms. Without stopping, I flashed it at the attendant, took a tag and found an empty booth.

Peeping back through the curtains, I could see him. He had his back to me, pretending to look at clothes. Women's clothes.

I was willing him to turn, but he didn't, just hanging up a blouse and leaving. By the time I got out, he'd gone.

Walking towards Regent Street, I looked into a couple of other shops, but no. Completely gone.

Before I knew it, my tailing had turned into browsing. I was looking at dresses. I mean *really* looking. What was I doing? Only a woman detective could turn a surveillance operation into a shopping trip.

My sister was coming round for dinner, I had food to prepare, my feet ached and it was rush-hour. Totally misnamed. If there's one thing you can't do, it's rush.

Cabs were occupied, buses stationary, pavements packed. I even considered the Underground, but one look at Oxford Circus, with people being sucked down like dirty dishwater, and no. In the end I had no choice but to board a non-moving bus and stand, arms aching, sweat trickling, for forty-five long minutes.

Finally, Victoria. I filed off, weaved my way through the concourse, queued up, fed the barrier, rushed down the platform looking for space, squeezed myself in between two sweating suits, and gripped an inch of handrail.

Eventually, we started. Then stopped. Then started. Then stopped. All the way to Herne Hill, where half the living dead decanted, and mercifully, I got a seat.

Then came that tunnel again. A slow, sweltering black hole. Worse still, the idiot driver had forgotten the lights. And I was very, very close to panic.

Counting backwards could be the answer. I closed my eyes. One hundred, ninety-nine, ninety eight … still dark, still hot, still suffocating …

Seventy-three, seventy-two, seventy-one … God, we've ground to halt again.

Sixty-eight, sixty-seven … If I knew the words, I'd be Hail Marying.

Fifty-five, fifty-four, fifty-three … Hang on, I *do* know the words. *Hail Mary full of grace, Hail Mary full of grace,*

Hail Mary full of grace, Hail Mary full of grace. We're moving again! Oh, thank you Mary. You're full of … grace. Just keep your bloody eyes closed, Pamela: keep praying, stay calm.

Light again! I could feel it on my eyelids. We were coming out.

Daylight in Penge. Truly wonderful!

People piled off. I was near an open window, feeling the breeze.

By the time we got to Shortlands, I had grave doubts about the whole project, and with fifty other shattered souls, slumped my way down the steps, through the barrier and into the station forecourt. Cars were pulling in, cars were pulling out. Worn-out wives, harassed husbands. Everyone wondering if life is worth living.

That's it! Enough! I'm not spending another day on this bloody project.

I fished out my mobile. *One Missed Call: Anna.* I probably missed it in the tunnel.

I hit the green button and got straight through.

'Hi, love, sorry I missed you. You OK?'

'Yes, fine. Thanks for lunch, by the way.'

'My pleasure, I enjoyed it.'

'Mum, I've been thinking. I'm up for that job.'

CHAPTER TEN

The weekend was uneventful, yet pleasant. I spent what was left of Friday, plus a good deal of Saturday, with Liz, my sister. Then Sunday it was gardening. Pruning and tidying, I found myself thinking about Stephanie. Should I simply come clean, tell her all about Paul's fling and then call it a day?

I was deadheading a particularly vicious rose when my mobile went, and, by the time I'd pulled off my gardening gloves, I thought I'd missed it.

'Hi, Andy,' I said.

'Oh, Pamela,' he said. 'Thought I'd missed you. How's things?'

'Not bad,' I said, brushing a wayward wisp of hair from my face.

'How about you?'

During the awfulness that was the Su A affair, DI Andrew McCullough was the one policeman who stood by me. He didn't have to – supporting a private investigator is never going to be a good career booster for a copper. As a rule, they don't like us. Especially if they are poking their noses into police business. But in Andy's case, even when it was all over – me proved right, and the police proved wrong – he didn't just walk away. Victim support, confidante, legal advisor. He was a bit of everything.

So could he, after a year-long absence, come round for a cuppa? Of course he could. I owed him that, at least. But it still surprised me: Sunday, not weekday, house, not office. Somehow, it just didn't sound social.

I went inside, kicking off my garden shoes and making straight for the mirror. Tangled hair, no make-up, sloppy Sunday.

I showered, changed and did some swift restoration. Fifty-five year-old bodywork, thirty-five minute repair, and the bell goes. Oh well, he'd seen me looking a whole load worse.

We pecked a kiss at the door, then it was kitchen, kettle, tea bags and finally, with Andy doing the carrying, took a tray into the garden.

One parasol, two chairs, tea and biscuits. Perfect. But I still wasn't certain. If this wasn't going to be work, what exactly was it going to be?

Andy's a solid man: late forties, but good for his age. His features, too, are young: sandy hair, blue eyes, a few old freckles. We talked about his career, which was on the up, Anna's wellbeing, which was improving fast, and my work. And that's when he brought it up.

'Yes, I er, know a little bit about that one,' he said, at the mention of Stephanie Hutchinson.

'You do?' I said, more than a little surprised. I mean, it wasn't a local case, nor was it particularly big.

'Yes,' he said, picking at the palm of his hand, 'It's, er, what I wanted to talk to you about.'

I was speechless. Why would he want to talk to me about a non-local three-month old case that the police weren't really interest in?

'You see,' he said, 'I've been asked to … well, ask you to back off.'

49

'Sorry?'

'I think you should drop the Paul Hutchinson case.'

I suppose, once my jaw had picked itself up of the floor, I could have given him a number of very justified answers, along the lines of *'It's none of your damned business*. But knowing how policing works, and given his sheepishness, I confined my answer to a single word:

'Who?'

'Don't you mean why?' he asked.

'No, Andy, I don't. I know perfectly well why well-meaning coppers like you warn off private detectives like me. You may recall we've been down that road before.'

'True,' he said. 'But you may also recall who stuck their neck out – told you to keep going. This time I'm not.'

I looked at him, and he looked at me. There was absolutely no way we were going to have a full-blown row about this.

'You still haven't answered my question,' I said.

He said nothing, just chewed his lip.

'Who, Andy?'

'Well, it's not coming from me ...'

'Obviously. I mean, with the greatest of respect, you're just the messenger, aren't you. Someone else is pulling the strings. Who, and how high up?'

'Very,' is all he said.

Once our little chat was over, a little less comfortably than it had started, I went back to the garden chairs and sat back down.

So who could it be? Not the Met. I would guess another of Her Majesty's very secretive services – able to harass at Heathrow and pry in public. An agency with the power to snoop on someone like me and pressurise a cop like Andy: MI5. It just had to be.

But why did they send round a friend? Why not the heavies?

Sitting there, the sun losing its heat, my next move was now clear. There was only one person who could decide whether I should or shouldn't continue with the Stephanie Hutchinson's case. Stephanie Hutchinson.

Tomorrow, Monday, I'd be putting in a call to Asif Farooki at the Pakistan International Bank. I had this hunch about this case only he could confirm. Then I'd complete my final report, warts and all, drive down to Brighton and give it to Stephanie in person. That much, I owed her, at least. She, and only she, would be deciding the next move.

CHAPTER ELEVEN

I hate Skyping. I *do* get the point of it: phone plus body language. But when I try anything more complicated than emails and Amazon things keep popping up telling me I need to download stuff I don't have, including a younger brain. Or that something's wrong with my attachments and that my software is out of date. Actually, I did use to have up-to-date software, trustworthy attachments and even a younger brain. But her name was Anna and she moved out!

After ten minutes of blank screens and submarine sounds, completely proving my point, Asif Farooki, CEO of the Pakistan International Bank, finally appeared.

'Brilliant,' I shouted. 'You're there!'

'I have been for a while, Ms Andrews,' he said calmly, in sombre suit and silk tie, 'as have you.'

I went cold. For the past five minutes, Karachi's answer to Omar Sharif had been watching me sweating, swearing and attacking a keyboard. And the little picture of me, in the bottom left-hand corner of the screen, gave an indication of the wrinkly, putty-faced apparition he'd been looking at. I tried to profile myself to the left, my stronger side, only to disappear off screen-right. So then I tried to adjust my hair, only for my wrong hand to come in and touch the opposite side of my head. Not a reflection, but a parody – a mirror from hell.

I cut my losses, concentrated on him, but did make a mental note. Old-fashioned phone calls in future.

I asked him how he was. He said he was fine. He then asked me how I was and I said fine too. Preamble-wise, that was about it. The awkwardness of Skype, at least, cuts the conversational crap.

'Mr Farooki,' I asked, 'Were you aware that on Paul's previous visit there was a woman with him?'

He smiled, but said nothing. Clearly he was.

'But you didn't see fit to mention it?'

'His wife was sitting next to you.'

'Fair enough, but you had plenty of other opportunities to tell me.'

'Why would I? It was only the once. Anyway, these things happen.'

'Did you meet her?'

'No.'

'How do you know about it then?'

'Paul told me.'

'When?'

'Look, it was nothing. Just something he told me over a drink.'

I found myself picturing the scene. Hotel bar, pricey booze, cheap talk.

'Did he say anything else about her?'

'Not that I would tell a lady, no,' he said.

I kept my temper. Just. I'm not going to be patronised, nor am I a *la*dy.

'Mr Farooki, we're talking a woman's life here, and possibly a man's death.'

He failed to respond.

'So, you know absolutely nothing about her – this other woman, I mean?'

'She's English,' he shrugged. 'Oh yes, and she's younger than he is, or was.'

'Was?'

'Was, as in when it happened, I mean.'

'Did he ever give the impression that it was a long-term thing?'

'No.'

'No he didn't or no it wasn't?'

'No he didn't.'

I scribbled something down in my notebook. Not because I needed to, but because I needed time. He was getting to clamming-up point.

'Mr Farooki.'

'Yes.'

'Do the police know about this?'

'I've no idea,' he shrugged. 'I certainly haven't told them.'

'Well, perhaps you should. It might save an awful lot of people an awful lot of time.'

His jaw tightened. A slight tick appeared above his left eye, or I suppose it could have been his right. Either way, clearly he didn't like being told what to do. Not by a woman, anyway.

'Mr Farooki,' I said.

'Yes … *Ms* Anderson.'

'That's not the main reason I'm calling you.'

'Oh,' he said, rather superciliously.

'Is there legal action going on? Between your bank and the advertising agency, I mean.'

He said nothing. The smirk was gone. Clearly there was.

CHAPTER TWELVE

Brighton at night: brassy front, classy rear. Having driven back and forth past Stephanie's flat three times, I eventually found a parking spot halfway back to London. I then walked back to her flat, arriving about ten minutes late.

She greeted me warmly. That trip to Karachi had changed many things, not least our relationship. But given the information I was about to impart, it needed to have.

We settled down, got past the chitchat and I handed her the A4 envelope.

'My report,' I said. 'It's not conclusive, obviously. I've listed the main possibilities, the evidence for each, and their potential outcomes.'

She took it from me, but didn't open it. 'Do you want me to read it now?'

'No, not if you don't want to. I can simply tell you. If you want me to, that is.'

'There aren't any surprises, are there?'

'It depends what you call surprises.'

'Go on.'

'Well, as you know, there's absolutely no evidence of kidnap or anything. So that's a good thing.'

She looked at me but said nothing. Perhaps she caught a look in my eye. Had she guessed that there was a not-so-good thing to follow?

'You see,' I continued, 'there's one aspect of this case that conforms to a pattern – one of the classic reasons why somebody would just disappear. And it would suggest, on the positive side, that he could still be alive.'

She still just looked at me. She absolutely knew there was something else coming.

'In that report there are four scenarios,' I said. 'And one of them, I'm afraid, is the possibility that he has another woman.'

She exhaled heavily, swallowed deeply, but still said nothing. Then she just looked down at the envelope.

In all her sleepless nights, in all her empty days, that possibility must have crossed her mind. OK, there was plenty ruling against it: the untouched bank account, the lack of sightings or phone calls. But it still would have been there: a cruel, painful possibility.

I let her gather her thoughts before continuing.

'On his previous visit to that hotel he definitely shared a room with a girl.'

She was still looking down at the envelope, so I went on: 'In there is a photo of that girl. Her name is Poppy Foster. She's a 24 years-old ex-film graduate working at Effigy Postproduction. There's a strong possibility they met on the job he was working on – again, this would conform to a common pattern.'

Finally, a little croakily, she spoke, asking me how I knew all this. And I told her, including the fact that I'd met this Poppy, and that I was quite prepared to meet her again – put the facts straight to her.

It was painful stuff. I also told Stephanie that I'd considered omitting his little fling, or affair, or whatever it was, from my report. But I felt, on consideration, that she needed to know. It was what she'd paid me for, after all.

'Well,' she sighed, 'As you say, at least it means he's …'

The word she missed out was, of course, 'alive.' An interesting reaction. It was clear, from her intonation, that she was more concerned about Paul's safety than his fidelity. Would she rather he was hitched up with some 24-year-old, than being held up by a bunch of abductors? It sounded like it. I found this both indicative and touching.

'I get the feeling you think it could be unrelated,' she finally said.

'Well,' I replied, 'you could argue that it fits the profile. After all, if a man isn't using his bank account it suggests he has another one. And if he has another one, he possibly has another life, too. It's not unknown, you know.'

'But surely I'd have—'

'Known about it, have had some evidence?

'Yes.'

'That's something I want you to think about.' I then paused, thought for a second. Should I say it? Yes, I should.

'You know the flowers, Stephanie? On your last meal together? Well, it does suggest premeditation, doesn't it?'

She looked down a little, at nothing in particular. Her eyes narrowed a little, her jaw tightened. In the cocktail of emotions she'd been going through, anger had just made its first appearance.

'Look,' I said. 'I'm only throwing up possibilities here. There are no conclusions in that report. And for what it's worth, that wouldn't be my number one bet – well, not on its own, anyway.'

'What would be, then? She asked, looking up.

'You may recall that Asif Farooki was a bit cagey about what was going on back in London?'

'Yes,' she nodded.

'It appears there was a big bust up between Paul and the ad agency and now there's legal action brewing. From the Bank's angle they have an unfinished commercial – not signed off by the Marketing Director, but from the agency's angle they've done their job, pretty much, and want paying. It's a mess. Mind you, I do wonder if it's a contrived mess.'

'How do you mean?'

'Well,' I'm not sure Farooki was that sold on the idea in the first place. He was clearly pulling the strings. Possibly sees it as a way out.'

'And you think that could be the reason for Paul's disappearance?'

'*A* reason, maybe. Possibly a combination of the girl and the job, and the stress of it all. Which is exactly why I want to speak to her again.'

Stephanie said nothing.

'This girl needs surveillance, at least,' I said, nodding towards the envelope.

'I'd do it at cost,' I said. 'I hate unfinished business. This thing needs sorting.'

'Oh, I couldn't let you do that …'

I took a sip of coffee, bought a bit of time. 'I'm sure we can come to some sort of arrangement, but there's another thing.'

'What's that?'

'MI5. It's in the report. Someone's been tailing me, you too. And I'm betting it's them.'

'Why?' she said, looking horrified.

'Because they still believe this is to do with terrorism.

'Do you?'

'No. But they've warned me off. Frankly, it's made me all the more determined to carry on. You see, I'm not the kind of person who just gives up. And nor, I would imagine, are you.'

CHAPTER THIRTEEN

I was born in the wrong century. Or, the right century, but then it changed. It's not just the Skype and the hype, it's pretty much the everything. Take Sushi Bars, for example. A couple of months earlier, on one of our meet ups Anna had suggested trying one. Now I have enough trouble choosing from one, motionless dish, let alone fourteen circulating ones. And, having made the wrong choice, I don't like being re-confronted with my moving mistake every forty-five seconds. Like gastronomic lost luggage.

So it was probably a blessing that, when it came to our next encounter with Poppy Foster, Anna would be doing the lunching, and I'd be doing to the tailing.

The plan was simple. Anna would ring up Poppy and set up a meeting. There were many reasons why I'd guessed she'd say yes: not just a shared industry and a similar age, but the concern for Paul and, of course, out of sheer curiosity.

That stage had been successfully completed and stage two, their actual meeting, was now under way.

And that was why I was sitting on yet another bench, in yet another square, in Soho. I say square, but St Anne's Churchyard isn't really that. In fact, it's not even a churchyard because it doesn't have a church. But it does have a tiny bit of grass, somewhere to sit, and a perfect view of Soho Sushi.

Anna's brief had been simple. Soften up Poppy with a bit of small talk and industry gossip, get around to the subject of Paul Hutchinson, then hit her with something subtle like: *'Tell me, Poppy, were you and Paul having an affair?'* That should take her mind off the conveyor belt.

And at that point Anna would do exactly as I'd taught her to do. Forget the notebook and look at the face. It's not about words, it's about eyes. From then on it would be down to whatever she could get out of her before she ups and goes. Like the book: eat, shoot and leave.

Anna may get lucky, she may not. Either way, that's when I'd take over.

The question was, once they had eaten, shot and left, what would Poppy do next? My hunch was that she'd try to make contact with whomever she was sharing her little secret with. Paul, possibly. One thing she wouldn't do was phone. Why? Because she'd think her phone was being bugged. And why would she think that? Because Anna would tell her so. She'd say that *my* phone was being bugged by MI5, because I'd been to Karachi – just as she had. *And* because I was involved in the Paul Hutchinson case – just as she was.

So given all that, what would Poppy do next? Well, if she couldn't talk, she'd probably walk. Which is exactly where I'd come in – tailing her.

Now personally, I didn't think Ms Foster was on MI5's radar at all. Her visit to Karachi had been before Paul's case had even kicked off and there was nothing suggesting she'd even accompanied him on that flight. After all, Stephanie had records of Paul's bank transactions, and whoever bought Poppy's tickets, it wasn't him.

The only reason I'd found out about Poppy's involvement was because I'd been to Karachi and questioned the hotel's manager. Almost certainly MI5 hadn't. More likely they'd be relying on the police over there. International diplomacy, you see. But the police in Pakistan weren't that interested in Paul's case. They'd made a few enquiries, checked the CCTVs and left it at that.

Sitting there in the late sunshine, with Soho's dayshift changing to nightshift – daytime to goodtime, I suppose – and with nothing but a couple of copulating pigeons for company, I had plenty to ponder.

While I was tailing Poppy, would someone be tailing me? Probably, but so what? I'd be saving Her Majesty's operatives a favour. They should have been following her all along.

Then there was the biggest question of all. If this was going to be an even vaguely successful surveillance I'd probably end up doing something I hadn't done in years. Travel down into the bowels of London's transport system. And that was something I really wasn't looking forward to.

About an hour after they'd disappeared, Anna and Poppy reappeared. Obviously the encounter hadn't ended too bitterly otherwise they would've left separately. On the other hand, their demeanour, checking phones and slinging bags on shoulders, seemed both brief and perhaps slightly awkward.

Anna turned north, towards Oxford Street, and Poppy south, towards Piccadilly. If she were making for home, to Hammersmith on the Piccadilly line, this was precisely what I'd expect her to do.

I got up from my bench, scattering a few pigeons, walked across the patch of grass, went through the gates, crossed Wardour Street and, giving no acknowledgement to the passing Anna, started tailing.

Out into the top end of Shaftesbury Avenue, our route was taking us directly to the Underground. Very soon I was going to have to face those demons.

We were almost at the entrance, with Eros dead ahead, when she stopped. So I stopped too. Then she turned, causing tuts from two tourists immediately behind her.

I ducked into a shop selling Union Jack mugs and plastic policeman's helmets. Against my wishes, I found myself scrutinising a tee shirt. It was telling me that someone's friend had gone to London and all they'd brought back was this lousy shirt. Hilarious.

Poppy passed back in front of the shop, I gave it a beat, then followed. We were now heading in the exact opposite direction, towards Leicester Square. She ahead, me cautiously behind, we passed silver-painted Michael Jackson's, parked-up rickshaws, and punk-for-the-day tourists.

I can't deny that I'd been relieved when Poppy didn't drop down into Piccadilly Underground, but now my heart sank all over again. It was just a stay of execution. She was heading straight for Leicester Square Tube.

Descenders pushing down, ascenders pushing up, and me squeezing down between: sweating, fretting and feeling like vomiting. I honestly wasn't sure I could do it.

Milling, swirling ticket hall: queues shuffling, barriers snapping. One-by-one, people were taking their turn: offering up cards, squeezing through, walking to the precipice and sinking down. Into hell.

Poppy joined the back of a Northern Line queue. I stood at the edge of the hall and let her get ahead.

I started to walk forward, but then stopped. My phone was vibrating. I took it from my pocket and looked at it. Unknown number. I pressed green and put it to my ear. Poor signal, too much noise, I couldn't hear anything.

Poppy was now at the barrier. Whether I intended to or not, I seemed to have joined the queue. With phone still to ear, I shuffled forwards.

'Hello,' I said.

'Hello,' replied a muffled male voice.

Almost at the barrier.

'Hello,' I repeated.

'Hello,' he repeated.

Oyster card ready, decision time: Speak or go back?

I bottled it, making the ridiculous decision that the phone call could be more important. Turning, I fought my way back. Against the tide, people were swearing, pushing and shoving.

Back in the relative sanctuary of the ticket hall, I took a deep breath.

'Hello?' I said again.

'Hello, is that Pamela?'

'Yes, um, hang on. I've just gone into the Underground. I'll walk back up.'

With phone to ear, I made for the steps.

Daylight.

'Hello,' I repeated for the umpteenth time.

There was a busker nearby, I still couldn't hear.

I pressed the phone to one ear, plugged my finger in the other, and walked.

'Who's that?' I said.

'It's Bernard.'

'Bernard?'

'Yes, Bernard Simmonds. You know, from … we met the other day, and—'

'Oh yes, Bernard …'

'I hope you don't mind, I got your work number off the internet …'

'No,' I sighed. 'That's what it's for.'

'Well, I was wondering … I was thinking perhaps we could meet up. You know, for a bite to eat or something?

'Er … I suppose so, yes,' I said. 'But I'm a little busy right now. Do you think I could call you back?'

'Oh yes, sorry …'

'No, no, it's good to hear from you. I'll call you back later. I've got your number now.'

'Fine, Okay.

'Bye.'

'Oh, goodbye,' he said.

I looked up. The entrance was packed, Poppy long gone. Would I be able to push my way back through that lot and find her? Could I even stomach trying? I decided the answer to both those questions was no.

Deflated, I walked back down Charing Cross Road. Probably a wrong decision. And definitely, I'd let myself down. What's the point of a detective who can't tail people? What's the point of a detective that's scared of the dark? Private Dick? Perhaps I should use the female equivalent. Also four letters but a whole load more vulgar. A whole load more apt too.

CHAPTER FOURTEEN

Anna's a good daughter. She could've made a bigger deal of it. I'm sure I would have. But she'd just shrugged and said 'Shit happens.' Not exactly the way I would've put it, but hey-ho!

It was a Thursday night and she'd come round to give me some moral support. Pinot from me, kindness from her.

I still felt lousy though. I'd asked Stephanie for three more days and she'd agreed. I'd spent the first mapping out, the second fouling up and now, the third, just morose. I'm good at that.

Stephanie had already had the report so there'd be nothing to add. Unless I was going to add a postscript about my survey of overpriced tourist tat. So it seemed my investigating days were over. Divorce work apart, that is.

'Look, Mum,' said Anna, picking up her glass and taking a sip, 'You've taken this a whole load further than the police did, the Poppy thing, the legal action thing.'

'Oh, come on, Anna. They could've got that if they'd wanted to.'

'Yes, but they didn't, did they? They completely missed it, barking up the wrong bloody tree again.'

She was right about that, at least. Not just the wrong tree, but the wrong forest, terrorism-wise. Yet the case was still a total mystery, as baffling now as it had been when Stephanie had hired me. My copy of the report would be confined to my unresolved file. And I didn't even have an unresolved file.

For her part, Anna had done well. She hadn't held back, she'd questioned Poppy about her relationship with Paul and she'd got a straight answer. The trouble was, Poppy's straight answer was a no. According to her, she'd travelled to Karachi to deliver the work in progress, explain it, and take the next stage of the brief. This was because Paul would be passing all that information to Asif Farooki, his CEO the very next day.

This all sounded unlikely in the extreme. Why wouldn't Aussie Sam, her immediate boss, do it? Or Head of Production, Nick Summers? Or what about sending it electronically? She had answers to all this, of course. Nick and Sam were busy and the material needed explaining. OK, so what was wrong with Skyping? Actually, I knew exactly what was wrong with Skyping, but I'm a middle-aged technophobe, not a twenty-something film graduate.

I could *kind of* imagine her bosses not really wanting to do a trip to Pakistan. It's hardly a top business destination, but then there was the ridiculous room sharing thing. It all sounded a little unlikely to me. According to Poppy, strictly speaking, she simply hadn't. Paul had booked a suite, not a room, and she'd slept the other side of an adjoining wall. Apparently, before leaving London, she'd tried to get a separate room, but the hotel was fully booked. So it felt safer kipping down next to him rather than booking an un-recommended hotel in another part of town – in a city not famous for its open-mindedness towards women.

Plausible? Just. Or at least, plausible enough for me to inform Stephanie. She could then make her own mind up. I pass information, not judgement.

So perhaps it wasn't a totally wasted week. After all, I'd be sending DC McCullough a quick update too. Whether he, or even MI5, would be in the slightest bit interested in Poppy Foster I couldn't say. But at least we'd be furnishing the authorities with the facts. It was over to them now.

'So where do you think Poppy was going?' asked Anna, snuggling back into the sofa.

'Not home, that's for sure. My guess is that she started walking towards her normal station, Piccadilly, and then, either absent-mindedly, or because she hadn't thought it through, decided that Leicester Square was a better bet.'

'Because of what I'd said?'

'I'd be surprised if it wasn't. Think about it: Poppy tells you she's got nothing much on that evening and that's she's going straight home. Then you bring up the whole Paul thing and suddenly she's off somewhere else.'

'On the Northern Line instead of the Piccadilly?'

'Yes. Not that that helps much. Morden to Manchester with about a hundred stops in between.'

'Well,' she said, 'Don't beat yourself up over it Mum. If it's any consolation, I wouldn't even have got as far as the steps.'

Kind words from Anna, but no, actually it was no consolation at all. The fact that my daughter had been equally screwed up by that woman-hating psychopath certainly didn't fill me with joy.

We both took thoughtful sips before she spoke again: 'So who was it?'

'Who was what?'

'That person. The one that called you at the barrier?'

'Oh just some man.'

'Oh *yes,*' she said, showing sudden interest.

And that was it. Suddenly, all talk of Poppy Foster was gone. What does he look like? What does he do? How tall? How hunky? Did I use to fancy him? Oh, yes, and as an afterthought: is he married? I fielded the questions while she almost squeaked with delight. The thought that her old mother could be attractive to the opposite sex seemed to come as a huge surprise.

'So will you call him back?' she asked, curling her legs onto the sofa.

'I doubt it.'

'Oh don't be such an old spoil sport. When was the last time you had a date? In fact, come to think of it, have you *ever* had a date, apart from Dad?'

'Of course I bloody have! The world didn't start when you popped out!'

'Yes, but I mean this century.'

And with that, I hit her with the cushion.

Despite Anna's enthusiasm, I had no intention of taking the Bernard thing further. But the following day he phoned again. Ten out of ten for persistence, I suppose.

I'd just passed the dairy products aisle at Sainsbury's when my mobile rang. Putting a pack of Benecol into my trolley, clenching a shopping list in my teeth, I fished my mobile out: *Bern S* it said.

I briefly considered pressing the red, but opted for the green. I can't really say why.

'Hello, Bernard.'

'Oh, er, is that Pamela?

'Yes.'

'Oh, um, I was calling because I couldn't remember giving you my number. But obviously ...'

'It's still stored from your last call.'

'Of course, stupid of me … well, I was …'

There then followed a short silence. At a guess, I'd say he was summoning up a bit of courage.

'Well,' he finally said. 'I was wondering if we could meet up … for a sandwich or something.'

'… OK,' I said, astonishing myself, 'when's good?'

'Monday?'

'… Let me think …

At that point, I heard a scream. Then something crashing to the floor. I looked up.

Just along the aisle people were hurrying towards or away from something, but I couldn't say what.

'Hang on, Bernard,' I said, 'I need to go.'

Mobile still in hand, I left my trolley and ran. All I could see were the backs of people. They were looking downwards. As I got closer a woman turned from them, pulling a girl away. The girl was sobbing.

I pushed my way into the gap and looked down. The source of the crash was immediate: a basketful of shopping strewn across the floor. But the *reason* was a few feet further on. Thick blood was creeping across the floor.

Looking up a little, it was oozing from a machine, sliding down its legs, dripping from its base: a bread slicer.

Three uniformed staff, nearest the slicer, stood motionless. As did everyone else. Someone was going to have to do something. And that someone, clearly, was me.

'Excuse me,' I said, pushing forward.

Walking right up to it, making sure I wasn't treading in the blood, I paused. Whatever it was would be inside the machine's lid.

Hanging from the side was a polythene bag dispenser. I ripped out a bag, put my hand inside it, and, using it like a glove, slowly lifted the lid.

At that instant, I couldn't say for certain what it was, but I was pretty certain it wasn't human. Pigs liver, definitely. Steak, possibly. The presence of a single staring eye suggested fish, too. But more than anything, blood. Lots of it.

I turned back to the crowd: 'It's okay everybody. It's, er, animal.'

I then turned to the staff: 'We probably just need a clean-up, but I'd contact the police first, just in case.'

Then I remembered my mobile.

Sorry, Bernard, are you still there?'

'Yes. What on earth's happening?'

'Oh, nothing much. Where were we?'

'Monday. You were going to tell me if you were free on Monday.'

'Oh yes …'

Then I thought about it. Perhaps Monday wasn't such a bad idea after all. Only a couple of days away, it kind of made it more casual, unplanned.

'Okay, I said. Monday it is.'

'Good, great! Would one be good?'

'Yes, perfect.'

'And, um, what sort of things do you like?'

'Anything but liver, Bernard, anything but liver.'

CHAPTER FIFTEEN

Driving home, two thoughts. The strange bread slicer business and the Bernard thing. Of the former, I decided it was probably just a crank. Possibly some anti-meat eating thing. Of the latter, perhaps I'd just ring back nearer the time and cancel. Come up with some silly excuse.

But when I got home, putting the shopping away, I mentioned this to Anna and she nearly hit the roof: 'You just *have* to go, Mum. You should be *flattered.'*

Well perhaps I should. But then, as I was filling the fridge, she added 'at *your* age,' and it rather took the gilt off. As for her next offering: 'You just *don't know* where these things can lead to, Mum,' I knew *exactly* where these lead to. Which was precisely why, *at my age*, I was worrying. She even started talking about what I should wear. To a sandwich bar!

In the end she just wore me down. And just to make doubly sure I was going to go through with it, she said she was now *definitely* staying for a few days. Thanks for that, Anna.

In truth, her extended stay with me wasn't entirely altruistic. She'd arranged one of her occasional old friend's get-togethers and was using my place, *our* place, as her Bromley & District crash pad. You know, they call Anna's lot the boomerang generation, but I'm not so sure. Boomerangs come straight back. Dog and stick generation would be more apt – sniff around a bit, *then* return. I wasn't complaining though. The time will come, not so far away, when visiting me will be an absolute chore. I had to take what I could, when I could. And anyway, despite her one woman pro date campaign, I felt a whole load better for having her around.

That old expression: *Boys mess up your house, girls mess up your head,* didn't really work in Anna's case. That weekend, head-wise, she did more tidying up than messing up. Just a shame that the other half of the saying was equally untrue. Picking up clothes, washing up mugs and mopping up bathrooms, it was like she'd never been away.

The days that followed were pretty uneventful. I did mention the bread slicer incident to Anna, but only after a day or so. I'm not sure why I waited. To make light of it, I suppose. Not that there was much to make light of in the first place. She didn't think much to it either. Just pulled a yucky face and said it was probably just some kid.

I also picked up a couple of new cases: one from a divorce lawyer, for good ol' partner surveillance, and one from a business, following an industrial injury claimant. But for all that I still couldn't get the Hutchinson case out of my mind.

But I kind of drew a line under it when, on the Monday, I called Stephanie for what would be, or at least *should* have been, the last time.

She hardly said anything. She was at work at the time and it was probably difficult for her to talk. There again, she'd hardly be bubbling over, would she? The fact that your husband *may* not be having an affair after all is good news, but weighed up against the fact he was still missing was hardly cause for celebration.

Towards the end of the week I got an email from Andy McCullough thanking me for the information about Poppy, but the interesting part was right on the end:

'Thanks for your help on this one, but I'm pleased you've finally seen sense and dropped it! Keep in touch. Andy. X'

Touching that he cared, but telling too. By implication *'finally seen sense'* would suggest that, had I not dropped the case, I could have been in some kind of danger. Interesting.

But not as interesting as the final thing that happened that week. Amongst Saturday morning's junk mail: takeaway pizzas, mini cabs, double glazing, was a piece of folded A4 paper. At first I thought it was blank. Then, when I unfolded it, it had just two words above the fold: *'Don't Make,'*... and two words below: *'A Bloody Mistake.'*

I flattened it out, reread it, then reread it again. *'Don't Make A Bloody Mistake.'* How weird.

CHAPTER SIXTEEN

'I'll show you mine, if you show me yours.'

Yes, it had occurred to me that Bernard Simmonds, together with David Ford and Joseph Radcliffe, owned the first set of male bits I'd ever seen. And yes, I had wondered whether it would come up. The topic, that is, not the bits. It wouldn't normally, would it? Not too many first daters have shared trouser-dropping and skirt-lifting experiences have they.

We were sitting in a Wardour Street café, next to the rain-streaked window, perhaps a little misty-eyed, recalling our school days. The forgotten friends and sworn enemies, the hopscotch and the marbles, the Love Hearts and the Sherbet Fountains. Then he brought up our walks home. In little groups, via the swings and roundabouts of Farm Lane Rec, we would dawdle our way back to Pinky & Perky, and meat and two veg.

Well, one day, on that journey, behind that park's wooden shelter, we revealed all. The boys went first, exposing their little willies, and then came me, willieless, instantly regretting the challenge. Only Sally Turnbull was saved – by Mr Parky, the imaginatively named park keeper – who came running at us, scattering us to the four corners of the field. And even though I'd half expected that recollection, I still blushed into my coffee. Bernard, I think, felt bad for mentioning it too. Ridiculous really. All that time ago, such innocence, yet perhaps a tiny bit inappropriate on a first date. If that's what this was.

Originally, the idea of meeting in a café had appealed to me. A posh restaurant, in the evening, would have felt wrong. I didn't want date, I wanted casual. And I suppose from Bernard's perspective, it made sense too. You bump into someone in your lunch hour and assume it's their lunch hour too. You also work in that area, so you assume they do too. If you're going to drop by again, why not same place same time? Of course, in my case, it wasn't quite like that; I'd just been visiting. But as I said, it suited me just fine.

So I'd put on a simple skirt and blouse combination, which wasn't glam enough in Anna's opinion, then I'd added a nice new raincoat from Boden which, being a (hopefully) up-to-date version of a tied-belt detective's mac, seemed somehow appropriate. Then I'd taken the train from Bromley North to Charing Cross. Now given the change at Grove Park, this was far more tedious than going to Victoria, but it did involve fewer tunnels. Finally, it being a wet day, I'd hailed a taxi on The Strand and asked for the top end of Wardour.

It was still bucketing down as our cab pulled up. I paid him off, opened the door and ran for the café's awning. No Bernard. So I poked my head inside. Nope. Had he forgotten? Maybe I'd misread the situation. Perhaps it was just an *'I'll see you when I see you'* type situation. After all, it was only a sandwich bar. On the other hand, no, he'd rung me twice. It was a definite date.

Had it been a big posh restaurant – the one thing I didn't want – at least there'd be reserved tables. All there was here were a few of bits of outside/inside garden furniture, all occupied. No obvious ladies toilet to hide in either. So simple choice: lone gooseberry inside, drowned rat out. With umbrella up, I took the latter.

I looked at my watch. Ten minutes late, which *I'm* allowed to be, by the way, but he definitely isn't. Another five minutes went by. Then another. I decided I'd give him till half past, no later.

At twenty-eight minutes past he finally came into view. Half-running, half-zig-zagging between brollies, with drenched suit jacket pulled over his head.

Full of dripping wet apologies, he told me he'd had an appointment which had overrun and, all taxis being taken, had decided to cut his losses and just go for it, all the way from Holborn. I told him not to worry, it was fine, which it wasn't, and we dribbled our way inside.

Luckily, one of the tables had become empty, so we squeezed between the raincoats, excusing ourselves profusely, and sat down. We exchanged a few wooden words about the terrible weather and craned our necks to choose from a chalkboarded list.

Bernard then had to squeeze back out, queue up, buy the sandwiches and hand the paper plates back over hunched-up heads and ducking shoulders. In truth, I felt so sorry for him, yet still cross. Sopping wet and over-late, his date was a bloody disaster.

Or was it? We soon settled down to a long and comfortable conversation about our present-day selves.

He already knew loads about me, courtesy of two-year old media coverage: a divorcée, living in Bromley with grown-up daughter. But I knew nothing about him. Unsurprisingly, he, too, had baggage. At our ages, hasn't everyone? Ex-wife in Watford, bills for marital home, grown-up sons he seldom saw.

'So where do you live now,' I asked.

'Just around the corner, in Brewer Street,' he said, thumbing over his shoulder. 'Flat above my business.'

'And what's that?'

'Editing … ads mostly.'

I told him that that was coincidental. I also asked him if he knew a girl called Poppy Foster. He didn't, but he did know Effigy Post – one of the biggest in London, he said. He also told me it wasn't that coincidental. 'Every other person round here works in post,' he said. And whereas they were a 'fully fledged post house: audio through to 3D animation,' he was 'just a humble film editor.'

'Sounds interesting, though,' I said.

'Not really, endless re-cutting. It's like the old joke: *How many advertising executives does it take to change a light bulb?*

'No idea,' I shrugged.

'Nor have they,' he smiled. 'Or the other answer would be "they'll know when they see it." And *that's* the problem. In the old days it was all Sellotape and scissors. You just couldn't carry on like that. Nowadays they just go on and on changing their mind.'

'In the old days,' I repeated, wistfully.

'Aye,' he said, before drifting off in thought for a second.

'Talking of which,' he finally said, 'You were a bit of a teacher's pet, as I recall.'

'I *was not*!' I replied, perhaps a little over indignantly.

'You were: Class 3 inkwell monitor, from recollection,' he said, laughing.

'God,' I said, hand to mouth, 'So I was.' I then rolled the words a couple of times: "inkwell monitor", God, it sounds positively prehistoric. What with your Sellotape and scissors, and my inkwell monitoring, we must sound like a right couple of old cronies.'

'Well, I suppose we are,' he said. Then, realising what he'd implied, he swiftly added: 'Or at least *I* am. You still look pretty damned good.'

'I'll take that as a compliment,' I said, and I suppose it was.

'Anyway, Bernard,' I said 'You were hardly going to get that job, were you, flicking ink pellets all around the room? I got big black stains on my school blouse because of you. Mum tried to bleach it, but they still didn't come out. Got me in loads of trouble.'

'Sorry,' he said.

'Bit late,' I laughed. 'About forty years.'

He then frowned and said: 'From painful recollection, that got me caned.'

I thought for a second: 'Amazing, isn't it. Even that's changed. Words, I mean. Getting caned is now something people do on Friday nights.'

'Yes,' he said, smiling, 'So it is.'

And that bought us back to the here and now, with me asking him what it was like living in a place like Soho, where people come to get caned just about every night of the week.

'Well,' he said, looking down at his coffee cup, 'I suppose, like the job, it sounds great, but all I can say is never, ever live above the shop: work, work, work.'

'Shi …! He nearly exclaimed, looking at his watch, 'Work!'

He suddenly got up from the table: 'I'm, er, really sorry, but …'

'Oh, that's OK,' I said, getting up too.

Then we looked at each other.

'I'll be in touch,' he said. 'If you want, I mean.'

'Oh, um, yes,' I said.

Then we shook hands. No kiss on the cheek, just a shake of the hands. Which was just perfect.

He rushed to the door and looked back. 'Um, oh yes, goodbye. It's been, well, great.'

'Yes,' I said, 'it has.'

Around me, the place had totally emptied. Queues gone, tables cleared, gushing Gaggia silenced. An hour of my life had just dissolved away, with the man whose inkwell I once filled.

CHAPTER SEVENTEEN

'So, would you go out with him again?' asked Anna, sipping at a mug of tea.

'Well,' I replied, 'It didn't exactly feel like *going out* in the first place.'

'That's a good thing, isn't it?' she said.

'Maybe.'

'So would you?'

Good question. I thought for a second, took a sip myself. 'Yes, if he asked, I probably would.'

'Oh, he'll ask,' she said.

'How do you know?' I replied.

'Intuition,' she said.

Since when was my daughter such an expert on men? Since when was I not? More to the point, since when was I the child and she the parent?

She meant well, was really excited about it. It's just a shame it wasn't the other way around. You see, we'd never discussed this, but since that terrible case, Anna hadn't had a single man in tow. Not that having a man in tow's everything. Far from it. But if you're not going to have one, it should be because *you* don't want one, rather than because some sick psycho has put you off. I didn't blame her, of course. But it didn't help my feelings of guilt either. There again, I'm a Mum. Guilt, I suppose, is what I do.

Just as she was asking me what he was wearing, and I was telling her that it was a wet suit, which briefly confused her, my phone started vibrating across the table. I picked it up. *Bernard.*

I hit green, got up, and wandered towards the kitchen. Again, the fact that it was me with the hush-hush call somehow made it feel all the more wrong. So I restricted myself to a business-like 'Hi,' a couple of 'OKs,' a 'Fine right,' and a 'See you then, then.'

By the time I sat back down she'd guessed and was back in squeaking mode.

'Where's he taking you, Mum?'

'Oh, just the opera.'

'The opera! Oh My God! You *love* opera!'

'Well, to be fair, it's no big deal. It's all very last minute and …'

'Last minute? When is it?'

'Well, he's got a pair of tickets for Boheme on Thursday and …'

'Thursday! *This* Thursday? Boheme! You *love* Boheme!'

'Yes, but it's not like that, the tickets were going begging – for a client who cried off.'

No matter what I said, I couldn't dampen her enthusiasm. Exclamation marks and OMGs flying all round the room. My sensible, thirty year-old daughter had turned into a pre-teen.

In the end, exhausted by the babble about what I could and couldn't wear, say and do, I decided to wave the white flag and simply go to bed. So I kissed her goodnight, traipsed upstairs, undressed and, on the way to the mirror, picked up the remote, switched on my bedroom TV, listened out for tomorrows' weather and started to unmake-up.

'A London businesswoman was gunned down in broad daylight today,' said a rather breathless reporter.

I turned and looked at the screen. The reporter was standing at the end of a taped-off row of Victorian terraces in an otherwise deserted London street. *'Rosemary Denton, the MD of a London post production company, was murdered today outside her Fulham home.'*

Then up came a photograph. Very clearly it was the woman Anna and I had met just a week earlier: Rose Denton, Managing Director of Effigy Postproductions.

CHAPTER EIGHTEEN

Generally, I don't read newspapers, but the following day I did. And amongst the many emotions I felt, was guilt. Not at Rose's death, of course. That was obviously nothing to do with me. But towards Anna.

Introducing your daughter, even briefly, to someone who is then gunned down in the street isn't my idea of perfect parenting. It brought back memories of the way I'd introduced her to the Su A case.

Back then, my ex had ranted at me down the phone about getting Anna involved in a case with a psychopathic sex offender. According to him, I was just a glory hunting, wannabe TV Cop. Actually, at the time, I hadn't the faintest idea this man was a psychopathic sex offender. But his accusations cut deep. Anna was missing, presumed dead, and a part of me, quite a big part of me, agreed with him.

Of course, the Paul Hutchinson case was very different. Neither Anna nor I were in the news, so my idiotic ex knew nothing of our involvement. More importantly, there didn't appear to be anyone especially nasty involved in it. It's true that Rose Denton's murder *was* in the news, and her murderer probably *was* the kind of person you'd keep from your daughter. But Paul Hutchinson and Rose Denton were two different cases. We were only involved in the former.

In the meantime, what could the papers tell us about the latter? Well, it would appear that, at 7:53 am on Tuesday

24th June, Rose Denton had opened her front door. No one seemed to know exactly why. She already had her coat on and her bag with her, so it could be that she was leaving for work. Or it could be that she was just about to leave when the bell rang. And given that her front door had a spy hole, it could also be that she knew the murderer. Who that person was, we obviously didn't know either, but one witness reported seeing a male of average height, with a scarf around his head, walking briskly from the scene. Given that the weather had been cold, this hadn't seemed too odd at the time.

Three different people, including the person that had seen this man, reported hearing gunshots, but there had been disagreement about exactly how many: two, three or even four shots were reported. All we did know was that two bullets had been administered to her temple at very close range. Clearly murder had been the intention, and possibly the murderer was a professional. No weapon had yet been found.

Rose Denton had staggered two steps forward then crumpled to the floor, dead. In a rather poetic postscript, given her name, one newspaper reported that the rose bed, next to her front door, was filled with her blood. Our dear old free press: don't you just love 'em?

Speculation as to a motive for the murder varied, but top of everyone's list seemed to be no motive at all – i.e. mistaken identity. After all, why would a single, middle-aged woman, whose main interests were her work and her garden, be a target for an assassin?

The other main theory seemed to suggest that it could be the same 'crazed' gunman who had killed Jill Dando, the well-known TV presenter, in 1999. There were a couple of similarities. The location – they even published a map showing how close (six streets) the two shootings were – and the fact that she'd possibly known her assassin. But suggesting that two people were murdered by the same perpetrator simply because they share a postcode is like suggesting two different scientific experiments must produce the same results because they share a fridge! And what, in the intervening 16 years, was this 'crazed' gunman supposed to have been doing? Sitting around being 'un-crazed' presumably.

Even more ridiculously, they were suggesting some kind of non-existent 'showbiz' connection. But while it's true that Jill Dando was a household name, Rose Denton certainly wasn't. Effigy Postproductions, of whom she was Managing Director, may have been a major player in film and TV – they'd even won an Oscar for one of the films they'd worked on – and Rose would probably have to attend industry functions. Most papers were making great play of her holding up an award at some advertising award ceremony in London. But none of that worked for me. Being boss of a TV company doesn't make you a TV personality.

But good journalists don't let minor details like the facts get in their way. Frankly, I was only surprised they hadn't also suggested that the murderer preyed on women who had short surnames starting with the letter D!

Strangely, or perhaps not so strangely, they'd missed one big trick. After all, one of the abiding theories behind the Dando murder was that it was in some way tied up with international terrorism. In Dando's case, it was Serbia. Yet not a single paper had tied Rose Denton's death in with the disappearance of Paul Hutchinson. Personally, just as with the 'crazed stalker' theory, I wouldn't rate that angle anyway. After all, terrorists from totally different backgrounds and with totally different beliefs (Serbian / anti-Muslim; Pakistani / pro-Islamic) don't tend to work together, do they – especially sixteen years apart!

Mind you, that wouldn't necessarily stop some resourceful journalist eventually making the connection. There's nothing like a conspiracy theory to get the tabloids going. And it took Anna, almost reading my mind, to voice that very point.

'Why do you think that they haven't made the connection yet?' she asked thumbing her way through the papers.

'Possibly because there isn't one,' I said.

'But they did meet, didn't they – on the day he disappeared?'

'Yes, but that was almost three months ago. Just think of the number of people she probably meets on a daily basis. And him, come to that.'

'So you think the press may never make the connection?'

'Oh, they will. It might take time, but they will.'

She thought for a second and said: 'Effigy Post aren't directly involved in all this legal stuff, are they?'

'No, it's between the Agency and the Bank – it just happened to kick off in their premises.'

'So do you think the police will connect the two?'

'Definitely. Probably already have. But it's all very tenuous.'

'Will they want to interview us?'

'I doubt it. If they *do* think there's some kind of connection, they're more likely interview some of Effigy's staff who were around when the bust up happened.

'You mean Aussie Sam, etc.?'

'Yes. But I can't think why they'd ask us. We came along three months later!'

I must admit I was playing things down here. Yes, we came along three months later, but so did the murder. And I was being just a little bit economical with the truth regarding being interviewed too. There was indeed an outside chance the police would want to speak to us. And, once those two cases became connected, there was an even greater chance the tabloids would too. I just hoped not. I really couldn't go through all that again. So in the end, I did the exact opposite of what I'd done the night before.

'Right,' I said, closing the paper. 'Time for action. I'm going upstairs for a bit of scrubbing up. Tonight's the night!'

You know, had it not been for the fact that this whole date thing afforded a bit of distraction, I'd probably have cried off. But changing plans now would send Anna all the wrong messages. It wouldn't stop her poring over the papers, of course. But with me upstairs and her down, at least it might cut out some of the questioning *and* add to my whole nonchalance thing.

I suppose, kicking off the day with a bath is not that normal. But dates aren't normal are they? Not for me, anyway. Nearer the time, I'd probably shower as well, but for me, bathing goes with leg shaving. The big question was: what does leg shaving go with? Time would tell. I wasn't taking any chances.

Buffed legs, plucked eyebrows, sizzled-off lip fluff. Like an oven-ready chicken I was stripping myself down before dressing myself up again. Anyway, another reason for bathing first was that I'd managed to book a last-minute hair appointment.

When I got back, Anna had migrated all the way from the kitchen to the lounge and from papers to laptop: deep in concentration, with slatted sunlight streaming across her.

'You like?' I asked, pirouetting at the door.

'Yes, she said. 'Nice.'

Nice was obviously as nice as it was going to get, so I went upstairs, spent ten minutes prodding at it in the mirror, both self-titivating and self-doubting.

From then on, my wardrobe system was simple. Anna remained downstairs at the computer, while I went halfway up and down the stairs trying things on. Standing behind the banisters, I'd hold up my arms and go: 'Ta Daaa! What do you think?' Most of the time Anna's answers were 'OK', which generally means '*Not* OK'.

It soon became apparent that our opinions differed. She thought I should flash the flesh and I felt I shouldn't. She chose a low cut clingy thingy ('I thought operas were all heaving bosoms, Mum.') whereas I favoured smart and simple ('Yes, but that's on the *stage*, Anna.')

In the end, I won. My date, my bait. The only concession I made was an extra button undone on my blouse, which would probably be done up well before the train pulled into Charing Cross anyway.

I finally made it out of the front door to only moderate approval, feeling especially guilty about leaving her behind. Mind you, I could hardly take her with me, could I! Then I walked to the station, got on an on-time, near empty train and sat down. Next to me was a discarded Evening Standard. I picked it up.

Headline: *'Rose's Death: Missing Man Connection.'*

CHAPTER NINETEEN

Just beyond the barrier: Bernard. Suit, tie and this time, dry. We shared a light, almost non-touching embrace-cum-peck on the cheek, combined with a 'you look nice.' *Nice*, hopefully, was the new great.

We started walking and talking, but there seemed to be this slight space between us. A sort of awkwardness. It was as if we should be holding hands or something. But I suppose that's normal on a first proper date. I did find myself wondering if he felt just as awkward too.

We got to Covent Garden, found the cloakroom and then the crush bar. He got the drinks in and, even though I'm not a great fan of standing and drinking, it somehow worked. Despite, yet again, that slight space between us.

The bar filled up with people with velvet jackets, long gowns and loud voices and, almost inevitably, the subject of Rose Denton came up. Not an ideal topic for a first date, but almost inevitable. You see, Bernard's little business used Effigy Post quite a lot and, even though Rose, as their MD, didn't need to have any day-to-day contact with him, the whole thing had hit him quite hard.

We discussed the sheer awfulness of it and I found myself learning quite a lot about the whole industry. Apparently, there are two types of editing. Bernard's type, which involved taking the raw footage and turning it into a story, was pretty much as I'd always imagined it to be.

Apparently, most of the companies that performed this function were like his: small, boutique-like, and living off the reputations of their editor / owners. Effigy Post, by contrast, was huge.

Effectively, they took the rough-cut that Bernard produced and, via a lot of expensive gizmos, turned it into a finished product. All very interesting, but it shed no light on why she, or anybody else at Effigy Post, could have been involved in Paul's disappearance. Or, come to that, why anyone would want to murder her.

For my part, I filled him in with some bits about her death he possibly didn't know about, though judging by the headlines, he soon would.

So did he think a dispute over a TV commercial was worth murdering for? Absolutely not. Especially, as Anna and I had already discussed, the dispute didn't even involve Rose Denton's company. He, like just about everyone else, was as mystified by her death as he was by Paul Hutchinson's disappearance.

Getting this discussion out of the way was something that just had to be done. A necessary evil, I suppose. We just about managed to conclude it before the curtain was called and the bar emptied.

By his own admission he knew little about opera and nothing about La Boheme. So walking from bar to box, I filled him in. I must admit that when I told him the story it didn't sound that great: a group of artists living in Paris, one of whom falls in love with a girl who then dies. There again most operas sound worse than they sound – if that makes sense!

The view from our perch was inspiring, in a civilised way. Slightly side-on to the stage, looking down to the orchestra pit, and above the murmuring, fanning crowd. And the performance, once it started, was magical.

Yet that non-contact distance remained. There were chances to touch: Rodolfo's accidental brush of Mimi's 'tiny frozen hand', the uplifting parade in the snow, the heart breaking denouement. Yet that gap remained. And apart from the lightest of touches on my shoulder, as he ushered me into the foyer, after final bows had been taken, still nothing.

Rain hadn't been forecast. There again, in life, plenty of things aren't, are they. Yet as we prepared to leave the main doors, thunder started to rumble and raindrops pitter-pattered outside. Suddenly, commotion – albeit a civilised, middle-class commotion. People in front were changing minds and turning back, people behind were buttoning up and pushing on. And we were caught right in the middle. With extendable brolly to the fore, we just went for it, and that was how it happened. Two people, one umbrella, clenched together. Almost a cliché.

We found a little restaurant nearby: wooden tables, waxy candles, rainy windows, and though the service was non-existent, the food ordinary and the wine awful, everything else was just wonderful. Everything else? Well, I suppose there was only one other thing. Our fingers did finally touch, and on the subject of clichés, it did seem as if we'd known each other forever. There again, we kind of had.

Finally, the question. Did I want to go back to his place for a coffee? It was a question so ridiculously loaded, we both almost laughed. You know, I honestly felt that he felt that I felt it was a question expected of him. I'm not convinced he was any more comfortable with it than I was. Either way, it was a no-no.

A second date and way too early. Anyway, I'd had no sex since my ex, and precious little then, come to think of it. So where was the hurry?

And if, on some future occasion, I did go back to his place, I'd be staying the night. Quickies, at my age, were out. In the meantime, Anna was at home, which meant I had to be too. After all, what would she think? Reversal of roles, eh? Me, worrying about Anna, worrying about me.

'No, I must be going,' I said, looking at my watch. 'Last train.'

He could have said something about getting a taxi. I'm sure his business had cab accounts. But he didn't, just said OK. Then squeezed my hand, asked for the bill, paid it, and we left.

Outside the restaurant, the rain had stopped. We no longer needed it. Arm-in-arm, we walked.

He saw me onto the train. It was late, he was concerned. Like I was some kind of kid. Silly really, he wasn't concerned yesterday, hardly even knew me. As it turned out, the train was pretty full. But I did get a seat, and closed my eyes … and felt contented.

When I reached Bromley, I texted him to say thanks and cabbed it home. He texted back, also said thanks, plus an XX

Anna was up and waiting. Again, role reversal. One proper date and I'd become a teenager! She asked loads of questions, of course. When I'd first told her about the date, her questions had been all jokey, but now she really was interested, which I found touching. After all, with this kind of stuff I was really going to need her seal of approval.

It didn't stop that whole guilt thing though. Date-wise, it should have been me asking the questions and Anna telling the story.

But what was creeping up on me was something slightly stronger than just guilt. It was worry. You see, having read the Evening Standard on the way up, then spent time thinking about it on the way back down, all the stuff they'd written about bloody doorsteps and bodies on paths had me thinking.

What about that odd supermarket incident? And what about that strange note that dropped through my letterbox? Was this indeed turning into a repeat performance of the Su A affair? After all, I'd had death threats on that one too. Was *'Don't make a bloody mistake,'* designed to warn me off? Could it somehow be related to Rose Denton's murder?

Probably none of the above were related, given that Paul Hutchinson's disappearance and Rose's murder weren't related either. But it still had me worrying.

Thank God I was off it now.

CHAPTER TWENTY

The following day Anna was up bright and early, leaving for London. My turn for slopping around. Once she'd gone, I got the house back in order, dressed and took my time getting to work: chatting to the woman next door, buying a local paper from the shop, and idling with the man who owned the pet shop downstairs from my office.

I didn't have too much on: catching up with emails, doing a bit of paperwork and, as for ongoing cases, looking into an incapacitated claimant who seemed to be able to paint his ceiling, and checking out an impoverished divorcee who somehow ran a Porsche. Yet my first phone call wasn't about any of that. It was on the case that just wouldn't go away.

Clearly in distress, Stephanie had read of the supposed connection between Rose Denton's murder and her husband's disappearance. Frankly, it was the last thing she needed. People who put bullets through people's heads are not the kind of characters you want your husband mixing with, even, or perhaps more so, with him being a missing person.

I calmed her down and then turned it into a positive. Well, sort of. Without doubt, I told her, the police would be putting more resources into his case now. Where murder is concerned, no stone would remain unturned, and they'd be looking for any links they could find. Personally, I didn't think they'd find any, but that wasn't the issue. The issue was getting to the bottom of Paul's disappearance. And that, the police would surely now do.

But as it turned out, this wasn't the only reason for her call.

After a bit of hesitation, she cleared her throat and said: 'And, er, Poppy rang.'

'Poppy?

'Yes. She told me there was nothing going on between her and Paul.'

'She said *what?* But you don't even know her, do you?'

'No, but she said she really had to clear his name on that score … and hers. Said she felt bad that anyone would think that of her.'

'What did you say?'

'I didn't quite know what to say. In fact, I think I said something stupid like *"Oh, er, thank you."* I mean, what are you expected to say? You don't expect a woman who's been having an affair with your husband to just ring up, do you?'

She was right, you don't. If there was one area I knew about, sadly, it was adultery. "Other" women ringing up out of the blue and apologising was rather out of character.

'Do you believe her?'

'Well yes, I think I do.'

I must admit that given what I'd just heard, perhaps I did too.

'Did she say anything else?'

'No, that's all. It was really strange. You know, awkward.'

I thought for a bit, trying to get into the mind of someone who'd ring up like that. She'd certainly have needed to psyche herself up first.

'Tell me, was this before or after the news about Rose Denton.'

'Before. The day before, in fact. Monday night.'

Again, I found myself thinking. Poppy rings up Stephanie, to tell her she's *not* having an affair with her husband. The very next day Rose Denton, Poppy's boss, is murdered. The other piece of this strange jigsaw is the fact that the very last place Paul was seen alive was the company where Poppy worked and Rose was boss. It all seemed connected, but how? Then another thought flashed through my mind.

'Did she ring you on your mobile?'

'Er, no, my landline.'

'Are you ex-directory?'

'Yes.'

I didn't take that thought any further. Didn't need to. Stephanie wasn't stupid. She'd probably have thought about it herself. Why would Poppy even *have* her husband's home number?'

I thanked Stephanie for ringing, told her not to worry about Rose's death, that I was sure it was unconnected, and asked her if she'd like me to ring Poppy one last time. She ummed and ahed about it, but then said yes, if I didn't mind, she would. So once we'd said goodbye, I got myself a coffee, readied myself and dialled.

'Hello Poppy, it's Pamela Andrews here …'

'Just leave me alone. I'm not interested.'

And that was that. Dead phone.

I tried a couple more times but it was switched off.

Like everything else in this saga, I just couldn't make a connection.

CHAPTER TWENTY-ONE

We met, again, at Charing Cross Station. But this time it seemed different. Different because it was Saturday, different because it was casual, and different because it was … well … different. The beginnings of previous liaisons had been tentative, cautious. That space between us thing. This time, no space. Just a smile, a hug, and a kiss.

The suburban trains that trundled into the station hadn't travelled far – fifty miles, tops – but to the people arriving behind us, feeding their tickets into the barriers, it must have looked as if we were long-lost lovers, separated by continents.

'The Parks,' was how Bernard had described the walk. From St James's: all ornamental and formal, to Green Park: cool and shady, to Hyde: open and breezy. Even fast paced, and we certainly weren't that, it would have taken two hours. We took all day, or what was left of it.

Waddling ducks, wagging dogs, weaving roller skaters – all of them, like us, enjoying the day. We bought overpriced ice creams, lunched on the Serpentine, and had tea, on the way back in Mayfair. On the way back? Mayfair isn't on the way back. Not to Charing Cross. It's on the way back to Soho … and Bernard's flat.

It wasn't put quite like that. 'Would you like to see where I work?' was his line. But in his case: work, rest and play. One place.

At street level and with window frontage, I suppose you could describe Bernard's work premises as shop-like. Certainly, they must have been retail at one stage. Locked up for the night, the large glass frontage shone brightly across the darkening pavement. Etched into it, almost barbershop-like, were the words: Simmonds Editing.

He unlocked the glass doors and we walked straight into the unfussy reception area. 'Welcome,' he said, holding up his arms, 'My world.' He then nodded towards one of the adjoining doors. 'The coal face,' he said.

We walked over to the door, pushed it open and switched on the lights. Similarly empty, similarly sparse, it contained just a desk, a keyboard, a screen and chair. 'Editing suite,' he said, then gesturing towards a big leather sofa behind us: 'And that's where we deposit our clients. Empty today, thank God.'

Although he had told me how different his company was to Effigy Post, this room, to me, looked remarkably similar to the one Aussie Sam had been sitting in.

We left the suite, walked back across the reception, through another door, down a white-walled corridor, taking us past toilets, a small kitchen and then up to another door. 'And this,' he said, 'is my other life.'

Using the same set of keys, he unlocked the door, pushed it open and switched the light on. Ahead of us, a rise of stairs. We took these to the top, he opened another door and in we went.

Bachelor pad. Spacious, neat, tidy. Walking through, I noted stripped flooring, a huge leather sofa, a contemporary glass table and two bean-baggy things. Not perhaps the sitting room of a fifty-something, but then again he seemed a young fifty-something – and this *was* Soho.

I wandered to the window and looked out. Evening was gathering over Soho: neon already pulsing, streets already clogging. Dead opposite, an oyster bar; to its left, a strip joint; to its right, a gay bar. What a place to live.

Turning back, I followed him across the lounge and into the kitchen.

Turning up the faders he revealed white worktops, a steel range, a juicer, a whisker and, big-to-small, utensils on the wall. Everything neat, everything tidy. But without, definitely, a woman's touch.

My mind went back to something he'd said when we were strolling through the park. I didn't quite get it at the time. 'You know,' he'd said, 'Perhaps everyone needs a little chaos in their lives from time to time.' Now I did get it. *'A little chaos? Maybe, Bernard, I'm your girl.'*

'Drink?' he asked.

'Thank you,' I replied. Well, I was going to need one (or two, or three) wasn't I? Rusty on the inside, flabby on the out, God help me, and perhaps forgive me, for what I'm about to do, *maybe*.

I was fully prepared: overnight undies, new toothbrush, deodorant and even condoms. And maybe, just maybe, I even wanted it. But could I go through with it?

'Look,' he said, whilst uncorking the wine. He was nodding towards a photo on the wall.

I walked over to it.

'Well, well, well. Our old class.'

Perhaps a strange choice for a kitchen, I thought. There again, I'm not a man, am I.

I scrutinised it. There was definitely something odd about it, but I couldn't quite work out what. I was certainly in it: front row, pigtailed, seated, third from the left. So was Bernard: back row, pudding-basined, dead centre. But like I said, something didn't quite work.

He handed me the wine. 'Cheers,' I said, taking a sip. It tasted good.

He came right up behind me and, hands on my shoulder, issued a challenge: 'Who can name the most, then?'

Unsurprisingly, one by one, I got most of the girls and, just as unsurprisingly, he got the boys. But at twelve all, racking our brains and running out of memory, he won with a tiebreak. 'Mrs Underwood,' he said, pointing his glass at a tall woman to our right. 'I've no idea why she's in the photo, she only took us for a few months.'

'Wonder why?' I asked.

'Maybe she just moved on.'

'Winner takes it all,' he said. Which was, in hindsight, a cheesy line.

He then turned, walked to the table, put his glass down, came back, took my head in his hands and looked at me. And I looked at him. Then he leaned forward put his arms around me and kissed me on the lips. With full wine glass still in my hand, I didn't quite know what to do. You know, I hadn't realised this before, but the position of your arms affects the performance of your lips. Arms out doesn't work.

'Just a second,' I said.

He realised, took my glass, turned and put it next to his on the table. He then came back and, with my hand as free as his, we kissed properly. Actually, my hand wasn't quite as free as his and he soon began to stray – first upward, then downward.

I can't deny, it felt good.

After a few seconds, I might have been a little breathless, but not speechless. And I wasn't going to have sex beneath Mrs Underwood.

Reading my mind, he whispered 'Bedroom?'

I didn't argue.

We did all the standard stuff: he leading, me kicking off shoes, us collapsing onto his bed. Then it was more kissing and more handiwork: not just his hands doing the work, but mine too. If I could have stood back and thought about it, I would have amazed myself. I was doing all the stuff I hadn't done for years. I suppose, like riding a bike, you don't forget.

After buttons and zips I realised my bag was in the other room.

'We'll need …' I breathed.

'I've got …' he said, turning over and reaching into to his bedside cabinet.

With his back to me and his head down in concentration, he fumbled under the sheets. If it hadn't been so downright funny, like a naughty boy piddling, it would've been a complete turnoff. Happy with his work, eventually, and with me stifling a laugh, he then rolled back over and started kissing me again. It's not easy kissing when you're giggling, but I just about managed it.

And then, I'm afraid, my phone rang. In my bag. In the other bloody room.

How could I best describe the stage we were at? Well, we were well past smoulder, but not yet aflame. At least, *I* wasn't.

'Leave it,' he whispered.

I sighed, took my fingers from his back, laid my arms by my side and, I suppose, desmouldered. And merely not answering the phone wasn't going to relight *my* fire.

It's different for men, I think. Their mechanism's far cruder. Like one of those huge switches you see in Frankenstein movies. Throw the lever and bingo, all the bits spring into life! Women, by comparison, are more complex – driven by funny little algorithms and complex formulae, and sometimes too complicated for their own good.

Bernard rolled off and sighed.

I heaved myself up, put on my blouse, pulled up my knickers, and got out of bed.

All this hasty re-clothing wasn't for the purposes of modesty. It was because my fleshy folds, in a horizontal position, don't look too bad. Standing up they do.

Of course, the phone had stopped ringing well before I'd put bare foot to contemporary carpet. So I padded to the lounge and fished out my phone. *'1 missed call. Anna.'*

I hit the call button, it rung twice, and Anna answered. She sounded breathless:

'Mum, have you seen the news?'

'No,'

'Paul Hutchinson. He's turned up.'

Seconds later, I was sitting on his sofa, with Bernard by my side, his laptop in front of me, and Anna in my ear. It was open at the main story on the BBC's webpage.

A man, his head covered, is flanked by two men in camouflage fatigues and black masks. The middle man, clearly a hostage, is wearing a soiled shirt and an old pair of suit trousers. The man to the left of him is holding a Kalashnikov and the man to the right, a viciously serrated commando knife. All three men are standing in front of a black banner with white wording on it – in either in Arabic or, possibly, Urdu. After a brief pause, the man with the gun barks out a few words. The man with the sword pulls the bag off the man's head.

Unshaven, blinking into the light: Paul Hutchinson.

CHAPTER TWENTY-TWO

'*Now* you know why we were telling you to drop it,' said Andy McCullough.

He was sitting on my sofa. Next to him was a rather expressionless, wax-faced man that he'd introduced to me simply as Mr Fisher.

'So you've known all along,' I said.

'No,' said Andy, shaking his head emphatically, 'but we had a few hunches.'

In front of us, deposited by Mr Fisher on my coffee table, was a black laptop.

He leaned forward, smoothed his hands across it, opened it carefully, perhaps creepily carefully, and entered a password. He then cued up the first frame of the clip that had been on the news, though not before I'd briefly noted an MOD crest, and hit play. The same ninety seconds of horrific action followed.

'What do they want?' I asked.

'Twenty million,' replied Mr Fish.

'Dollars?

'Pounds.'

The night before, sitting with Bernard we'd discussed it at length. Then, finally I'd dressed and left. It hardly needs stating that we never went back to bed.

Originally, I was going to stay for food – post-coital pasta, I believe. But in the end, like the passion, it never happened. So he'd just walked me back down to Charing Cross, we'd shared an unconvincing goodnight kiss, and I got the train home.

As soon as I'd got back, I switched on my computer and watched it all again. And again. And again. Then I phoned Anna.

Eventually, after going over and over it until we were both sick to death of it, I wished her a goodnight, of which there was little chance, and we went to bed.

Lying there that night, everything was mixed up in my head.

I'd completely misjudged the case. What had I said about the police? *Not just barking up the wrong tree, but running around the wrong forest.* Well, it was me doing the running around and the barking. They were dead right and I was dead wrong. But the other thing keeping me awake, somehow all mixed up together, was the whole Bernard thing. Maybe Anna's call had been a good thing: a rude, or perhaps not so rude, awakening. Did I really want all that at my age?

I must have eventually nodded off because I had this dream. It was sort of connected to that old school photo on Bernard's wall. Except it wasn't a photo, it was a video. We were all in a line, jostling, laughing. All in black-and-white, getting ready for the photo to be taken. But then I noticed Mrs Underwood. She wasn't moving. She was standing behind us. Decapitated.

I'd awoken with a jolt. Sweating. Then I'd turned over, thought for a while, and turned back.

You know, I could still smell him. Bernard. Even back home in my own bed, even hours later.

I looked at my bedside clock: 3:33. Fluorescent numbers, burning into the blackness. I closed my eyes and turned back over. Purple neons, swimming like jellyfish, slowly faded away.

Back in my own darkness, with curtains softly breathing, it was all just a dream. But Paul Hutchinson wasn't. He was real. A genuine, living nightmare.

'Are you OK, Pamela?' asked Andy, bringing me back to the here and now.

'Oh yes, sorry. I was just thinking.'

'About?'

'This case, I suppose.'

'That's why we're here. To share your thoughts: every single detail, everywhere you went, everyone you met. Particularly in Karachi.'

And that's exactly what I did. From the meetings with Tariq Ashkani, the hotel manager, to my discussions with Asif Farooki, the bank's CEO, and from Superintendent Sharma to Commissioner Martin Hague.

'Do you know where this place is?' I asked.

'Yes, about two miles from the airport. You can even hear a plane taking off if you listen carefully.'

'So near the hotel, too?'

'Between the two, roughly.'

'Why do you think they filmed it there? In the open, I mean?'

Andy smiled. I could second-guess them, but he knew the way my mind worked too. You see, the image in front of us, to the experienced eye, posed a few questions. Why film up against an outside wall of some kind of derelict shed? To the bottom of the frame was scrubby wasteland, to the top, a corrugated roof. But more to the point, to the extreme left and right, on the very edges of frame, distant traffic was flashing past.

'Because they could,' he said. 'It's a statement – showing just how much in control they are. Also, moving around makes them more difficult to track down. That's probably the reason we've drawn a blank so far.'

I begged to differ. The reason they'd drawn a blank so far was because they'd spent their time following me in London, rather than these guys in Pakistan. I didn't say that, of course.

'So is it about money, or politics, or both?'

'What's the difference,' he shrugged. 'Profits, prophets?'

'Okay,' I asked, addressing Fisher. 'So why follow me?'

'Why not?' he replied.

I suppose the whole point of having a blank face is that you can't read it. If anything, it was Andy giving the game away – looking the more uncomfortable. Did he even *know* his colleague had been tailing me? It seemed not.

'Because,' I said, 'Given what we now know you would've been better concentrating your efforts on Karachi.'

'But we didn't know that then, did we? We had reasons to believe he was mixed up in terrorism, but we also had no access to Pakistan. You'd just come back from Karachi, visiting the people and places he'd visited. So like I said, why wouldn't we?'

I left it at that. I'd gained the tiniest new piece of information. *'Mixed up in terrorism'* he'd said. Not just a hapless victim. It went against everything I'd been told. Nobody had been able to come up with a reason why he'd just disappeared, less still that he'd been 'mixed up' in anything. Now it seemed it was always there: being considered as a strong possibility. The only other thing I discovered related to the kidnappers. Apparently the video wasn't originally emailed, but dropped off anonymously, as a tape, at the offices of *The Karachi Mail.* So these guys hadn't been stupid enough to leave any kind of electronic trail.

After they'd left, I rang Anna. I wanted to warn her that she might get a visit too. On the other hand, she might not. I'd been to Karachi, she hadn't. If anything, it would be poor Stephanie who'd be getting the pleasure of their company. Mind you, that might be no bad thing. She'd need to keep herself busy. And on that very subject, within minutes of them leaving, she was on the line.

'Hi, Steph,' I said. 'I was just thinking about you.'

'Thanks,' she said.

'You're not by yourself, are you?' I asked.

'No, no' she said. 'I've got a police woman here with me. Valerie, really nice, really helpful.'

Stephanie then told me about how having someone else around the house was helping her through it, but from the sound of her voice, she was clearly very distraught, only just keeping the tears at bay.

'So where's Valerie now?' I asked.

'She's had to go off for a meeting. I'm sure she's got lots else to do.'

I'd like to have said, yes, I'm sure she has. But her main job is being with you, the victim.

'Look, Stephanie, would you like me to come down?'

'Well …' she said. Then, after a long pause, she said: 'It's just …'

I knew exactly what it was *just.* After all, I'd been there. It was *just* hell on earth: being the first item in every news bulletin, having the world's press on your doorstep, desperately wanting the phone to ring with news – but dreading it as well.

'No problem,' I said. 'I'll come down tomorrow.'

CHAPTER TWENTY-THREE

Tired of traffic jams, paperwork to catch up on, I decided to travel to Stephanie's by train. You see, in the amazing world in which I now find myself, I can use my nifty little laptop to complete and send reports, and my niftier little smartphone to attach photos. All of which has been taught to me by my even niftier, even smarter, Anna.

And you know, smart phones might have been designed with detectives in mind. Not just the calls, but the GPS and the in-built camera. OK, you sometimes need big bulky SLR for telephoto work, but if you're in a shopping mall or a suburban street, you can't beat a mobile. Everyone uses them, so no suspicions.

Of the two cases I needed to write up on, I had some perfect shots of the first: a man with an industrially damaged back giving his daughter a flying angel, and a great clip of the second: a penniless father picking up a blonde woman in a silver Porsche.

But although my 21st Century technology was up to it, the 19th Century transport system seemingly wasn't. On a baking hot day, with no air conditioning, the first leg of my journey dawdled its way up through a dusty, rusty South London, in humid haze of sepia sun. Frankly, I could've been back in Karachi. Then a change of trains at London Bridge, and back down again, forking west through a melting Croydon and into a sweltering Surrey. By the time

I reached Brighton I was finished, work-wise, energy-wise, though the taxi, at least, was bearable. Mind you, by then it was late afternoon.

I'd already phoned ahead. Victim support, unsurprisingly, was long gone. In a way, this may be no bad thing. I had a couple of things I wanted to sort out. Things that could be better done without police presence.

First up was the press. I'd already made up my mind about how I'd deal with them, before, hopefully, even setting foot in Stephanie's door. And with this plan in mind I asked the cabbie to drop me off at the end of her road. The last bit, I'd do on foot.

There they were, miserably camped outside Stephanie's Regency railings, kicking their heels, chewing on gum, dragging at fag butts, and generally looking bored.

I immediately recognised one of them, a persistent, Gollum-like creature called Eddie, from my own brush with the tabloids some two years earlier.

'Hi,' I said.

He turned, saw me and his face lit up. Most of the others weren't immediately sure who I was, but it didn't stop them defaulting into instant, click-and-take mode: film first, think later.

'*Pam*ela!' he said, 'What brings you here?'

'You lot,' I replied.

Suddenly, a scoop. Not only hostages, terrorism and shootings, but now a (briefly) famous detective who'd worked on a well-known missing girl case. At this rate they'll be able to cover an entire edition with one story.

'Shortly,' I said, 'I'm going to stand on that doorstep with Stephanie Hutchinson. You can take all the photos, and write all the words you want. Then we're going in the house and you lot are going home.'

None of them said anything. They didn't have to. Their looks did the talking: *'Like hell we are!'*

'OK,' I said, pulling out my phone and holding it up: 'Before I go in I've got an announcement to make. You may recall that the Su A case was one of a number that were looked into at the time by Lord Justice Finlayson: harassment, phone tapping, invasion of privacy. Some of your friends lost their jobs over what he uncovered. Now, on this phone I have his number.' This, of course, was a complete lie.

'It's up to you, but if you take down my address, every day you'll get an email. In it will be a quote from Stephanie. I can't guarantee it'll be earth shattering: something about how she's missing Paul, probably, but it'll sell papers. We'll also send photos. Again, nothing special, just snapshots. Now, I said everyone gets these mails, but that's not strictly true. Anyone of you seen outside this house won't. All you'll receive is a summons. Got it?'

With that, they all fished out their grubby little notebooks and took down my address. Carrot and stick. Works every time.

'Now,' I said, pushing through them, 'Stephanie's going to answer the door, you're going to take your pictures, then you're going to leave us in peace.'

And that, pretty much, is what happened, with their photo opportunity being all the more dramatic for Stephanie – almost breaking down when she saw me and burying her head into my shoulder.

We then went inside, she offered me a tea, which I accepted, and we sat down together, stirred, sipped and talked. More than anything else, talking was what she needed. And more than anything else, talking is what I *do*.

She did have a mother and a brother to confide in, but mothers fuss, and in her case she clearly wasn't that close. As for brothers, they do have broader shoulders, but not for crying on. Anyway, he was in Australia and wouldn't be over until the end of the week. And the point is, very few people have been through what she was going through. I just so happened that I was one of those very few.

At times she just wanted to talk about the past. At other times she wanted to talk about the future: the worries and the 'what ifs.' I just listened, didn't offer false hope, but did stay positive.

A few things became clearer to me too. The bank, it now appeared, had received prior threats about all this. Just how explicit these had been, whether they'd actually specified an employee being kidnapped, wasn't clear. But what was becoming clearer, was that this was why the police, from the beginning, thought it was terrorism. It's just a shame they hadn't told us a bit earlier too. Either way, that vague threat was now a grim reality. Using the same coded password as before, the kidnappers had now turned their threats into figures: twenty million dollars. That was the price they were putting on Paul's head.

Clearly these people weren't stupid. They knew the British government wouldn't pay up. The Brits just don't do deals with kidnappers. Neither, in this case, would the Pakistanis. Why would they pay up for one Englishman when they suffer multiple atrocities all the time? But the bank? That might be different.

Twenty million dollars, to them, was peanuts. So they might just consider coughing up, even if it was via the back door. And the bank, more than anyone, was who we needed to appeal to. That's the way I saw it anyway.

And with this in mind, once I played a combination of big sister, agony aunt and shoulder to cry on, I suggested that at some time during the week, we should make contact with Asif Farooki. The Met would be listening in, off course, as would MI5, GCHQ, Interpol, Uncle Tom Cobley and all. But so what? Yes, I'd said I'd stay out of it, but that was then, this was now. Neither governments would be negotiating with them, so that just left me, us. All I cared about was Stephanie: giving her support, giving her a few crumbs of hope, keeping her in the loop. In a way, it was like the emails to the press: keep her busy, do something constructive, make her feel we were getting somewhere.

So on the Thursday afternoon, after we'd pinged off the latest email, we Skyped him. And after much delay and interference, possibly caused by MI5's snooping, his image finally blinked up.

He was the very picture of sympathy: sombre suit, dark tie, pudgy fingers forming a steeple in front of him. Clearly he'd prepared for this part, but that was fair enough. He didn't even have to do it. He could easily have fobbed us off with some excuses about it being a police matter now.

'Let me start,' he said, with brow knitted, 'By saying that all of us here at the bank have the greatest of sympathy for your predicament, Mrs Hutchinson. We'll do everything we can to help.'

'Does that mean you might be prepared to …?' asked Stephanie, rather cutting to the chase and perhaps asking him the one question he really couldn't answer.

'Well,' he said, taking a few seconds to consider his response: 'Like I said, we'll do everything we can. There are many issues to consider here. But the main thing you need to know is that we're on your side. We feel very responsible – and take our employees welfare very seriously.'

He was hinting, heavily, that the bank might indeed pay up. What I didn't tell Stephanie was that this could well all be a giant bluff. Could, for instance, MI5 be using Farooki just to slow things down, to buy some time? Then there were the Pakistani authorities. Could they be pulling the strings, instructing the bank to go through the motions just to flush out the kidnappers, before a full-blooded attack?

And if that meant wiping out Paul along the way, so be it. The CIA would be listening in too and they *didn't* take hostages. This was international terrorism, for god sake.

As the video conference progressed I found myself considering all these and many other issues. The video we were now making would be dissected by dozens of countries – from Israel to Russia, from Syria to China. And should any of them feel they could benefit by it, they'd leak the pictures to whomever they saw fit – from ISIS to Al Qaeda, BBC to Al Jazeera. Conversely, they may all just sit tight, altering their strategy as they went along, seizing opportunities as they arose.

Of course, I kept all this from Stephanie. If all she wanted to hear were positives, then that's what she'd hear. Anything that got her through the night.

We only spent about fifteen minutes on the call – with Asif, almost politician-style, signing off with a rather over sincere: 'I promise, Stephanie, I'll do everything within my power to bring this episode to a satisfactory conclusion.' We then offered thanks, he offered sympathy, and the screen went blank.

We both sat there for a few seconds and then I gave her a hug. I'm not sure if it was a hug of hope or hopelessness. I suppose it was just a hug.

I suggested we eat something. So we went to the kitchen, prepared some food and talked. Then we sat down and ate. In all the time I'd been with her recently, it was the first time I'd seen her actually eat anything. Then we sat on the sofa, drank a glass of wine and talked more – slowly but surely moving off the case. It was also the first time she'd talked about anything other than Paul. Eventually she nodded off. Her first sleep, too.

Friday morning, time to leave. Her brother had already touched down and would be arriving in a few hours – she'd be in good hands.

Standing at her front porch, a taxi ticking at her railings, I felt I'd done a decent job. In fact, in many ways, I'd made a better fist of victim support than I had of investigation. Certainly, she was in better shape than when I'd arrived.

I told her to keep sending me the updates, which I, in turn, would forward to the press. They were proving to be useful on two counts. Firstly, you simply can't have too many articles and photos where missing people are concerned. The public's eye is both voracious and all-seeing. But it wasn't just the exposure thing, it was the therapeutic thing too. For Stephanie, effectively, they were daily diaries: keeping her busy, keeping her sane.

We kissed goodbye, just as we'd kissed hello, but minus the paparazzi at her gate. I got into the cab, waved and we turned left and made our way along Brighton's rather blousy seafront.

Getting comfortable, I found myself thinking. You see, there were still things that just didn't add up about this case. The murder of Rose Denton for a start.

Since when did Islamic militants, or even plain old what-it-says-on-the-tin kidnappers, employ contract killers? And if they do, why? What did the MD of a media company have to do with it? Of course, that could just be a coincidence. The trouble is, I tend not to believe in coincidences. I'm a detective.

So what did we actually have here? A married man shares a hotel room with a girl. This happens a long, long way from home. The girl insists there's no affair. The same man has a meeting 'closer to home' back in London. This meeting turns out to be at exactly the same company that the girl works in. It all turns nasty and legal threats are made. The man completely disappears. The girl's boss, who wasn't even present in the meeting, is then mercilessly gunned down in a London street. Finally, a long, long way from home again, the man reappears. This time as a kidnap victim.

All unconnected? It seemed that way.

CHAPTER TWENTY-FOUR

Over the next couple of days I kept in touch with the news, remained in contact with Stephanie, yet nothing. That could be good or bad. We all wanted Paul's release, but given previous such cases, were quite happy to do without a follow up video. So no news, in a way, was good news. But the waiting, in some kidnaps cases, can go on for years. For those in wait it is debilitating in the extreme. Even I was finding it difficult, so God only knows how Stephanie was coping.

By Tuesday, I'd had enough. Suffocating suburbia, claustrophobic weather. I needed to get out and go somewhere. I needed hustle and bustle, I needed life.

Anna and London, would come to my rescue. So I phoned her up, and she said yes, of course she'd love me to pay for lunch!

Before I even got there, I got what I was after. The distraction of people. You know, it was over twenty-five years since I'd regularly commuted to London, and in that time almost everything had changed. Back then, train doors would slam rather than slide, staff would smile rather than scowl, and commuters could smoke but couldn't phone. But probably the biggest change was illustrated by the girl sitting opposite me. She was pretty normal really: skirt, blouse and cardigan, just as I had been a quarter of a century earlier. But I didn't have a tattoo on my wrist and a stud in my nose; I didn't pay for water, a bottle of which she swigged from, but *did* pay for a newspaper, a copy of which she was browsing. Most of all, I didn't plug myself into one form of media whilst reading another and watching a third.

At London Bridge, she got off, leaving her *Metro* on the seat. I reached over and picked it up. Although it wasn't the main news, turning a couple of pages, it was still *in* the news. There they were. Paul and Stephanie: on holiday, in happier times. Accompanying this picture, in big bold letters, was *Steph's Agony*. I hated it, but knew from bitter experience that the oxygen of publicity was better than the suffocation of silence.

I left Charing Cross thinking about Stephanie's situation, but, on entering Soho, soon started thinking about mine. There was the street corner where I'd had a surprise encounter with an old school friend. There the café where I'd stood in the rain outside, but time had stood still on the inside. There was the little restaurant where we'd both touched hands, but I'd felt guilty. And finally, there was Bernard's place, where I'd lost all inhibitions but, found only, well, regret. Fifty shades of it! Even the name of the café Anna had suggested we meet up in, Café Boheme, was an aide-mémoire to my little non-affair.

I got there first, finding myself an al fresco seat in Old Compton Street. It was a warm day and the world was walking by: dress-to-impress gays, in-a-hurry businessmen, take-your-time tourists.

Anna turned up a little late, something she'd successfully achieved since the moment she left my womb. She looked wonderful, though. Which, thinking back all those years, was ditto.

She hadn't made much of an effort on the clothes front – sloppy top, skin-tight jeans, sunglasses on head – she didn't seem to need to in her job. Mind you, at her age, anything looks good: dress down, dress up, it didn't seem to matter. At my age it's the opposite.

We kissed, we sat, we talked. About the case, to start with. It was on everybody else's lips and minds, so it was always going to be on ours. But unlike my internalised agonising, our talking actually helped.

She told me all the things I should've been telling myself: yes the situation was dreadful, but in my line of work, all clients' problems are. That's why they call me. If I didn't like it I shouldn't be doing it. And as our food arrived: simple, snacky, croque monsieur and fries, she advised me not to get so emotionally involved. Client's problems, she said, not mine. Again, complete role reversal, and advice I'd given to many a young cop in my time.

But for all the fact that her advice was obvious, it worked. Sitting in the Soho sunshine, I felt the weight of the world lifting from my shoulders. Mind you, the chilled pinot might have been a factor too. It was all just perfect.

Anna did tell me one thing I found quite strange though. Apparently Poppy Foster had rung her too. She hadn't said why she was ringing, but did sound pretty stressed. Anna tried to find out what the problem was, even suggested meeting up again, but Poppy seemed to change her mind. Just clammed up and put the phone down.

'So you've no idea what it was about?'

'No.'

'Did you try to ring her back?'

'Yes, but it wasn't her normal number – it was withheld.'

I was thinking deeply about this, dabbing a couple of crumbs off my plate, when my own phone rang: *Bernard.*

Keeping it brief, I just said 'Hi.' This was followed by one 'yes,' two 'mms,' and an 'I'll think about it.'

In the meantime, from his end, all I got was the unsure sound of prevarication. But if you cut the crap, basically, he was asking me out again.

Amazingly, Anna, a table width away, guessed. Furthermore, from my few mumbles, managed to pick up that I was turning him down.

'So you're not going to see him again, then?' she said, after I put my mobile down.

There was no point in pretending. She could read me like a book, or perhaps, in her case, a Kindle. So I exhaled, sighed and simply said: 'No.'

'Why?' she replied.

Now that was a very good question indeed. After all, he was my age, good company, decent looking and, though it shouldn't be a factor, he wasn't poor either. What was there to not like?

'Oh I don't know,' I said 'Perhaps I'm not …'

Perhaps I'm not what? Now believe it or not, I was about to say that I wasn't ready. Not ready! For what! At my age, if I wasn't ready now, when would I be? When I'm in a bath chair, I suppose.

'It's not because of me, is it?' she asked, eyeing me over her shades – and hitting the nail, bang on the head.

'No, no.' I replied, perhaps a little too hastily. 'I mean, why would it be because of you?'

'Oh I just wondered, you know, if you felt you shouldn't be going out with a man just because I wasn't.'

'God no,' I laughed. 'Anyway, I haven't definitely made my mind up yet. I er … told him I'd think about it.'

And that was pretty much that. I did say something about not wanting all the hassle, which had an element of truth in it. Also, in a way, I suppose I was saying I didn't fancy him. But that wasn't really true, was it. Anyway, we then moved onto other bits and pieces, time flew by and our lovely lunch was soon over.

Walking back over Leicester Square I decided to go for it. I pulled out my phone, dialled, waited for him to answer and simply said: 'Yes, Bernard. Friday would be great!'

CHAPTER TWENTY-FIVE

This time, even more than last time, I was worrying about what to wear. The opera may be posh, but at least it's fairly quantifiable, dress-code wise. As for our weekend walk, that had been casual. So what would a Soho member's club be like? I didn't have Anna as wardrobe consultant, but did at least ask her. 'Some people put on a bit of a show, I suppose,' she'd shrugged, 'some just chill.' So there I had it: show or chill. Both sounded worryingly young.

I kicked off with a Top Shop stretchy jeans and sparkly top combination. Nope, too flashy. Anyway, sideways to the mirror it looked as if they'd come from Bottom Shop. So I tried my little black Monsoon number. It was alright, but at my age, was it just a little too little? Finally, I settled for wafty slacks, a lemony top and a pashmina over my shoulder. If that all sounds a bit Marks & Spencer, it was. But safe. Also, if I positioned the shawl carefully, it covered the tops of my arms. Floppy trousers I can live with. Everything else should be unfloppy.

Bernard picked me up at Charing Cross. He wore smart jeans and a check shirt, which was nice. Almost as Marks & Spencer as me. But you know what? Despite the fact we matched wardrobe-wise, that barrier was back. And I don't mean the one that snatches the tickets.

Our kisses were mere pecks, our steps tentative. We seemed separate again, awkward again. But I suppose if that gap was back, a least it was a known gap. One we'd bridged before, and perhaps, one we could bridge again.

Soho, as we walked up through it, was preparing for Friday night: workers leaving, partygoers arriving, steady drinkers staying. We walked up through Chinatown, with its steamy windows and flattened ducks, across Compton, with its stumbling drunks, along Greek, with its tables, chairs, bars and beers – and on to our Soho Square destination.

The Square House was a beautiful place for beautiful people. In the middle of a row of Georgian houses, it may have been square dimension-wise, but it certainly wasn't going to be attitude-wise.

Ahead of us, as we walked towards its door, were a group I was hoping, absolutely praying, weren't going into the same establishment (they did). Boys in pencil jeans, girls in clingy nothings. So there's me in wafty and floaty and there's this lot, apart from being 25 years younger, dressed as snakes. To say I felt intimidated by what I might find behind that door would be an understatement. I was petrified. What are you doing to me, Bernard?

He stood back and, ever the gentleman, let me enter first. For once, I'd have gone for a non-gentleman, allowing me to turn and run. With the door half ajar, for the benefit of the teenagers ahead, I breathed in, as if that somehow made a difference, and went for it.

First impressions: not as bad as I'd expected. Oak-panelled entrance hall, old-fashioned reception desk, pretty-boy receptionist.

There was even a group of oldies, standing at the desk. I say oldies, but the women were still ten years my junior and the men, though my age, were wearing a selection of inappropriately young suits. One tight-fitting and narrowlapelled, the other sagging like an elephant's crutch. Oh well, at least it was droopy and floaty, I suppose.

We squiggled signatures in the reassuringly leather-bound visitors' book: me as a guest, Bernard as a member, and gave in coats. And I made straight for the sanctuary of the Ladies. Once inside, I was pleased to find no adolescents preparing for dressing-up parties, no teens in tears, and no cackling coke heads. In fact, blissfully, no one. I made straight for the mirror.

Over the years, I've used toilets to *com*pose more than *dis*pose. Sanctuary rather than sanitary. And looking at my reflection, as I composed, how did I look? Old. On the other hand, I looked me. And me was all I could ever be. All anyone was ever going to get.

So final repairs done, I pushed the door open and left my refuge. Time for trial-by-twenty-somethings.

My heart sank again. Bernard was talking to a tall, pencil-slim girl wearing a skirt the size of a hair band. 'This is Betsy' he said, as I walked up.

'Hi,' I said, as she flicked a look. I'm surprised she even bothered. Next to her I was invisible.

'She's going to show us to our table,' said Bernard.

I didn't know we even had a table. She walked ahead of us, mounting some creaky stairs, and from where I stood, or perhaps climbed, she was showing us more than a table. The soles of her stilettos and the derriere of her knickers were a perfect, vermillion match.

She escorted us through rooms that adjoined other rooms and stairs that met other stairs. Everywhere we went it was buzzing: drinkers and talkers, pissheads and posers. Some looked vaguely familiar, most, didn't. Yes, it was Soho: scruffy, yet smart. And yes it was louche. But not quite the seedy side I'd known. Less shame, more show. More money, too.

As we continued, some rooms had crappy old furnishings and tarnished mirrors: the kind of stuff I threw out years ago. Some were modern and bright: bleached wood bars, chrome stools. And one was even set somewhere between brothel and boudoir: dusty pinks and gold chintz. This, being Soho, was no doubt an attempt at irony.

Each area threw up the unexpected: a piano in one, an old skeleton in another, the kind of jumbled mishmash I'd love to have had parties in when I was young, but could never have afforded.

And on the subject of the unexpected, suddenly we were outside. A rooftop terrace, warm night, glittering people, tinkling conversation.

Despite the showiness of it all, not everyone was flashily dressed. Thank God. I was now really relieved I didn't try to compete. Yes, there's twenty-somethings in look-at-me leggings and sparkly vest tops, or camouflage combats and painful piercings. But there were summer frocks and sensible skirts too. I even spotted another pashmina!

Betsy pointed to our table, or perhaps *pouted* to our table, said 'Ciao,' and left us.

We picked our way through the throng, with Bernard shaking hands here and there. I even noticed an actress from 'Enders and had to fight the urge to ask for an autograph: presumably not the done thing hereabouts. But finally, glad-handing completed, we arrive in our spot.

Perfect: Balcony's-edge, stunning view. We were not especially high up: just three or four floors, but with the lights of Soho Square twinkling through the canopy of the trees, it was truly magical.

Before sitting, we paused and looked out. You know, despite the hubbub, I actually heard birdsong. Not a nightingale singing in Berkley Square, maybe, but close enough, and beautiful enough to be anywhere.

I don't think I was expecting waiter service, but we got it. A handsome boy in a navy apron, white shirt and black plimsolls: the elasticised type I hated at PE, somehow managing to buzz back and forth with perfect timing.

We briefly touched on the Paul Hutchinson affair, but only briefly. Frankly, I'd definitely had enough of it, he'd probably had enough of it too, and, being a Friday, the world outside had had enough of everything.

Drinks were poured, canapés brought, and conversation flowed – and slowly all my fears, including my wardrobe worries, were melting away.

We started on a sombre note – the whole Hutchinson Denton thing – but soon moved on: places we'd been, people we'd known. Mine revolved mainly around the Met, Bernard's around advertising.

The thing about men, for me, is that they must be amusingly amusing, *or* seriously serious. What I mean, is I could never get involved with a man who wasn't funny, but thought he was. Or didn't have the answers, but thought he did. Amusing is good, serious is fine too, but trying too hard to be either is a no-no. Bernard, I felt, found the right balance.

I told him some stories about my policing past: Christmas snogging in the cells, bums-on-photocopiers, that type of stuff. But if I'm truthful, I didn't think they were that funny. Mind you, he certainly laughed. But then he came up with a story that topped the lot.

Men, I think, are good at anecdotes. It's something to do with claiming territory, corralling up the group. And being able to spin a yarn demonstrates the yin and yang of maleness too, because they're bloody good at lying as well.

I suppose the other reason the story worked was that it was set at night on the Riviera, and we were sitting at our table, in a similarly dreamy setting. I must add at this point that, given my little secret I also felt it opened up the slightest of opportunities, but more of that later. Oh, and the drinks helped too.

'It's all about a put-down line,' he said, picking up his glass. 'Probably the best one-liner I've ever heard a girl give.'

He then took a sip and continued: 'You see, every June, I'm lucky enough to go to the Cannes Film Festival. The advertising one, that is, less glamorous, but more fun.'

'Sounds terrific,' I said.

'Oh it is, believe me. About ten years ago, I was down there with Cynthia, she used to come down for a few weeks too.' Cynthia was his ex, and the resigned little shrug he gave suggested he didn't really want to talk about that aspect of his life, so I just let him continue with his story.

'One evening we were invited to this glitzy do, but Cynthia wasn't really feeling up to it. She used to get fed up with all the shop talk. I couldn't really blame her, she only really went down for the sunbathing and stuff. Anyway, this particular evening I was walking along La Croisette, that's the posh promenade there, and I had one of our assistants with me. She's a girl called Ella, and as I say, Cynthia was back at the villa …'

'Oh, yeah,' I said, suspiciously.

'It wasn't like that. Ella had been invited down there by one of our clients. That's the way it works, a sort of thank you for all the hard work you've put in for them over the year. Now Ella's a pretty girl, bright too – you know: very sharp. So we're walking to this function, past all the big hotels: Carlton, Majestic – I'm in a tuxedo and she's wearing something slinky. Now back then, I was in my mid-forties and Ella would have been mid-twenties. So there was a big age gap. So we're walking past a group of very drunk lads sitting at a bar – that's not unusual, most

delegates down there get absolutely plastered, especially the young ones. They obviously weren't going to a function or anything because they were just wearing shorts and T shirts and stuff. Anyway, just as we walked past, one of them shouted over to Ella, and asked if she fancied a drink. That's already a little insulting – to me more than her because you don't offer drinks to a girl who's already got a partner, do you?'

'No,' I agreed. I'd like to have added you simply don't shout across the street to a girl, period. But I let him carry on.

'Then one of the boys shouted something about giving her more than just a drink, which drew howls of laughter from his mates. Ella just stopped, turned, and gave him this look. Then this lad pushed his luck even further. Sitting amongst his mates with his legs apart, you know, the way boys do, he used his lager glass to point to his groin *"Nah, tell yer what, luv"* he said *"Why don't yer sit on me lap?"* More laughs from his mates, but Ella just glared at him. I tried to get her to move on – beginning to sense trouble – but she was having none of it. *'Just fuck off,'* she said and turned to go. Of course, they all jeered even more. But one lad *really* pushed his luck: *"Nah,"* he said, *"Never mind me lap. How about me face?"* Cue huge howls of laughter all round. So Ella stopped dead, turned, and with utter composure, replied: *"Sit on your face? Sit on your bloody face? Why, is your nose longer than your dick?"* Like I said, just about the best put-down line I've ever heard. And one big guy was made to look very small indeed.'

I wanted the night to go on forever, but of course it couldn't. And at the point in the evening, when he looked at his watch and said: 'I suppose we should leave,' I hadn't even thought about the time. Or the 11:58 from Charing Cross.

'You can get a cab from my place,' he said.

Of course I could. It made absolute sense. I mean, why wander around London looking for expensive black cabs when his business has a safe, tried-and-tested cab account?

'Fine,' I said.

He paid the bill and we fought our way downstairs. The place, by now, was really rocking. Jostled and squeezed, pushed and shoved, we had to battle every inch of the way.

Every so often Bernard would meet someone he knew and there'd follow some confined-space air kissing or nose-to-nose back slapping. It was all an act, of course, but given the raised eyebrows he was offering me between bouts, at least it was an act he was aware of.

At one point, a young guy with skin tight jeans and a pork pie hat called out: 'Hey, Bern,' offering a ridiculous double-barrelled six-gun greeting. Bernard didn't return the fire. He just replied with a 'Hi, Jasper,' and gave me a look suggesting that replying with real bullets would have been preferable. But all industries have bullshit, and this was no better or worse than the police.

On reaching the reception, we handed in our tickets, and I made straight for the ladies.

It had turned into the kind of hormone hell I was dreading earlier. Mind you, by now, everyone was so pissed it didn't really matter.

Having waited for ages for a cubicle: one of the girls in front was wearing Lycra cycle shorts under a chiffon ra ra, which must have taken some pulling down and peeling off, I claimed one, peed, came out, completely gave up on the mirror / basin front, and buffeted my way back out again.

We left the club and, arm-in-arm, walked around the now less tranquil square: no birdsong, just distant drunks, and were soon back amongst the neon and the noise of Old Compton. We pushed through crowds, cut through alleys, and found ourselves in Brewer Street, from which Bernard's is just a short stroll.

On reaching his office, he unlocked the door, pushed through ahead of me, upped the dimmers and ushered me in. Now, if we were getting a cab, why not use the reception phone? But we weren't getting a cab, were we?

Through the reception, down the corridor which leads to his flat, key into door, push open, up the stairs, into flat.

Coats off – no coffee, no questions – into bedroom, fall on bed. Kisses long, deep and alcoholic. I pulled myself away, already breathless.

'Give me a second,' I said, leaving him, fingertips last.

I padded to the bathroom, unzipping as I went, closed the door, switched on the light, stood at the mirror and dropped my clothes – or most of them. My little secret. Not so much Pamela's, as Victoria's, High Street, Bromley (Moulin Rouge Collection).

Looking back was a different me. And you know, in many ways that's who it was for: me.

You see, I'd thought about it a lot. Well, I would, wouldn't I? And somehow I felt the outfit could make it easier. I'm not exactly sure why. Maybe it's something to do with deflecting the reality of it all. There again, maybe it was simply to do with covering up a flabby tummy! Either way, not so much Dutch courage, as Basque – although I'd certainly covered the booze angle too.

I slinky-slunk back – at least, I imagine I slinky-slunked – and pushed the door open. And stood before him. He was in bed. Silent. Only a sheet covered the lower part of his body. Yes, it would appear my outfit did indeed please him.

He looked at me: a tiny smile.

In exaggerated cockney, he softly said: 'Over 'ere darling – why don't cha …'

'Why?' I asked, taking two steps forward, 'Is your nose bigger than your ...'

I reached forward and slowly pulled the sheet back.

'*Oh,* Mr *Sim*monds,' I said, in mock disbelief, '*Clear*ly not.'

Still surprising myself, never mind him, I climbed on top of him. This time there'd be no pulling out, so to speak.

Girls on top, woman in pleasure.

HRT, now *that's* the real secret.

CHAPTER TWENTY-SIX

Over the next few weeks I became Bernard's Soho whore. Or perhaps, in newspeak, his milf. Many positions, same location. And I loved it.

As the mild astonishment wore off – I was no longer surprised that I was prepared to expose the bits I did, and that he even found them sexy – I simply became comfortable with it, with him, with me. A shared hobby, I suppose, where all the bits fitted together and complemented each other perfectly.

The sessions, always after business hours, were arranged around his work, rather than mine. I had the time, he didn't. You see, I didn't have much on (I'm talking work here) during those summer weeks – apart from boring old office stuff – so in a straight contest between filing and, well, that other 'f'-ing, it was no contest at all.

But it certainly wasn't just the sex. It was the buzz and the booze, the neon and the nights: pubs full of drunks, people full of crap, all mixed up with ordinary, out-for-a-bite suburban couples. Within a short walking distance I had the shopping of Oxford, Regent and Bond Streets, the restaurants of Mayfair and Soho, the street theatre of Covent Garden, and people-watching everywhere. Not just walkable, but wonderful. So a typical West End afternoon and evening would go: shopping and sex and pubs and food (mix and match accordingly) compared to my suburban world of sales ledgers, slippers and beans on toast. Which would you choose?

And all the time, that picture, that photo. Sometimes, with Bernard editing away downstairs, I'd put down my magazine and just look at it. Or in the middle of the night, if I got up for a glass of water or a pee, it would just be there, in the moonlight, looking back at me.

What was it that made it so strange? Well firstly, I'd never have a photo like that in my house. There again, blokes are different aren't they? They even have football teams on their walls. But it was more than just *what* it was, it was *where* it was. There was definitely something odd about it.

I could've asked Bernard, I suppose, but I didn't quite know what to ask. I'm sure, if I'd said I found it spooky, if that's the right word, he would've moved it. But it wasn't for me to rearrange his flat. Or his life.

And what a life! Sometimes, post pleasure, we'd forget the crazy world outside and just lie in bed and talk. Now I'm told, by women more experienced than I, that men are not supposed to be interested in that. After sex, I mean. Well, Bernard was. Interested *and* interesting. So life, overall, was good.

Did I have any misgivings? Yes, of course. The same old thing, really. Guilt.

Let's take Stephanie first. Despite my best efforts, with every passing week, her story was losing its legs. The great British media, as ever, was moving on. And yet, in a way, the situation was getting worse. The same deafening silence that made it less interesting, also made it more ominous.

All the information I was getting, from both the media and bits and pieces of inside knowledge, suggested that the kidnapping was originally money-motivated, rather than politically-motivated. And the bank, according to both Stephanie and DCI McCullough, hadn't yet coughed up.

No doubt they were being leaned on *not* to, but whatever the reason, their lack of action suggested the worst. Whereas, political hostages, as long as they can be kept alive, have an ongoing worth: traded or exchanged, paraded, prodded, and used for propaganda, criminal kidnappings don't. And when it's simply about money, and the payee won't pay up, it's curtains. So in the opinion of those in the know, Paul was probably already dead.

And yet, despite all this, and the terrible silence and the conclusions being drawn from it, Stephanie was bearing up pretty well. So I shouldn't have been guilty, but I was. Which brings us to Anna.

I should've told Anna about all the sex and stuff, but hadn't. It may be about the only thing in my entire life I've kept from her. When I say kept from her, I don't mean I didn't tell her anything. She knew Bernard and I were an item of sorts. And had she asked for slightly more detail I honestly would've told her. You see, I could never lie to Anna. But she didn't ask. This may have been down to embarrassment, but I honestly don't think it was. The reason I didn't tell her what *I was* doing, was because it was what *she wasn't* doing. Worse still I was doing it just around the corner from where she worked, *and* only admitting to about twenty-five percent of it. The twenty-five percent that didn't involve sex.

But I did catch up with her every week for a sandwich and a natter. This made me feel all the more guilty because she thought I was making a special effort. I wasn't, of course. Had it been necessary, I'd have made any kind of effort: gone to Timbuktu to meet her. But it wasn't, and I didn't. And therefore I felt guilty.

There was one weekend when we did spend some time together. One of her old school friends was getting married so she needed a Bromley crash pad again. We spent lots of time talking about how she looked and lots of time talking about how she felt (about yet another friend getting married off) and absolutely no time talking about me. Perfect. It made me feel a whole lot better.

I waved her off, at about midday, looking wonderfully wedding-like and received her back, at about midnight, looking terribly vomit-like.

The next morning I was up bright and early and she wasn't. This gave me a chance get a Sunday paper, make a proper coffee, sit down in the lounge and not think too much. I'd flicked, scanned and read most of what I wanted from the paper and was considering going for a late morning jog, my ageing body requiring greater maintenance of late, when from the bottom of the stairs I heard a soft croak: 'Morning.'

I looked towards the hall. Bird's nest hair, half-closed eyes, sleepy yawn. My lovely daughter.

'Morning,' I replied, 'How are you?'

No clear answer.

'Fancy a coffee?'

Silently, she walked to the kitchen, grated a chair out from under the table and slumped herself down. Presumably that meant yes.

I got up, walked to the kitchen, banged out and re-scooped the cafetiere, switched on the kettle and had a one-way conversation about how last night had gone.

Just as I'd walked back to the lounge, my phone rang.

Anna, who was within leaning over and groping distance, picked it up – her first meaningful contribution to the day – mumbled a hello then held it up in my direction and yawned: 'Mu-*um*, it's for you-*oo*.'

I felt like saying it would be, Anna. It's my bloody mobile. But I didn't, of course.

The other thing was the sighed 'It's Ber-*nard*,' as she handed it over: the whole line delivered in the same, bored *'it's-him-again'* way I used to use when she had some guy in tow.

I walked over to her and took the phone from her limp hand. I then made the coffee, took it to her, and continued my conversation, walking on past her to the privacy of the lounge.

Bernard was phoning me back regarding a bit of a do I was thinking of setting up. I'd had this thought. I felt it might be good for Stephanie to come over to stay with me for a weekend. If Bernard came over for a meal that evening it would make three, and if Andy McCullough joined us, it would make four.

I wasn't, for one minute, trying to match Stephanie up with Andy. Far from it. Apart from anything else, he was nearer my age than hers. Anyway, more to the point, it would've been totally inappropriate. Paul was missing, not dead. If this whole episode ran to form, he would either turn up as a corpse, or not turn up at all. Either way, it would be some years before she would be able to come to terms with the situation. So the reason I'd thought of Andy was: A) to even up the numbers: B) because he and Stephanie had already met, whilst working on her case: C) They'd therefore have loads to talk about, and: D) he lived within a cab ride of my house.

I was on the phone a while, but when I got back Anna hadn't even moved – clearly incapable of even plunging and pouring.

I sat down and did it for her.

'Mum,' she said.

'Yes, my petal,' I answered.

'I know I shouldn't ask this.'

I found myself thinking: then why ask it, Anna?

'But are you two … you know …?'

I didn't entirely get the question. But I suppose she was asking how serious we were.

'What I mean is,' she continued 'Do you two … you know?

To say I was shocked would be an understatement.

'That, Anna, is none of your business,' I said.

'Oh,' she replied, matter-of-factly. 'So you do.'

'Look Anna, when, where, and *if* we have *"you-knows,"* assuming *"you-knows"* are what I think it is, has got absolutely nothing to do with you. Ding-dong, Anna, this is your mum speaking.'

Now that first statement wasn't strictly true, was it. The '*you knows*', would've started a damned sight earlier had it not been for Anna's phoned intervention. So the 'whens', at least, were influenced by her, she'd saved me from second-date sex.

But I didn't mention that, of course. What I did do, was get up, go to the sink and busy myself, which is something I've always been good at when I'm annoyed.

Having gathered my thoughts, I then went on the attack, which is something else I'm good at when I'm cross. And when I'm in the wrong.

I told her that her generation put far too much emphasis on the whole physical side of a relationship. 'You're all just sex mad,' I said. Now how hypocritical was that? Worse still, I very much implied, though didn't actually say, that Bernard and I *weren't* having sex. Four houses down, in the Montcrieff's back garden: they're our local grow-your-owns, I could swear I heard their cockerel crow three times.

'You're the one making the big deal of it, Mum' said Anna, once I'd completed my mini-rant, and far calmer than I.

'I was just kind of interested in where you were … well, sort of up to. You know, relationship-wise.'

"Up to!"…

'OK, OK, calm down. I'm sorry. I was only interested in how big a deal he is. You know, how serious.'

That was a good question.

You know, when I'd embarked on this little affair, I certainly hadn't been looking for serious. There again, what we look for in life, and what we get, are often quite different.

I looked back at Anna. She was sitting there, hungover, nursing a mug of coffee. I felt sorry for her. She was only showing interest. Time for truth. For her, for me.

I walked back over to her and put my hand on her shoulder.

'Mind if I sit down,' I said. 'I'm afraid have a confession to make.'

I told her everything. Not the intimate details, obviously. More the fact that I'd spent almost every afternoon in Soho, about a quarter of a mile from where she worked, yet told her nothing. She was brilliant about it. Better than I would've been. But even with the guilt, it was good to talk. It always is. Yet I still couldn't help feeling it was all the wrong way round. I should've been the sounding board, she the sound.

Finally, after we'd discussed this for a good hour, plus loads more coffee, she simply got up, kissed me on the cheek and said 'That's great, Mum.'

I didn't answer. I didn't feel it was exactly 'great,' but I was pleased to have her approval.

'So there'll be a spare bedroom.'

'Sorry?'

'Well, I was listening to you talking – you know, to Bernard on the phone. That was one of the reasons I asked in the first place. You see, I was wondering if I could come, too. With Zack.'

'Who the heck's Zack?'

CHAPTER TWENTY-SEVEN

I liked Zack from the moment I met him. And the moment I met him was when he stood on my doorstep, slightly apprehensively, next to Anna.

He didn't push forward and introduce himself, which would've been quite acceptable, but hung back. This allowed Anna to half enter first, and do the introducing. Actually, even that wouldn't have been strictly necessary. Anna had a key, so she could've let herself in and then introduced him. But I was glad she didn't. It seemed significant, somehow: daughter, plus boyfriend, plus gladioli, all together on my little doorstep. Similarly, it was all very sweet when Bernard, getting up from the sofa, shook hands with Zack. It was a world I'd somehow missed out on. Partner shaking hands with daughter's new boyfriend. Almost Victorian.

'I'll get the tea,' I said, once coats and jackets and overnight bags had been dispatched. And when I got back, Hobnobs and all, there we all sat: a blissfully average, semi-detached scene. But even before that, the ordinariness of it all had been set.

Bernard, in his first visit to my little world, had arrived the day before.

I'd met him at Shortlands Station, walkable to my house, in the middle of a simple, sunny afternoon. He also brought flowers and they too were gladiolas, bless him.

We kissed, sensibly, and he gave me the glads. I thanked him, and off we strolled into the sunshine. We crossed with the lollypop lady, plus mums and kids and bikes and buggies, then cut through the park, past dogwalkers and joggers and children on swings. Everything pleasant, everything as it should be. Finally, it was down my road, with its hedges and roses and turtlewaxed cars, through my rusty gate, where I took the lead and grappled with keys.

I pushed through the door, de-alarmed and Bernard tentatively followed. He then took off his shoes, unzipped his overnight bag, and put on some slippers. Yes, he'd actually thought to bring them with him. So double bless him. Somehow, this felt even more significant than the daughter / boyfriend scenario that would follow. Like some kind of ceremonial thing.

Then, after I'd made a coffee and put the flowers in a vase, I showed him around – me doing the cheesy TV host thing: *'da dah'* at the entrance to each newly Hoovered room, with him standing there mumbling appreciatively in his significant slippers.

We went upstairs first, which included my bedroom and we *didn't* immediately have sex. This, again, was significant. Back downstairs, into the lounge, where he laughed at the rather embarrassing photo of me as a police cadet. Thinking about it, was this so different to his old school photo? Maybe men simply go for the teams and trophies, whereas women go for the families and selfies. Then we went back to the kitchen, sat down, drank tea and talked. It was all so much more civilised than all that rampant stuff. Less exhausting, too. I even got out the biscuits: Digestives for me, Rich Tea for him, I was saving the Hobnobs for best, and we didn't even dunk. All very refined, in a *Brief Encounter* sort of way.

That evening we went to the pictures. I say the *pictures* rather than the movies, because it was the Odeon Bromley rather than Leicester Square. A comedy called *Hope Springs*, starring Meryl Streep and Tommy Lee Jones, and was about an older couple who'd been married so long their relationship had turned into dust. They shared hardly any words, few interests and absolutely no intimacy. Of course you can have intimacy without sex and you can have sex without intimacy, but they had neither of either. So we laughed a lot – smugly, probably. I mean, we hadn't known each other for ten minutes, yet did all of the above, copiously. Oh well, it was only the movies. Sorry, the *pictures*.

The intension had been to go to a restaurant afterwards but in the end, having eaten too much popcorn and jelly babies, we cancelled our table, went home and had beans on toast on trays. If I tell you no more than that, it's because there isn't any. The '*you knows,*' in Anna-speak, were no more important than the tea, slippers and baked beans.

The next day, being a Saturday, we went to the Glades. Now the Glades Shopping Centre is a mandatory sentence for Bromley couples. If your relationship survives the Glades test it survives anything.

Bernard did all the things men do best, like sitting in chairs next to changing room curtains looking embarrassed and bored. He also complimented me on absolutely everything I tried on. Ill-fitting, unflattering, anything: they all got the thumbs up.

At one stage, I bumped into a woman I knew from Keep Fit. I was proud to introduce Bernard as 'my friend.' Such a lovely term. Two words, yet so many possibilities. Bernard, again, did what men do best: held the shopping. Which brought us back to Saturday tea time, Anna, and Zack.

The name Zack Jones, to me, sounded like some kind of pop star. But he certainly wasn't flash. The other image it conjured up was that of a clothes label. But though his narrow jeans and cardie were fashionable, they were neither dandified nor daft. Overall, he seemed straightforward and simple. In a good way, of course.

Like both Anna and Bernard he worked in media, running a small business doing corporate videos: anything from events, to conferences, to pitches and presentations. I suppose it was inevitable that he'd be doing something like that – practically everyone in Anna's little Soho circle seemed to. But apparently it was a far cry from either Anna's researching or Bernard's editing. That said, the three of them had enough in common to start talking shop, and I was relieved when Andy McCullough turned up. With us both coming from a policing background, at least it balanced out the conversation a bit.

Actually, the timing was just about perfect, too, allowing Andy the chance to ease us into the Paul Hutchinson situation before Stephanie arrived. There's no doubt that the kidnapping could become the elephant in the room, so we just had to broach the subject. It would have been ridiculous not to. So the fact that we'd already aired the subject would definitely help.

Stephanie turned up at about half-past eight, having somehow finished a full day's work and then driven up from Brighton. Even that helped, I felt. Our shared enemy, the M25, proved to be a perfect ice breaker. Oh yes, and she'd brought some gladiolas too. 'Glads All Over,' I joked, to laughs and groans all round.

We all got on very well and, over a few drinks, did indeed broach the subject of Paul's kidnapping. Stephanie did really well, I felt, striking the right balance between hoping, moping and simply coping.

Food-wise, none of us were veggies, so I'd gone for a large beef hot pot with shallots and red wine, plus garlic bread. I'm no cook, but it seemed to work OK, having been

145

able to pre-prepare it, so I didn't have to spend too much time in the kitchen.

The bedding arrangements were all pre-organised too. Andy would be cabbing it home, Stephanie would have the spare room, and Bernard would be in with me. Which left Anna, Zack and just one remaining bedroom. They'd already worked this one out between them. Anna would get the room, and Zack the lounge sofa.

Now this wasn't my idea, but it kind of felt right. Yes, yes, I know I was being hypocritical, but it was the first time I'd even met the lad, *and* it was *my* home. It was quite sweet that they were being so old fashioned about it, too.

Either way, it never really mattered because of what happened next. That was to change everything.

We were just finishing the meal, talking about the dreadful cost of housing, when Andy McCullough's mobile rang. He excused himself, picked up his phone, stood up to leave the room and then paused. His face visibly paled. Clearly, this was important.

'Do forgive me,' he said, squeezing between his chair and Stephanie's, then walking towards the dining room door, but not actually leaving the room.

Apart from a single 'Yes,' he remained silent. Whatever it was, he simply needed to listen.

Sharing a few raised eyebrows – a policeman's lot is obviously never done – we all stopped talking. We did pick up our conversation a bit, but it was stilted. Bonhomie and policing don't really mix. After about thirty seconds he put his hand over the phone, and said: 'Do you mind if I leave the room?'

'No, no,' I said. 'Would you like to go …?'

'No,' he said. 'The hall will be fine.'

He left the room and closed the door.

I tried to get our conversation back on track whilst also straining to hear what Andy was saying. Probably everyone else was too.

A few seconds passed, the door opened again and Andy put his head round it. We all froze. Somehow we all knew that something big was breaking.

Andy looked at Stephanie and said: 'Could I have a word?' and with napkin still to mouth, she got up, excused herself, and joined him. After a couple of whispered words at the door they left the room.

Any chance of our conversation continuing was gone. We sat in silence.

I then coughed, got up and busied myself by clearing the plates up. 'Lovely meal,' they all said.

I couldn't take the plates out because the hall, with Andy and Stephanie in it, were between me and the kitchen. So I piled the plates up in my place and sat down again.

After a brief, silent pause, Andy and Stephanie came back in. They had their coats on. Andy, slightly to the fore, said: 'We need to leave. I'm really sorry. It's been a lovely, but we really do need to leave.'

I got up from the table and joined them. Almost immediately a blue light arrived outside, followed by the sound of car doors opening and closing.

'Are you OK,' I asked Stephanie. It was a ridiculous question. Clearly she wasn't.

They moved back out to the hall and I followed a pace or two behind them. Andy opened the front door for his colleagues, which left Stephanie, briefly, nearest to me. She was looking down. She didn't want to catch my eye.

I moved closer, touched her on the arm. She turned to me, but still couldn't look. We embraced and she sobbed.

'He's still alive,' she whispered.

'But …'

CHAPTER TWENTY-EIGHT

So here's what had happened. MI5, or MI6, or Interpol, or whoever, had seen a new video. Now before even telling you about it, it's worth thinking that through.

How could a government agency get hold of a terrorist video before the rest of the world? If the bank offered the kidnappers the best chance of extracting money, why would you show it to the government first? At the very least, it suggested inside information. Either the kidnappers had been infiltrated, or were in direct contact with the authorities.

But back on the subject of its content, the good news was that Paul was still alive. That was about as far as the good news went though.

Emaciated and hollow-eyed, he was a shadow of his former self. That was precisely why, incidentally, Stephanie had to go off with Andy McCullough. Paul was so changed, so defeated, that they needed confirmation that it was actually him. Unfortunately, it was.

Technically, it would have been simple enough to have sent the material to my house. But there were a thousand good reasons not to. Quite apart from the inappropriateness – it was a dinner party, for God's sake – there was the victim support issue. If she was going to see this stuff, she needed to be in the right place, surrounded by the right people, at the right time.

They'd set something up at Bromley nick, which I must say, for a government agency, showed remarkable forethought. Dragging her all the way up to London, or all the way back down to Brighton, wouldn't have been ideal. Once Stephanie was made aware of what was going on, which was precisely what Andy was doing in my hallway, the poor woman needed to confront the situation as soon as possible.

So what exactly was that situation? What was on this video? Before telling you, I'd like to point out that I'm not glorying in this stuff. Nor, on the night, did any of us even attempt to view it. Assuming it was out there somewhere on the Internet, I'm sure Anna could have found it.

I simply went back in the room, told them as much as I knew: that another video was emerging and that Paul, crucially, was still alive, and we kind of left it at that. We discussed it for a bit, deciding that, overall, it was more positive than negative. But it obviously put a huge dampener on things.

We all helped to clear up: I think everyone felt the need to keep busy. Then we retreated to our respective beds and, in Zack's case, sofas.

I warned them that I'd probably be getting phone calls later, and that there was every chance Stephanie would be back at some time in the night. Her car was still outside, so she'd have to come back anyway. She was also over the limit, so she wouldn't be driving back to Brighton anyway. She'd probably want the company, too. And that was precisely how it turned out.

She phoned me at about one a.m. to tell me she'd seen the material – and yes, it definitely was Paul – and that she'd answered all their questions and would be back soon. In the end, she arrived at about two.

Needless to say, none of us were asleep. I came down as soon as I heard the car doors slamming: Bernard following behind. We passed Zack, non-sleeping on the sofa, followed by Anna, offering to get some coffee going.

Like so many things around that time, when Stephanie came back in, a balance needed to be struck. We were all interested, obviously. But there's a fine line between concern and curiosity. Tired and beaten, the one thing she didn't need as she sat down on that chair was us in her face.

Zack had already disappeared to the toilet, presumably dressing, and Bernard had joined Anna in the kitchen. I sat next to her, prepared to listen, if she wanted me to, but not to talk, if she didn't want me to.

'He's alive, at least,' she eventually said, then sighed, 'So that's got to be good.'

'Yes.' I said.

She then put her to hands to her lips, prayer-like, and thought.

After a few long seconds, she said, 'It's a different place, but nearby. New Karachi, apparently.

'They know that do they?'

'Yes.'

I did a quick bit of mental geography. From the signposts I'd seen when we were there, New Karachi was to the north. At a guess, about ten miles from where the other video was shot.

'So it's outside again?'

'Yes,' she said.

I didn't want to deluge her with questions but if she wanted to talk, fine.

'They've given it a date: two weeks.' She then opened up her hands and looked down at her fingers. 'No one's going to pay thirty million, are they?'

'Thirty?' I said. 'I thought it was twenty?'

151

'It was. The price just went up.' Then she then looked at me. 'Doesn't make much difference, does it? Twenty, thirty. If no one's going to pay, what's the difference?'

'If it would help,' I said, 'We could speak to Mr Farooki again – tomorrow, I mean.'

She thought for a second, but said nothing. I took that as a possible yes.

'The knife,' she said, breaking her silence. 'It was on his neck.'

I didn't respond to this. There was no response.

'Sleep,' I finally said. 'You need some sleep.'

Just as we got up, the others came in. They may have been waiting for us to finish. Stephanie apologised for all the trouble, which was ridiculous and, head bowed, made for bed. Silently, we all did the same. I doubted too many of us would get much sleep though.

Bernard and I lay there, in the darkness, not saying much. Originally, tomorrow would have been a full day. I'd planned to go off to my sister's, introduce Bernard to the other parts of my little world. It was to be a big Sunday lunch with her extended family: children, grandchildren and us. But I couldn't see it happening now. I'd ring her in the morning, cancel and apologise. I needed to stay with Stephanie. Everything else could wait.

Somehow, I must have slept, eventually, fleetingly. I do recall the grey light, the echo of an early train, the beginnings of traffic, so it must have been very, very late. Or early, I suppose.

I had that dream again, or similar. A photo on a wall. Bernard's kitchen. I walked up to it. The same, but different. Bernard, Mrs Underwood, all my old school friends. And Anna. She was standing exactly where I was, in the line.

'Why are you me? I asked her.

'Because I'm dead,' she replied.

CHAPTER TWENTY-NINE

Like a hangover, but worse. That's how the next morning felt. An empty, numbing nothingness, but without even a headache to comfort you. Real pain is tangible, anguish isn't. Like a thick, poisonous jelly, it just clings.

It wasn't my pain, of course. And not Anna's, thank God. But just being in the presence of such suffering, being close to such hurt, is debilitating, exhausting.

Almost like ghosts, we moved but didn't speak. We did things because *not* doing things was worse. I sorted out bedding, others dressed, or cleared up, or packed their few bits. None of us turned on a radio. But no news wasn't good news. It was just no news.

Stephanie would stay, that was a given. Her brother had gone back to Australia and there was nothing but loneliness in Brighton. Plus, probably, the press again. So everyone else would go and it would just be the two of us again.

Anna and Zack left first, after coffee, but before any form of breakfast. It was totally out of character for Anna to be up so early. I doubt she'd previously even seen seven a.m. on the Sabbath before. OK, like the rest of us, I'm sure she'd barely closed her eyes, but at weekends she didn't need sleep as an excuse. All she needed was a warm duvet and the knowledge that there was no work. So I would imagine she'd got up for Zack's sake. There was no way he'd have slept either. Slap bang on the crossroads between upstairs and down, he didn't have a chance.

They were limited as to what they could say to Stephanie. We all were. You can't come up with some chipper line like *'Good luck,'* or reassure her with *'It'll all work out,'* because it almost certainly wouldn't.

In the end, standing in the hallway, Zack came up with a simple 'Good to have met you, Stephanie,' and shook her hand. For Anna it was slightly easier. She's a woman, she can hug, even kiss. That's where we're so much luckier. Hugs can say a million things, kisses a million more. You know, equipped with what little men have, I don't think I could have got through some of the things life has thrown at me.

Bernard stayed for a bit of breakfast, the three of us sitting silently in my conservatory. Funny word, conservatory. It means a place where you can keep things, save things, protect things. But there are some things you just can't protect yourself from.

Once we'd eaten: tasteless toast and lukewarm coffee, he offered to stay. But I didn't see the point. Somehow, it was always going to be just us the two of us: Stephanie and I.

At one point, out of her earshot, Bernard asked me what I was going to do. A good question. I suppose, if I was really pushed for an answer to that, I'd have said I was going to do what women do. Intangible, yet indispensable. You see, we'd grown close. Possibly, apart from Anna, I was closer to Stephanie than anyone at that time. There was Bernard, of course, but he was more a physical thing. And Liz was different again. Sisters are.

In comparison to me, Stephanie had no one. An only child with no father, a barking mother, and a Death Row husband. She needed me. But if Bernard had asked what she needed me *for*, I would have found it difficult to explain. After all, he's just a man.

Standing in the kitchen, he said goodbye to both of us. But then he added something interesting. 'Look after each other, won't you.' *Each other.* In one way, that was illogical. How, and why, would *Stephanie* be looking after *me*? But somehow, he was spot on.

Then, on the doorstep he said goodbye to me only. So two different goodbyes with the same person. But that's the way we are, us humans. Complex lot. All mixed up: lovers, friends, colleagues, parents. Different people, different goodbyes.

After we'd kissed, I watched him walk away. My man. Well, sort of.

You know, after Stephanie had finished needing me, I might need him. He was turning out better than I'd expected. Such an English expression, that. Not perfect, just 'better than expected.' At least something had.

CHAPTER THIRTY

'Would you like to see it?' asked Stephanie, sitting at the kitchen table, almost as soon as I'd got back in.

'Do you want me to?' I replied.

'Yes,' she said, 'I suppose I do.'

Whilst everyone was still in the house, as I said, it had been the elephant in the room, or perhaps one of them. We all knew that somewhere, just a click away, were those terrible images. Just as we also knew that the news, brimming with it, would be just a TV or radio channel away.

'I'm no expert,' I said. If it's not on YouTube or something, I might not …'

'I can find it,' she said. 'Fisher told me.'

'He was at the station, too?'

'Yes. They had their own copy. Clearer, I suppose. But he said that it was everywhere.' She then sighed, looked at her fingers and said: '"Global" was what he said, like it was some kind of brand, some kind of product.'

I shuddered at this. How crass. How stupid. At least Andy McCullough had a bit of warmth and a few people skills.

'Did he say how they'd got it?'

'Yes. Apparently it was dropped off at a newspaper, like the other one was. Different paper though. The editor decided to give it to the government first, provided they still got first options.'

'First options?'

'Yes,' she said, exhaling again, 'That's what he said.'

And there you had it. The exact problem: language. Words like 'global' and 'options' were completely wrong: too clever, too corporate. And people like Fisher: faceless people, government people, just don't get that, do they?

I went to the study, got my laptop, took it back and placed it between us. I switched it on and waited.

I couldn't think of how I was going to help. If MI5 had pored over every frame, probably benefiting from a higher quality version in the first place, what would I be able to add? Still, if it helped Stephanie …

I typed in *Paul Hutchinson Kidnap* and up it came immediately, on top of a row of clips that also included the previous video as well as a string of news bulletins.

The first thing that struck me was how utterly audacious this was. At least the first video had been filmed behind a shed. This one didn't even have a building for cover. They were standing, yet again, on a piece of wasteland. OK, they were clearly further out of town. But also very clearly, in the background, cars were streaming past.

'That newspaper he's holding,' said Stephanie, pointing at the right hand man. It's from a couple of days ago. It's the same newspaper the ransom was sent to: The Sindh News.'

Apart from the paper, the other thing that distanced it from the first video was the state of Paul. His face was drawn, his body thin, and he looked as though he'd aged about ten years. But they were taking a huge risk. The two men were masked, it's true, but the overall scenario was open for all to see.

The men, this time, stayed silent. There was no banner behind them either, just empty scrubland and a distant road. Then Paul spoke. It was almost a croak.

'You have ten days. Thirty million dollars. You will be told how to pay.'

The man to the left then raised his knife to Paul's throat, Paul closes his eyes, and the screen went blank.

After a few seconds Stephanie said: 'That's been edited for public consumption. On the real video it ...' her voice broke, she paused and bowed her head.

I put my hand on her shoulder. After a few more seconds she looked up. Not at me, but at straight ahead, at the screen. She swallowed, composed herself and said: 'On the real video they ... well... there's blood.' She paused again, swallowed again: 'It's not certain. Not lots, but, well, it does look that way.'

She was being incredibly brave. I left my hand on her shoulder and gave her the chance to compose herself a little. If composing were even possible.

If I were her, could I have done this? I'm not sure. There again, I suppose she was doing what she had to. If going through this video again could in some tiny way improve her husband's chance of survival, she'd do it.

'Do you have any thoughts?' she finally asked.

I did. A thousand. But many of them were simply about man's inhumanity to man, and the depths people will sink. But I didn't say that, of course.

'Were the police able to get any other clues?'

'Yes,' she sighed. 'Voice recognition. They said something ... in the section that's been edited, just before they ...' she then paused, recomposed herself and added: 'I didn't understand it, but apparently it's definitely the same men.'

'And this was filmed near Karachi, you say?'

'Yes, just outside.'

'If I find a map can you show me?'

'Yes,' she said.

Using Google it took seconds to navigate to the exact spot: a piece of non-descript semi-desert just north of New Karachi.

'They had their backs to this road,' she said, pointing to what looked like no more than a shadowed crease in the land.

I studied it for a while. Unlike the virtual maps in more inhabited parts of the world, we couldn't go right into human view. All we could do was hover above it and, road apart, there was little to be seen.

'What did the police say about what he said? How anyone's supposed to pay, I mean?'

'They're a bit mystified. Before this it was all via newspapers. They hadn't been giving details of drop offs or anything.'

'If they contact the government with that, they'll be wasting their time. By my reckoning there's only one other place with that kind of money.'

'The bank,' I said.

'Yes, so if they're serious they're going to have to contact them.'

I thought for a second. It suddenly occurred to me that they may already have.

'Look Stephanie,' I said, trying to sound a little more upbeat, 'We're all assuming no contact has been made yet. Or, if it has, the bank's refusing to cooperate. One or the other. But maybe not.'

'I'm sure I would've heard if …'

'Well, I'm not sure,' I said.

'How do you mean?

'Think about it, Steph. Every call you've made – to Asif Farooki – has been pored over by the British, the Pakistanis, the Americans, everyone. If Farooki told you that contact had been made, the deal would be off. They're not going to hand over Paul if they think the place is swarming with police, are they?'

She considered this, but didn't answer.

'The point is – either way – you're not going to know, are you?'

She looked at me. There was the slightest glimmer in her eyes. Maybe it was hope. 'Are you saying there could already be some kind of dialogue going on?'

'Well, there's absolutely no point in kidnapping someone – for money, I mean – and then *not* having some kind of dialogue, is there?'

'No,' she said, 'I suppose not.'

'My guess is that something has been going on between the bank and the kidnappers but now it's stalled. So, in a typical piece of haggling, they've upped the threat, *and* the price.'

She just nodded thoughtfully. She could see my point, I'm sure.

'So you think there could be something going on after all. Ransom-wise, I mean.'

'Reading between the lines, yes I do.'

I looked out of the window. Sunday afternoon. Sunny and cold. 'Tell you what,' I said. 'Let's go for a walk.'

And that's exactly what we did, starting with a short drive to the local woods, where we put on sensible shoes and took leafy paths under autumn skies. We passed families with friends, children on bikes, dogs on leads. All were meandering slowly, mulling over, taking time and chatting: what's been done, what's to come. We were doing the same: discussing sisters and brothers and daughters and lovers, but inevitably coming back round to Paul, and what to do next.

'Do you think it's worth Skyping Farooki again?' I suggested.

'If you think it'll help,' she said.

Of course it would help. Just doing something, just doing anything, just keeping her busy, it would all help. I didn't want to put her through more than she could take, but she seemed up for it. And even if all she was doing was keeping in contact, reminding him, it would be worth it. The closer the link: visually, verbally, emotionally, the greater the responsibility he'd feel.

Tomorrow, the bank would be open, Mr Farooki should be contactable. Stephanie would do the talking, I'd do the watching. She'd be more heartfelt, I'd be more analytical, circumspect. He'd be telling us there's been no contact. I was sure of that. But that's just words. And words lie. Body language doesn't. It was worth the call, worth the watch.

'I'd also like to catch up with everything,' she said. 'You know, on the news, about Paul. On the news, on the Internet, I mean.'

I thought about this. It was very brave. News could be cruel. Some of the web sites would be downright distressing. But I could see her point. If we were going to plead our case, we'd need to *know* our case.

However, the motives for her next suggestion seemed less clear. We'd just got to a crossing in the paths. Veering off left and right was the now darkening woodland, straight ahead was open parkland. We went straight ahead.

'And the other thing I was going to ask you,' she said, 'While I'm up here, I'd really like to go on Tuesday.'

'To Rose Denton's funeral?'

'Yes, if that's OK.'

'Fine by me,' I said. And I suppose it was. But why was it fine by her?

I honestly couldn't work out why she'd want to go to the funeral of a woman she'd never even met. Paul had, it's true, but only very briefly.

Meeting a *living* person that your husband had met, I could understand. After all, when it comes to keeping memories alive, any kind of contact with someone who can tell an anecdote or two, and provide a bit of insight, is worth being around. But dead people, dead bodies, can't do any of that.

So why would she want to spend an afternoon in a cold London crematorium listening to hymns, prayers and pulpit recollections of a life she knew nothing of? Wasn't there enough blackness in her life already? And if there were plenty of reasons why Stephanie *needn't* go, there was one very good reason why she *shouldn't*. Newspapers. The press would just love it. Did she really want pictures of her at Rose Denton's funeral? Did she really want the whole *'Dead Rose & Missing Paul'* thing reignited?

So as we made our way back to the car park, across a final squelchy field, I decided it was a point worth making:

'You know the press'll be there, don't you?'

'Yes,' she said immediately. It was clearly on her mind too. 'And I'm not looking forward to it, particularly.'

She then stopped and turned to me. 'But somehow, I just want to be there. I can't explain why.'

'OK,' I said, touching her on her arm, 'I understand.' I'm not sure I did though. But I left it at that. We'd go.

You know, at the very beginning of this case, when I'd sat with Stephanie in her Brighton flat, I'd briefly doubted her. Yes, the missing husband thing was obviously genuine, but was she being entirely open with me? I'd soon changed my mind, of course. She was obviously just an innocent, wrong place, wrong time victim. Now, some three months later, a few doubts were beginning to reappear.

And back at my car, sitting on the tailgate, pulling off my walking shoes and unbuttoning my coat, my thoughts turned to tomorrow's Skyping. Perhaps Asif Farooki's body language wouldn't be the only thing I'd be watching.

There were still things about this case that didn't quite add up. And one of them, perhaps, was Stephanie.

CHAPTER THIRTY-ONE

The following day panned out exactly as we'd planned it. We'd had an early night and some decent sleep: mine naturally, Stephanie's Tamazepammed, got up late, drank coffee, eaten toast, and set to work.

Obviously Stephanie had already been given an update by the police. But even though their information had been accurate, it hadn't been that enlightening. The forces of law and order, by their nature, are cagey. We needed to spread our net a little wider. I say 'needed to', but in actual fact, we didn't. All we were preparing ourselves for, later that day, was Farooki's conference call. We hardly needed to dissect every Tweet and blog for that. But we both felt it would be worth the effort.

Like Stephanie, I hadn't so much as looked at a front page since it had happened. Better that we did it together – her sitting next to me.

Before even starting, I put my hand on Stephanie's arm and asked her if she was sure she wanted to go through with it. Yes, she said, she did. I'd already decided to kick off with the BBC's website. It would be the safest place to start. Then we could move our way through the broadsheets.

This was exactly the path we followed and it soon became apparent that the story was pretty much as Stephanie had been told. As with the first video, a tape, rather than disc or USB, had been delivered to a local Karachi newspaper. The only differences this time were: A) it was a different paper, and B) rather than going for headlines, they'd acted 'responsibly' and handed it straight over to the authorities. I put the word 'responsibly' in quotes because the end result was anything but expedient. By the time the story had re-emerged from the corridors of power, the kidnapper's two week ultimatum was down to just eleven days. And those eleven had now shrunk to just eight.

After digesting the mainstream websites, we decided to delve further. Googling *Paul Hutchinson Kidnap* threw up half a billion results. I repeat: half a *billion*. You know, publicity's a funny thing. There's no happy medium. Like the rain on a farmer's field, or perhaps the attention men pay women, it's always too much or too little.

To think I'd spent the weeks prior to this event trying to keep this story in the news. Now, it appeared, it *was* the news.

I asked Stephanie if she was still OK with it.

'Yes,' she said, nodding.

The first logical step, I suppose, was to find out where the world's Twitterers and bloggers thought these guys could be holed up. Top of the Pops, it seemed, was Kirthar National Park: an uninhabited area of scrub and mountain, about the size of an English county. This was hardly an Earth-shattering piece of deduction, given that the video had been filmed on the road between Karachi and the Kirthar mountains. It also fitted the Al Qaeda / Islamic State brand image: jihadists living in some gun-toting, lawless wasteland. Except Kirthar wasn't.

Firstly, Kirthar was nowhere near the Afghan border and even further from Syria; secondly, there were no conflicts going on there; thirdly, it had no cave complexes or isolated villages, and finally it was tourist country rather

166

than terrorist country. A couple of helicopters carrying thermal imaging equipment could sort it out in no time. And delving deeper, we even found a couple of people who claimed to have actually seen them, including a passing driver who said he'd seen the video actually being filmed: *'There were two men in front of a camera holding a third man between them.'* Someone had followed this up by asking if they'd seen a car nearby. To which the Tweeter had said: *'No, just the three men in the desert in front of a camera.'*

Now this was possible, but extremely unlikely. The first question would be how they even got there. The second question related to the number of men. The blogger said three, but by my reckoning there were four. Very clearly, in the video, there was the shadow of a cameraman; three men being filmed, and one doing the filming, made four. Which leads us to speculation as to who these people were.

The world's conspiracy theorists were coming up with a right old mishmash: Al Qaeda, the newly emerging Islamic State, Israel's Mossad, Putin's Russia, the Chinese, the North Koreans, the CIA, and even MI5.

All the time, as we scrolled through ever more ludicrous notions, I was aware of Stephanie sitting next to me: her breathing, her hand movements, her little coughs. I could even pick up her slight sweating. On balance, it was a good thing she was doing this, but I had to be careful. A step too far and we'd call the whole thing off. Which is exactly what happened next: some idiot from Wisconsin saying he was looking forward to the execution video. That was it. Enough.

As I closed my laptop I said: 'Out there, Stephanie, are a billion people wishing you and Paul well, plus a handful of cowardly creeps who get off on cruelty. Forget them. Keep believing,' I said, 'you'll come through.'

I gave her a hug, then a kiss and got up. Then I went to the kitchen and switched on the kettle. She just remained there, sitting there, in front of the screen, in silence.

I must confess that I did find myself questioning what I'd just done. After all, we'd discovered little. But there are no easy options. No 'right' ways. Had she hidden her eyes now, she'd simply encounter this lot later, in painful dribs and drabs.

Stage two. Conference call. I'd already set it up the night before, ringing Assan, Asif Farouki's secretary, before going to bed.

We could do the Skype from home, but I'd decided not to. For reasons of image: professionalism, legitimacy, gravitas, it would look better from my office. Framed behind us would be bookshelves, certificates, and a well-known picture of me, Anna and Su A: the missing student who was famously *found* by us, but *not found* by the police. Having this stuff in the background may only be a detail, but details can count.

The next step would be to make *us* look the part. Again, it may sound ridiculous, but Steph would need to look soft, yet persuasive, pretty much as she always was, and I needed to look professional and business-like. In the end, given the head-and-shoulders nature of teleconferencing, I suppose there wouldn't be that much difference: pale lipstick and blouse for her, suited and Thatcheresque for me. Finally, we rehearsed exactly what we'd have to say, and our probable responses to what he'd have to say. This call, I felt, could be our last chance.

'Okay, Steph.' I said, standing in the hall, in front of my full length mirror, 'Time to go. My office awaits.'

And ready for battle, we left the house.

It was a beautiful day, but it didn't quite feel that way. The three journalists, propping up my front wall didn't exactly help. They immediately sprang into action: two going for cameras, one for his notebook: 'Any comment?' he shouted.

Our total silence, plus a steely look straight ahead, was all the reply they got.

Across the road and into the prim little park, the warm sunlight seemed sepia. There were chatting mums and playing kids, but somehow it all seemed sullied, tainted. A couple of women nudged each other as we passed. Even if they were sympathetic, the gesture somehow felt judgemental.

After we left the park we popped into the newsagent to buy some milk for the office. Mehmet was behind the counter. He served me and, even though we exchanged greetings, with Stephanie next to me, he made no reference to the situation. I couldn't really blame him. What was he supposed to say?

Almost as difficult, as we turned, was the paper stand stuck right in front of us. I know it sounds strange because we'd spent the morning trawling the internet, but we still averted our eyes.

Then it was out of Mehmet's, past Paul's Pets – the guinea pig-smelling pet shop immediately below my office – through the street door next to it, up the musty stairs, onto my landing, and into my rather neglected little office.

I opened the blinds to dusty sunlight, we took off our coats and, while Stephanie surveyed the walls (me as a copper, me with Anna), I switched on both the computer and the kettle.

We arranged two chairs in front of the screen, with Stephanie's being the more centrally placed, but also framing for maximum study / office effect. Then I got up, leaving her to the connecting: her generation being more computer-savvy than mine, while I finished making the teas.

I then re-joined her and made a landline call to the bank. While I was waiting to get through, Stephanie made adjustments to our framing.

I got through on the land line and was greeted in Urdu, but asked for Mr Farooki in English. I was put on muzak hold for about thirty seconds before a pronunciation-perfect female voice says: 'Hello Mrs Andrews, Mr Farooki will be with you shortly.'

'Thank you, Assan.' I said, before being looped back into the muzak. Finally, still holding onto the landline, the screen in front of us blinked into life and he was there.

Mutely, he cleared his throat. I wasn't sure if he could see or hear us. Then his secretary leaned into frame, did something with the keyboard. Finally, we were connected: picture perfect, sound clear.

He rigidified himself, became more statesmanlike, cleared his throat, and said: 'How *are* you, Stephanie?'

Prior to this introduction, I hadn't thought it possible that anyone could open such a conversation with a *'how are you?'* Yet somehow, in ultra-smooth manner, it worked. Somehow, it also contains an unspoken *'I* feel *for you, Stephanie. I'm* with *you, Stephanie.'*

After a longish pause she replied: 'Surviving, I suppose.'

'And you're staying with Pamela?' he said.

'Yes, she's being very kind,' replied Stephanie.

I'm not used to being talked about in the third person and felt the need to say something, so I simply said 'Hello.'

We were probably all feeling uncomfortable.

Stephanie broke the silence: 'Mr Farooki,' she said, exhaling, 'You know, I can't offer you anything except … well, the chance to save another human being's life.'

'Do call me Asif,' he said, warmly.

'Asif,' she said, letting the name resonate, 'If you can do this one thing, it will be forever. Not just a life or a lifetime, forever. Until my dying day, *all* our dying days.'

There was a silence. The words 'dying days' hung in the air.

Stephanie cleared her throat: 'Now Mr Farooki, sorry, Asif, how many people can say that? How many people have *that* kind of power? I beg you. Use that power. Save Paul.'

There was another silence.

'I have no power, Stephanie.'

'You have money.'

'I don't. The bank has.'

'But you control the bank.'

He noticeably relaxed, leaning back in his chair.

'I can't control the future, Stephanie. But I can change the past.'

'Sorry?' said Stephanie.

Farooki remained silent. He wasn't going to repeat it, I could tell.

'Sorry, Asif,' I said. 'Did you say you *can't* control the future, but you *can* change the past?'

He nodded, thought for a second, held up his hands and said: 'I've said enough. I've taken your comments on board, Stephanie, and I've said enough.'

And that, pretty much, was that.

Over the next few hours and minutes Stephanie and I went over it time and time again. What could he have possibly meant? Surely, if anything, the opposite was true: you *can't* change the past but you *can*, to some extent, control the future. Not only would that make more sense, it would fit this particular situation.

171

After all, if Farooki had said that, he'd effectively be telling Stephanie that he couldn't change the fact that Paul had been kidnapped, but he could control future events and hopefully set Paul free. But he didn't. He'd quite clearly said: *'I can't control the future, but I can change the past.'*

Obviously he was limited in what he could tell us. Half the world's spooks were listening in. We hadn't expected candour, we hadn't expected him to commit. All we were doing was pleading our case. But we hadn't expected riddles either.

After a bit, just sitting there, looking at a blank screen, it occurred to me that it could be some kind of Pakistani proverb, some kind of saying.

'Tell you what,' I said, as Stephanie came back with two glasses of water, 'Let's find out.'

And so we did. Sitting at that window, sunlight streaming, we lost ourselves – researching all kinds of incongruously beautiful proverbs, most of which, it seemed, were the same the world over, but none of which, it seemed, had anything to do with the controlling or changing the future or past.

And that evening, over a glass of wine, I said to Stephanie: 'You know, I've been thinking.'

'About?'

'Today's call.'

'Me, too,' she said. 'But what, specifically?'

'Well, maybe it's not all bad.'

'In what sense?'

'Well, he couldn't tell us he was doing a deal. With the kidnappers, I mean. That'd be like giving the police an open invitation.'

Stephanie just nodded. It was obvious.

'But on the other hand, if he *wasn't* doing a deal, he definitely *could* have told us,' I said. 'After all, what's to stop him?'

'Maybe he was just being kind, or perhaps, you know, a bit of a coward. Maybe he just couldn't tell us face to face.'

'Maybe. But he didn't.'

Stephanie didn't seem to share my token optimism on this issue, just looking down rather gloomily into her wine glass.

'Stephanie?'

'Yes.'

I put my glass down and turned to her: 'If you wanted to tell someone something, but you couldn't. If you knew someone was listening in. What would you do?'

She thought for a bit, a tiny frown forming. 'I don't know. Say nothing, I suppose.'

'What's the point of that?' I said. 'You're doing them a massive kindness. You're literally saving their husband's life. You want to tell them, but you can't. So what would you do?'

Stephanie said nothing, just thought.

'If it were me,' I said, 'I'd say something coded; something so ... so *enigmatic* that whoever was listening in couldn't possibly guess what it meant.'

'Maybe,' she shrugged, unconvinced. 'But if we can't understand either, like I said, what's the point?'

'Plenty. And you know what? This conversation proves it.'

Stephanie thought about this, but she didn't look convinced.

And I thought about it too. And you know what? I *was* convinced. Maybe it was just wishful thinking. Maybe I was being a hopeless optimist. But if I was, it ran completely against my normal character. Either way, suddenly, it was all making a whole lot more sense. With all this past and present stuff, he was trying to tell us something: But what?

CHAPTER THIRTY-TWO

West Norwood Cemetery. Grey skies above, the freezing dead below.

Black limos crept in. With engines idling and doors opening, the mourners decanted. In little huddles, dark-coated and hunched, they stood. A last cigarette here, a few stilted words there.

Others, separated by their sorrow, made their own way, slowly, to the chapel.

The demarcation lines were clear. Cars containing the real pain bore family resemblances: mother, father, sister, brother. An auntie, probably, too: as stooped and as old as Rose's mum. And an uncle, definitely: the spitting image of Rose's dad. Others, walking mostly, fell into looser categories: the friends, the neighbours and the difficult to define. A few dribs and drabs of the rich and vaguely famous, too.

An industry grandee, knighted for his service to advertising. A film producer, fresh off a set. A pop singer, so crass he almost waved as he alighted from his limo: not only blacked out windows, but blacked out glasses. And for me, that's the most loathsome showbiz convention of all. Sometimes, just sometimes, shades can be justified on such occasions: worn to hide genuine tears. But mostly, they're just funereal fashion accessories, worn for effect. The clue's in the name, guys. They're *sun*glasses.

And then there was the inevitable police presence. Assistant Commissioner Mark West, all buttons and epaulettes, was doing his best to stay visible, whilst a couple of covert coppers tried to do exactly the opposite. So just to spite them, expansively, I pointed them out to Anna and Steph.

Then, coalescing into the largest group of all, were her ex-employees. Probably, parked up somewhere in a West Norwood backstreet was the coach that had brought them there. That or a fleet of cabs. For them, I suppose, it was a bit like a works outing. Without, hopefully, the booze ups and the shagging.

Talking of which, I pointed out Poppy Foster to Stephanie.

'That's her,' I said, nodding towards the pretty blonde in the too-flimsy top.

Stephanie said nothing, just shivered.

I'd have liked to have been able to read both Stephanie's and Poppy's mind at this point. And for that reason, I'd also have loved Stephanie to have introduced herself. Poppy's body language would've been a statement in itself. But that was never going to happen, and I certainly wasn't going to suggest it.

Then, outside the railings and ostracised from us all, was one final group. They'd probably been there prior to the minister even bringing in his bible, and would still be there after the crematorium man has swept up the ashes. Unwanted and unloved, was a gaggle of chatting, snapping, scribbling hacks. Same old faces, but in slightly smarter clothing. And the following day we'd all be poring over their every word.

We stood a good distance from them and a bigger distance from the crematorium. Stephanie, Anna and I, suitably sombre, standing in the perishing outdoors, rather than the perishing indoors, because we wanted to be last in. The very back of the chapel would do.

'Hi, Pam,' said Bernard, who had somehow managed to creep up on me, almost making me jump out of my skin. I turned, smiled and we shared a brief, cold kiss.

'Sorry I'm late,' he said. 'Meetings!'

'That's Okay,' I said. 'At least you made it.'

Respectfully dressed, in a heavy overcoat, dark suit and black tie, he then greeted Anna and Stephanie and we started to stroll, silently, to the chapel door.

I was just about to enter when I got a text. I paused, took out my phone, but then didn't bother to read it. At least it reminded me to switch it to silent.

Inside, as hoped, we were at the back, filing into the last four spaces of a pew. We sat ourselves down, removing a programme from our seats in the process. I looked at it. On the cover was her picture. Kind but proud. Around this, aptly, was a tangle of roses, below which were the simple words: *In Loving Memory of Rose Denton*. I flicked through: prayers, hymns and tributes. Life in a leaflet.

To my left was Anna, to my right, Bernard. As people filed into spaces, I recognised a few backs. The straight neck and shoulders of Nick Summers, Head of Production. A few along from him was Sam, the Aussie graphic artist, with silly tight suit and even sillier pointed hair. Next to him was Poppy, his assistant. And one row in front of her, Julie, Effigy Post's receptionist: the last people to see Paul alive, this side of Heathrow, at least.

I noticed a couple of guys from the Pakistan International Bank and a couple of others from the advertising agency. Finally, in a box, in the aisle, and aptly I suppose, dead centre, was Rose.

'I am the resurrection and the life,' droned the minister. *'Those who believe in me, even though they die, will live.'*

My phone vibrated. Another text. I hadn't responded before because, apart from the fact we were entering a chapel, anyone I wanted to hear from was to hand.

This time, most of the congregation had their heads in the programme, so I decided I could surreptitiously take my phone out and check it.

'Elsie Turnbull,' said the text *'1888-1951.'*

I scrolled down. The next line said: *'First Row. Angel.'*

I tried to scroll down further, but that was it. Nothing more. A mistake, maybe?

I read it again: *Elsie Turnbull, 1888-1951,'* then, *'First Row. Angel.'*

Suddenly, the penny dropped. It was a grave. From memory, near the chapel door, in the first row of graves was a large stone angel.

The first hymn kicked in: *'Abide with me.'* We all stood.

I needed to get back to that grave. The chapel door was behind me. And out through that door was a corridor that lead to the chapel's entrance. As we'd walked through that corridor, from memory, there were toilets.

'Excuse me,' I whispered to Bernard 'I'm afraid I need …'

He got the gist and let me out. I nodded a thank you and quietly made my way to the back, pushing through the swing doors and walking down the corridor.

As I passed the toilet door, I pushed it. Probably unnecessary, but at least it made a convincingly squeaky sound. With the hymn still ringing out, they probably wouldn't hear it anyway.

Through to the outside. Dead opposite was a stone angel. No one was nearby, though some distance away a couple of undertakers were standing near long black limos. I made straight for it.

Old and lichen covered: *Elsie Turnbull, Born 31st October 1888, passed away 2nd April 1951.*

That confirmed it, but why?

Apart from the angel, there was nothing exceptional about the grave. Except, perhaps, for one thing. Amongst the weeds was a fresh bunch of lilies and on them was an envelope. I bent down and picked it up. Blank. I turned it over and opened it. Inside was a folded piece of paper. I unfolded it:

To change the past, speak to no one, email no one. Just wait.

CHAPTER THIRTY-THREE

Over the next couple of days I thought long and hard about what the note could mean. Very obviously, it was from Asif Farooki, or someone working for him. That was the reason he'd said the strange words in the first place. Proof that any note he left, any covert communication, would be Kosher – if you'll excuse that very un-Islamic expression.

But who left it? One thing I can say is that it was someone in or around that chapel. Why? Because I received two identical texts. The first text would have set it up perfectly because I was really near Elsie Turnbull's grave. But I didn't take the bait. They must have seen this and sent it again. For that to have happened they were almost certainly amongst the congregation or near the chapel, at least.

So who could it be? I couldn't say for sure, but I could hazard a few guesses. There were two or three guys from the Pakistan International Bank and they would be top of my list. Given that Farooki was behind it, using someone from his London branch made sense. It's also possible it was put there by someone from Effigy or even the advertising agency.

It was pretty clever way of getting a message to me. Emails are traceable and phone calls voice-recognizable, which just left two options. Texts, providing the mobile is immediately trashed and, best of all, the written word. So those were the mediums he'd chosen. But what was the purpose of the words: '*To change the past, speak to no one, email no one. Just wait.*'

Well, the purpose of the first part: '*To change the past,*' was to let me know who'd sent it. Farooki. The purpose of the second part: '*Speak to no one, email no one. Just wait,*' was to tell me to do exactly that. And if those words were for my eyes only, then so be it. Anyway, who else would I tell? If Farooki could save Paul, but only on condition that Stephanie wasn't involved, that was fine by me. I'd probably do the same myself. The last thing I'd want was a grieving, stressed-out spouse fowling things up.

So would I tell Anna? Absolutely not. I could trust her, of course. But I'd got her involved in a life-and-death situation before and regretted it to this day. The police, then? Even worse. I might as well sign Paul Hutchinson's death warrant as do that.

So over the next day or so, with my little piece of paper hidden amongst my utility bills, I got on with my life.

Stephanie, for her part, went back to Brighton. Her mother was going to keep her company. She was dreading this, but on balance, it was better than being alone. In fact, though I didn't say it, it could be the best thing possible. Her mum, apparently, was selfish, high-maintenance, and a complete pain in the arse. The last person you'd want around in most situations, but perfect when it comes to distracting you from life's real problems. Biting your tongue is definitely preferable to slashing your wrists.

For me, back to normal, meant Soho. There was one difference though: Anna now knew about Bernard. So all that secretive skulking was unnecessary.

So I met Anna for lunch, in a newly opened little Italian – all white walls and black pasta – that she'd been recommended to. It was good, but pricey. Not that it worried her much. Mum did the paying and Mum did the listening, too. Zack this, Zack that: Anna was bubbling. Which was terrific news, off course. Worth eating ink for. Perhaps I should've asked if they'd 'done it' yet. But no. Listen and pay: the parental way.

We kissed goodbye on Greek Street and I walked down a damp, camp Old Compton, crossed into Brewer Street, and pushed through the glass doors into Bernard's. The reception was busy: clients phoning, staff rushing. His little world was in a hurry.

Kirsty, behind her desk, looked up and asked me how I was, taking his flat keys from her desk drawer as she was doing so. Rather than simply giving me the keys, she got up and escorted me to the flat's door, mouthing *'important clients'* to me as we passed his office door. Once there, she unlocked it and simply left me to it.

Very quickly, I made myself at home: getting myself a tea, sitting myself down on the lounge sofa and flipping through a magazine. But I was soon drawn back to the kitchen. To that picture. What was it that was so strange?

Eventually, Bernard came up, tired and tetchy. He undid a button or two: his not mine, made us both a dry Martini and suggested we eat out. Great by me. So it was off to The Square House again. When we got back, we were both a bit woozy, so it turned out to be sleepover, but not leg over, so to speak. Probably for the best. Drink followed by sex normally precipitates pillow talk and loose tongues. Drink followed by snoring doesn't. So at least I wasn't unprofessional enough to tell him about the note.

I suppose, if I'd heard nothing within the week, given the deadline on Paul's life, I would indeed have to tell someone. That would probably be the police. What they'd make of my withholding that kind of information I could only guess at. Private investigators sitting on vital evidence whilst clocks clicked down? I'd be subjected to all that old *private investigator, public nuisance* stuff again.

The following day, Friday, I decided to leave Bernard to his work / stress / life balance and make for home. Originally, I was kind of hoping to make a weekend of it, but it wasn't to be. So I was up with him for showers, toast and coffee. We then descended the stairs together, where I kissed him goodbye in the still-empty reception, then left him to his deadlines.

Outside, it was damp and dreary. I pulled up my collar, put up my umbrella, and walked, back down through the alleys of Soho. Opening out into Leicester Square, I got that funny feeling again. So I stopped and turned. But there was nothing: no one. I was probably just imagining it. Turning back, if anything, most people were coming towards me. So I continued my walk: past St Martin's-in-the-Field, over The Strand, and into Charing Cross against a gathering tide of commuters.

Inside the station, brolly down, I looked up at the indicator board: *Orpington train – now! I hurried across the concourse but just as I got there, bleeps sounded, train doors closed and the barriers locked in front of me. Bugger!*

I walked back across the station, found a seat, sat down and waited.

The rush hour was building: trains trundling in, doors sliding open, people spewing out.

You know, sitting there, watching the oncoming hoards, I realised I'd been kidding myself. I'd told myself I was still using Charing Cross because it was easy. It wasn't. Yes, it was the nearest station to Soho. But to get back to Bromley North I had to take two trains, changing at Grove Park. Even after that I'd need a bus to get to Shortlands. Far more logical would've been to take the Underground from Leicester Square to Victoria, then go directly.

So why was I sitting here? Because it stopped me going underground twice: once for the Tube, then that long, dark tunnel between Sydenham and Penge.

Once my train arrived and the swarms had left, I found myself on a near empty, newspaper-littered train. Despite the fact that the train I'd just missed left on time, we pulled out about 15 minutes late. That's always the way, isn't it. We then edged across the rain-spotted river, slowed into Waterloo East, waited five minutes, rolled out at a snail's pace, over the blackened roofs of Borough, and eased into London Bridge.

A few people got off, even fewer dawdled on.

We then picked up speed a little, clickety-clacking through the flat-lands of Bermondsey. To my left, through dirty windows, Canary Wharf glistened. Golden towers, rising against greying skies, like some distant kingdom.

I closed my eyes.

Sunlight on my face, I started to nod off.

Suddenly, behind my seat, the carriage's dividing doors hissed open. This was not an Intercity, but a suburban tub: no restaurant cars, no buffets and half-empty. So why move, why come through?

I opened my eyes. No one had walked past me. Which meant he was still there, behind me.

Then I thought about it. I'd only heard one door. There are two sets of doors between the carriages. So he must be between them. It's cramped, it sways, so why would anyone do that? Even if you were getting off at the next station you wouldn't. There are no exit doors. So why?

No CCTV, that's why.

I have three choices: sit and wait, get up and move to another carriage, or turn and confront. Waiting gives him the initiative and running never works. So only one option.

I stand up, and with my back still to him, side-step into the aisle. Definitely someone there. I feel his stare. Prickly. That intuition thing.

Could it be the man who murdered Rose? Or the man who put the note on the grave? Or both?

We're nearing a station. That's why he's waiting. Whatever he's going to do, it'll be quick. Then he'll run. But that's not going to happen. Whether he likes it or not, he's going to be on camera.

I turn. I'm right. There's a shape in the chamber: the only unlit place.

We're nearing New Cross. I step forward. If it wasn't for the glass we'd almost be face-to-face.

The door behind him slides open. Is he going to turn and leave? I still can't make out his features. If anything, the light from the carriage behind him is silhouetting him more, making him less distinct. I think he has a scarf across his face though.

Neither of us move. Only the rocking and rattling gives us movement. What's he going to do?

Suddenly, the door between us opens. He flings something. It hits my face. I freeze, briefly panic, but whatever it is falls away. I look down: it's just a newspaper. But by the time I've realised, he's gone.

Do I pick it up or go after him? The paper can wait.

I lurch forward and hammer the door button. Nothing happens. I hit it again, and again. The door finally opens. I'm in the chamber. I move to the next doors. They should open automatically. They don't. I hit the buttons. Nothing. I hit them again. Still nothing. The door behind me closes. I'm now hemmed in.

It's dark. Moving floor. Noises from below. Air blowing upwards.

Back in my childhood. Ghost train: doors hissing, air blowing, echoing wails.

Sweating, feeling faint, drifting, I'm going to pass out.

Suddenly, the door in front of me opens. Empty carriage ahead. He's gone.

The train's stopping. Decision time.

I can run on to the next carriage, if that's where he's gone, then out onto platform, and give chase. Or I can go back into my carriage and find the newspaper. One or the other, but not both. I decide to go back.

The doors, typically, work perfectly this time. The paper's on the floor. I bend down and pick it up. Today's *Standard.*

I unfold it. Scrawled across the front page: *To change the past. Heathrow. PIA Desk. 10 p.m. Passport.*

CHAPTER THIRTY-FOUR

I didn't get there at ten, I got there at nine. And I didn't wait at the PIA desk, I waited on a nearby plastic seat. With a takeaway coffee and a paper: broadsheet, not tabloid – cover being more important than content.

In all probability, nothing would happen, and no one would turn up. Almost certainly, a pre-paid ticket was sitting at that desk. Just for me. And just as certainly, given it was the PIA desk, it would be for Pakistan. I'd checked the flights and there was one that fitted perfectly. 12:10. Two hours after check in. But if someone else was going to be making an appearance, I wanted to see them before they saw me.

As for what I should bring along with me, nothing on that note, passport excepted, suggested anything in particular. But there's travelling light and there's travelling naked. And I'm too old for that. So next to my knee, standing upright, with handle extended and essentials compressed, was my hand luggage. And if the whole thing turned out to be a fool's errand, I'd simply be wheeling it back home again. But somehow, though the person who'd set this errand up may be many things, I didn't think they were fools.

So what, and who, was I expecting? I honestly couldn't have said. But there had been many a Heathrow link to the whole affair: Paul's last sighting, the officious customs staff, and even Stephanie's references to 'baggage.' And where you find a link, you find a weakness. That's why I was waiting, and that's why I was watching. To get first sight, to get an edge. You see, I needed every tiny advantage I could get.

Watching the people coming and going was like one of those ever-building, time-lapse movies: families overburdened with bags, businessmen with nothing more than briefcases and phones, bleeping carts, flashing wagons. Even a couple of heavily, and reassuringly armed airport policemen walked by.

Most of the people who stopped at the desk, unsurprisingly, were of Pakistani origin, with one man, in particular, catching my attention. Given where we were, the lack of any kind of baggage, not even a briefcase, marked him out as a possible. A possible what though? Either way, after five minutes of hanging around, he simply left.

Then it happened. In many ways, I suppose, it was the last person I'd been expecting. In many others it was logical. So, so logical.

I recognised her not just from her walk, but from her coat and bag – the same one she'd taken before. I got up, walked over, pulling my bag behind me. She was at the booth, talking to a girl behind the desk, head down, studying documents. Tickets probably.

'Good morning, Stephanie,' I said.

The relief on her face was palpable. You just can't falsify that stuff. If you magnified my surprise tenfold, then added a dollop of relieved realisation that she wouldn't be going into the unknown alone – you'd have it.

Briefly, probably, she'd wanted to throw her arms around me. But my 'not now' expression stopped her. There'd be plenty of time for emotion. Now was a time for *not* attracting attention: show ID, pick up tickets, go.

Similarly, we kept it simple as we progressed through the system: check in, passport control, baggage check. But once in the departure lounge, we could relax, just a little, and compare notes.

'So how did they contact you?' I asked, as we put our coffee down on a still un-cleared table.

'A note,' she said, pulling up a chair.

'Just the one?' I asked.

'Yes,' she said. 'Telling me to come here – plus that thing about changing the past.'

This made sense. Kind of. No need for introductions for Stephanie. No need to ask twice. She'd drop everything. The keeping us apart and in the dark was logical too. Fewer conversations, less leakage. If either of us had uttered a word to anyone – including each other – the deal would've been off.

'How did you get it?'

'Through my letterbox.'

'You didn't see who put it there?'

'No. It was just there, on the mat, when I got back from your place.'

I thought about this for a second: 'So how would they know you'd got it?'

'It told me to leave a light on. In my lounge. All night. I can only imagine someone drove past that night to check it. Crazy really. I've left it on ever since, just in case.'

And so we settled down to discuss exactly what was going on. Certain things were pretty clear. The man behind this was obviously Asif Farooki. The code word proved that. It was obviously for our eyes only, too, and that meant everyone else – police, MI5, Interpol – were excluded. This all led to one, very obvious conclusion. The bank was going to cough up. And we would be part of that process.

'So why are we travelling together?' asked Stephanie. 'I mean, why not keep us separate all the way to Pakistan?'

'It would've drawn more attention. Travelling together is exactly what we did last time. The idea's to make it look like more of the same. We've even got economy seats again.'

'Aye,' she said ruefully. 'One-way tickets.

'Yes,' I agreed. 'But hopefully that's just because they don't know how long it'll take. Or perhaps to stop *us* knowing how long it'll take. The less we know the better, from their point of view. But either way, it won't be a money thing. A couple of first class seats aren't going to make much difference. Not with what they're forking out – *if* they're forking out. They're keeping it all low key. Just another trip.'

Stephanie thought for a while and then said: 'So, er, what's in it for them? All this forking out, I mean? Don't get me wrong, I'm not being ungrateful. I'm desperate. But Farooki isn't, is he? He's a businessman. Why spend all this money just to save my husband?'

'I've thought about that myself, and I think there are a couple of reasons.'

I counted on one finger: 'Firstly, paying out ransoms, sadly, is what big businesses do. Check it out: over a hundred million dollars in the last couple of years. And it's not just for the benefit of the staff involved. It makes sound business sense.'

'How? *Why?*'

'Well, put simply, if they didn't, they'd never get key staff in the first place. Not in dangerous parts of the world. On top of which, half the time it's tax deductible anyway.'

'Right,' she said, nodding thoughtfully. Clearly, having a tax deductible husband didn't particularly impress her.

'And the other reason?' she said, looking up. 'Number two?'

'Marketing,' I said.

'Marketing?'

'Yes. Just think about it. Farooki employed Paul to make them into world players, and that costs. It's not just the Pakistani market they're after, it's Islamic: worldwide.'

'So you're saying he's just using the same money in a different way?'

'Some of it, yes. The ads and the air time are obviously on hold for a start. He won't need them now, will he?'

She looked a little sceptical.

'Put it this way, Steph, have you ever heard of Terry Waite?'

She thought for a second. 'Do you mean ...'

'Yes, I do. And that kind of proves my point. He was kidnapped twenty-five years ago. You were just a kid, yet you know the name. Okay, so he didn't work for a bank, but that's not the point. The point is, PIA will be the good guys. Governments might not think so, but who likes governments? The bank will parade you two in front of a big new logo and some slogan they've just thought up: *"The Bank with Feelings",* or whatever.'

'So it all comes down to the job Paul was employed to do in the first place?' she said.

'Ironically, yes. Every interview, every photo, will have their logo behind it. Every headline, will put them in the public eye. A previously little known bank. *And* it'll keep them there. It's about marketing, and it's about money.'

I looked up. People had started to form a queue.

'So is that why we're involved: in the handover, I mean?' said Stephanie, 'For the PR?'

'If there is to be a handover, yes. It's all part of the deal. They get their exposure, the kidnappers get their money, we get Paul. Happy days!'

As we stood up and walked to the back of the queue, I'm not sure I really believed this. The next few days could be many, many things. But happy may not be one of them.

CHAPTER THIRTY-FIVE

I'd told Stephanie to expect more of the same. Not just the same flight, but same cab, same journey and same hotel. And so it proved.

Traipsing off the plane, we were greeted by a bearded man holding up a sign saying *Hutchinson and Andrews*. We sounded like solicitors, but felt like crap.

The driver needed neither directions nor money and the hotel receptionist, who immediately recognised us from our last trip, simply asked for passports. Our adjoining rooms were exactly the same as our previous stay, though one floor above.

Unpack, shower, go down together: that was the plan. The people we were dealing with seemed to be able to appear anywhere, at any time: in the cemetery, at the doorstep, on the train. So we had no reason to stay room-bound. We also had no reason to believe we'd be picked off individually. If they'd wanted to do that they wouldn't have put us together. But still, it was a case of safety in numbers, even if that number was just two.

I texted Anna a simple 'arrived OK.' She'd been one of only two people I'd told since realising what was happening, the other being Bernard. I couldn't simply *not* tell her, could I? What if something awful happened? Her mother meets her fate in some far flung land and she doesn't even know I'm there. So a half-truth would do. We were going back to Karachi to plead our case again. And that worked perfectly in another way, too. If anyone was listening in (and they certainly would have been) they'd hear exactly what our hosts wanted them to hear.

But perhaps the first big surprise after arriving was no surprises at all. Twenty-four hours of nothing.

On entering my room, I'd half expected an envelope on my newly made bed, or propped up amongst the rather twee beverage-making facilities. But no. Then, while we were downstairs having breakfast, I'd wondered if something might be pushed under our doors. Again no. So I checked at reception. Had there been any messages? Still no.

Perhaps we'd missed something. Was that whole 'change the past' thing supposed to contain some kind of cryptic instruction? Well if so it had gone straight over our heads. So with body clocks shot to pieces, we went to bed early. And guess what? I had that dream again.

Anna's with me, but I'm not her mother. She's just a school friend from long, long ago. We're in some kind of fairground at night. It's pretty. Coloured bulbs dance in the wind. I look down. I'm wearing sugar pink sandals. It's all so real. I can even smell the onions, taste the candyfloss.

We're inside an arcade. Brightly lit. Pinballs, flashing and pinging. But it's not an arcade. It's a House of Mirrors. I turn: I'm tall and skinny. I turn again: I'm fat and dumpy. Different mirrors, different people. I'm Anna, I'm me.

We start to walk. Through doors. They hiss. No longer House of Mirrors, House of Horrors. Blackness.

We're being followed, chased. Air blows and sirens wail, floors move and webs waft. But it's no longer a house of anything. It's a Tube train. Empty and dark, rattling and swaying. We're walking through it. Empty seat after empty seat. We reach the end door. It's locked. There's a photo on it. I walk right up to it. Anna's no longer next to me, she's in the photo, she is *the photo. But she's just a head, a severed head.* 'I'm in the wrong place,' *she says.* 'Change the past, Mum. Save me, help me.'

Cold, shivering, I wake up. Unfamiliar ceiling. Hotel room. Darkness. I'm clammy, sweaty. That's the air conditioning, of course.

I turn over, reach for the bedside light, turn it on: brightness. My eyes sting. I scrabble for my watch. 2:36: not even bedtime at home.

I propped myself up and thought about the dream. What did it all mean? Where did *that* all come from? Some things were obvious. The House of Horrors was the train. But that picture? It was horrific.

I calmed down a bit and thought it through.

It was simply to do with the hostage video and the picture on Paul's wall, that's all. But why that? What was so odd about that particular picture? Why did that keep turning up in my dreams, in my nightmares?

I punched my pillow, turned back over and closed my eyes.

Phone ringing. Where am I?

I open my eyes, saliva in my mouth. I must've nodded off again. I leaned over, scrabbled the bedside phone, looked at the clock. 2:57. What the f…?

'Hello,' I croaked, grappling the light switch.

'Mrs Anderson?'

'Yes.'

'Reception here. You car's arrived.'

'My car?'

'Yes. To take you to the airport.'

'The airport?'

'Yes. He said he was a little early, but he'll wait outside.'

195

'Right, er, thank you …' I nearly replaced the phone, then said: 'Oh er, have you rung Mrs Hutchinson, too?'

'No, but I'm going to do that now.'

'Thank you.'

The phone went dead.

I put the phone back. Settled back, thought.

Well, whatever it is that's going on, we're not being separated. But the airport? Can it be? We haven't even got tickets yet.

My mobile rang. *Stephanie,* it said. I hit the green button.

'Hi, you've heard?'

'Yes,' she said. 'What do you think's going on?'

'I haven't a clue. I think we should just do what they say. Dress, pack and go.'

'Right. How long?

'Twenty minutes?'

'Right,' she said. 'Twenty minutes.'

CHAPTER THIRTY-SIX

'We're not going to the airport, are we?' I said to the back of a driver's head.

I got no reply.

I'd already asked him where we were going when he was putting our cases in the boot. He'd simply slammed the boot and handed me two tickets. I'd looked at them: Karachi to London. But it didn't really answer the question. Departure time was 12:30 p.m. So why were we leaving the hotel in the middle of the night?

For about the first five minutes of driving I'd thought perhaps we were. Going to the airport, I mean. Then we'd started to veer off north, leaving behind the darkened city centre. So I'd said: 'We don't seem to be going to Jinnah.' Again, silence.

Stephanie had given a little shiver.

Two minutes later I'd asked, rather optimistically, who he was working for. No chance: just silence. He was good at silence.

He was local, for sure. But local plus Merc equals some level of English. Even for a cab driver. With that car, in that trade, he'd need it.

I put my hand on Stephanie's thigh. I could feel her fear, or anticipation, or both. The drifting street lights were getting gappier, the buildings between them shabbier. As habitation became sparser, the black voids were becoming more frequent.

Stephanie was looking out of her window; I was looking out of mine. In the space between us, on the seat, I moved my hand to hers and gripped it. It was trembling. It wasn't the car. Like I said, it was a Merc.

The buildings were running out. More voids, more blackness and less town. We'd been driving at a steady pace for thirty-five minutes. Mostly going north. If we were leaving New Karachi, it would make sense. As much as anything did. We'd be in the area where the second video was shot. That would mean, ahead of us, was Kirthar National Park. And that would make even more sense. Huge and uninhabited.

In front of us, just our headlights, converging into nothing. To my left, inky blackness, dark hills. Above those hills, the beginnings of dawn.

Eventually, we slowed down and went over some kind of grid. The road was even rougher. I was nervous, nauseous: tired yet wired. Another ten minutes of slower, darker driving went by and finally, we slowed to a stop.

I had no idea why, or how, he had chosen this spot. It all looked the same to me. A black nothingness. He hadn't been directed there by phone. Not that I was expecting he would be. That would have been asking for trouble.

He lit a cigarette.

'Could you smoke outside please?' I asked him.

He didn't, of course. But he did lower the widow.

So did I.

Outside, it was warm. A slight breeze. I handed Stephanie my water. She drank. I could see the bottle shaking.

Minutes went by. We said nothing, saw nothing.

I considered asking him what we were waiting for, but there would have been no point.

A few minutes went by. Then a car, in the distance. No lights, but definitely, it was a car. An SUV or a truck. It stopped. Just short of our headlights.

I desperately wanted our driver to switch to main beam, but there was no chance.

I nudged Stephanie, nodding forward. She stared, almost squinting. She too nodded. She'd seen it.

We waited.

'Okay,' said our driver, 'It's time.'

His English, as expected, was perfect.

The vehicle's doors opened. Yes definitely. I could see two people. They were standing next to it.

Our driver turned in his seat, looked at us.

You know, I'm used to detecting fear. In people's eyes, I mean. But there was none in his. So he was probably on their side. But was he on ours?

'The boot's open,' he said. 'Get out, both of you. There's a case in there, behind yours. Get it out, bring it to my door. Carry it between you.'

The central locking clicked.

We looked at each other: this is it.

We got out, Stephanie sliding out behind me.

I felt dust under my feet. The wind was warm.

'Are you okay?' I asked Stephanie, and she nodded.

'Shut up,' said the driver. 'We're doing this in silence.'

We went round to the back of the car. The boot was unlocked and slightly ajar. I lifted it slowly.

At first, all I could see were our cases, but then I noticed something behind them. Not a case, a holdall: big and green, with brown leather straps. We reached in, grabbed it and pulled it – across the top of our cases and onto the boot sill. It was pretty heavy, but just manageable. Zipped, but not padlocked.

I gave Stephanie a sideways glance, then looked back down. Two choices: exchange without checking, running the risk of handing over rubbish to an armed gunmen. Or take the chance of opening and checking it, running the risk of it being a bomb.

But thinking about it, how could it be? The driver was at the wheel, I was at the boot: a detective and an unlocked bag. He wouldn't take the chance that I might check it. It would blow us all up. So logic said it wasn't a bomb.

Then again, what if the driver wasn't involved? But that possibility didn't work either. In that case *he* could've opened the bag, blowing the car up even *before* it had reached us. Or taken the money. So by my reckoning: 1) The driver was *definitely* involved: 2) The bag *did* have money in it: 3) The bag *didn't* have a bomb in it. Mind you, that was just me being a detective, wasn't it?

I looked down at the zip. Long and snaky, like clenched teeth. I looked backed at Stephanie, looked back down and crossed myself. Suddenly, in the land of Islam, I was a Catholic again.

I then breathed in, grabbed the tabs and tugged.

Partly unzipped, no explosion. I was clearly still of this world, wherever *that* was.

So I pulled the zip fully apart. Yes!

Neatly stacked $100 bills. Used yet beautiful, powerful yet terrible. Each little stack, I'd guess, fifty grand. One, two, three four … ten across. And six down. That would be $3M. Ten deep? Thirty.

'Happy?' shouted the driver.

Now, he couldn't possibly have seen what we'd done from inside the driver's cab. So he'd guessed I'd check it.

There again, I'd worked him out too. So on guessing games, we were all square.

But to answer his original question: no, I wouldn't say I was exactly happy.

'Bring it here,' he said, 'Together.'

We humped it to the ground, grabbed a handle each, breathed in, and walked. It wasn't that heavy and I could have managed it by myself, just. So that clearly wasn't the reason we were both doing this job.

Our driver was leaning his arm on his open window, smoking, looking dead ahead. He didn't seem bothered. Or maybe he was. Maybe he was keeping his eyes on the situation ahead.

The men from the car (I was pretty sure it was a Toyota Hilux) were peeling apart, left and right.

We stopped next to our driver. He had no visible gun. There again, I could only see one of his arms. The one with the cigarette.

'Wait,' he said, putting his hand up.

Then he put his hand back to his mouth, took a last drag on his cigarette and flicked the butt into the night. Briefly, it glowed on the ground in front of us.

One of the men ahead of us raised his arm.

'Okay, walk,' said our driver.

We did as we were told, slowly. Nearer and nearer. Ahead of us, the two men. I could see what they were wearing, just. Fatigues, masks and boots. Just like the video. They didn't appear to have guns though. But they didn't appear to have Paul either.

The back door of the car opened. Two more men got out. This time they got out of the same side. That could mean one of them was bound, and that could mean one of them was a hostage. They started to walk away to our left, away from the others.

We stopped. I was still looking dead ahead, but Stephanie's gaze was drawn to the two who were walking. If I had been her, I would have been, too.

Could the two ahead of us have guns? Could our driver? If they did, we'd be right in the middle of a hail of bullets.

'Okay,' said the driver, 'Walk.'

We did as we were told. I fixed my stare on the eyes of the guy ahead – his only exposed feature. His hands were by his side, as were the other man's.

Nearer and nearer. I could even see the damp patch on his mask.

'Stop,' he said. 'Put the bag down.'

Slowly, we did as we were told.

'Open it.'

That meant bending down, taking my eyes off them, but I had no choice.

I was now glad I'd opened it earlier.

Slowly, again, I did as I was told.

'Walk back four paces.'

And yet again, we followed orders, backtracking, looking straight ahead: us, the bag, them. Separated only by darkness.

'You,' he said, pointing at Stephanie, 'Over there.'

He was pointing to our left, towards the other pair. He was going to split us up.

She started walking. I watched her. For the first time I noticed something. The eyes of the men I've been talking to are visible. But one of the two men Stephanie's walking towards is totally covered. A hostage, it must be. Paul, it just had to be.

She reached a point opposite the other two and stopped. Now we had mirror images. She was facing two men, I was facing two men. The only difference was the bag, separating me from my pair.

One of the men opposite me, the one who'd been giving instructions, walked forward, making for the bag.

He got to it, crouched down, looked inside and rummaged. He said something I didn't understand.

'Okay,' he said, re-zipping the bag and picking it up. 'Look over to your friend. When she raises her arm, it's done.'

One of the men opposite Stephanie called her over.

She walked forward, nearer to the pair.

'Stop,' he said.

She stopped. She was almost within touching distance of them.

She raised her arm.

Suddenly, mayhem! The hostage has his cover ripped off. There's some kind of struggle, commotion.

Deafening, blinding. Gunshots. Automatic fire. Crackling, shattering, lighting up the night. Silhouettes flash, appearing and disappearing. Blinding, then black. Then blinding. Then black again. Rat-tat-tat-tat. One of Stephanie's men is firing. It's the man who was covered, I think.

Chaos. The man near me, with the bag. He turns and runs. Everyone's running in different directions. Scattering, firing, shouting.

Stephanie's just standing there, I'm just standing here. The men seem to reform, they're scrambling into the Toyota.

It screeches away. Our Merc screeches up behind us: 'Get in,' shouts our driver.

'It wasn't Paul,' shouts Stephanie, scrambling across the seats.

We're still only halfway in, but the Toyota's gone – its red tail lights disappearing into the night.

'Not Paul?'' I repeat.

'Shut the fuck up,' screams the driver, throwing a sharp U and hurling me onto Stephanie's lap.

We snake away, straightening out, back the way we came.

'We aren't going after them?' I shout.

Foot down, engine screaming, clearly we weren't. Nor, given their armoury, would I particularly have wanted us to. But sometimes obvious questions, even stupid questions, need asking. And I had a million of them. After all, those shots weren't intended to kill us. Sprayed into the night sky, they were to distract us, confuse us, scare the shit out of us – and they'd certainly succeeded there.

So were those really the men holding Paul? Or had they just seized an opportunity? Had they simply hijacked a kidnap? And what about the man in front of me, gripping the wheel and flooring the peddle? Whose side was he on? Farooki's? The kidnappers? The kidnapper's kidnapper? Assuming all those people weren't all one and the same, of course. One thing I did know was that money-wise, deadline-wise, Paul-wise, we'd lost. The game was up.

'Are you Okay?' I asked Stephanie. Clearly she wasn't. It was another of those stupid questions.

She just nodded. We were both unhurt. That was something, I suppose.

As we were tossed about by the car, still shell shocked by the guns, Stephanie was able to shed the tiniest bit of light on what had happened. Almost at a whisper, to herself as much as me, she said: 'He pulled the gun ... said "hands up," what else was I supposed to do?'

'It's not your fault,' I said. And it wasn't. It was almost laughable, but not her fault. Hands up was the sign for OK too!

So whose fault *was* it? And more to the point, speeding back through the suburbs: what were we supposed to do now?

I waited a few minutes, till the lightless streets were grey again, till he'd slowed to a steady speed.

'Where are you taking us?' I asked.

Instantly, he veered over, slamming on the breaks and turned around. 'How many more bloody times?' he snarled. 'One more question and you get out here. Got it?'

Looking around the neighbourhood, yes, I got it.

A little later, silent, shell-shocked and tired, we finally pulled up to Jinnah Airport which, under the circumstances, I was happy to see.

'Get your bags and *go*,' was all the driver said, eyeballing me in the mirror, just willing me to say something, *anything.*

We slid ourselves out, walked to the back of the car and lifted the boot lid. As we hauled our bags to the floor the driver appeared by our side. He slammed the boot shut. The guillotine-like implication was clear: *"Don't even* think *about contacting anyone."*

Not that we would have. Wheeling our bags through the departure lounge, the sight of gun-toting police was enough to make us avert our eyes, hold our breath and simply hope. One of their cells could be even worse than our driver's proposed drop off point. The thought of just a single night made me shudder. And given what we'd just done, a single night would just be for starters.

So should we contact someone? Asif Farooki? Ring him? Tell him how we'd just blown his $30m? Hardly.

How about the British High Commission? Perhaps Martin Hague would like a call in the middle of the night. We could tell him that we'd gone completely against government advice, flown back to Pakistan and attempted to deal directly with terrorists. That would go down well.

No, in the end all we could hope for was a plane, some sleep, which would probably be impossible, Heathrow and home.

CHAPTER THIRTY-SEVEN

I'd been expecting the worst at Jinnah, but it didn't happen. Straight through the system smoothly. I suppose it lulled us into a false sense of security – *airport* security. You see, I thought Heathrow would be the same. It wasn't.

Queuing with papers and passports in hand, we were pulled out of line by armed police. We didn't even get the comfort of each other's company: I was dragged into one room, Stephanie another. It was the last we saw of each other.

'You're lucky,' said Fisher, his face expressionless. Very, very lucky.'

I didn't feel it. But I suppose we were. Lucky we'd been dumped in the airport and not in the desert. And lucky, as he put it, that even though we'd lost our heads, we hadn't lost our lives. But that wasn't quite the luck he was referring to.

'For now,' he said 'No one will know.'

I expressed no opinion on this. Looking a fool wasn't the biggest of my worries. Stephanie's wellbeing was.

Fisher leaned back in his chair – standard-issued and metal-framed – and said: 'You screwed up, *and* you donated thirty million to known terrorists in the process. So now there'll be more. More kidnappings, more murders. But like I said: for now, no one will know.'

'Why?' I asked

'Because it suits us. For now, you'll remain the famous Pamela Andrews: the detective that gets the police out of the excrement – rather than vice versa. For now, your screw up won't be featuring in tonight's headlines.'

'Am I supposed to say thanks?' I said, looking at him.

'No. You're supposed to say *nothing*. You see, the reason we keep things quiet is because sometimes it's safer that way. You should try it sometime.'

I let that pass. I could have told him that I hadn't once blabbed. But I didn't. As instructed, I said nothing.

'We've been telling you to keep out of this for weeks, months even. But no. You have to go and stick your highly paid little nose in.'

'I certainly wasn't highly paid,' I said 'I didn't do this for money. I did it for Stephanie.'

'Then you're an even bigger fool than I thought.'

'Maybe,' I said. 'But I didn't go chasing it. It came to me.'

'How do you mean?'

'I mean, I was given a note.'

And with that, I told him every last detail. The man at the cemetery and the man on the train. The code words *'change the past'* that proved, in my opinion, that it must have been Farooki's bank's money. The fact that no, I had no other proof, because we'd had no other contact. That I hadn't even had contact with Stephanie until we'd met at Heathrow Airport. Finally, I went into every last detail of the heist, even telling him about our journey back: sleep-deprived, scared, expecting at any minute to be pounced upon by the police. Or worse. And that even on the plane home, where every steward, every seat belt and table check, had us quaking in our flight socks. And that having landed at Heathrow, the last thing I'd expected was to be pounced upon and dragged into this little hole.

'Mr Fisher,' I asked. 'How is it we got all the way through the system at Karachi yet get pulled out of the queue at Heathrow?

His answer was no answer: 'I'm asking the questions.'

And so after it was over, with me neither officially cautioned, nor, astonishingly, even baggage checked, I walked to the Short Stay, got back in my car, and drove off towards Bromley.

But crawling around the M25, just as I hit the inevitable tailbacks at the M3 junction, I had this thought. You see, MI5 seemed to have been ahead of everyone. The Pakistan authorities, the British police, everyone. So, what if they were involved *before* all this kicked off? Before Paul was even kidnapped? What if Mr Paul Hutchinson, an international businessman – already travelling back and forth to Pakistan – was doing a bit of work for them on the side?

I found myself reimagining those words that Stephanie overheard. The ones Paul was saying on that final phone call. What if it were: *'I'll need some help with the Baggage Checking'* and that it was MI5 on the end of the line? If he was about to carry something through for them, those words would make a whole load of sense, wouldn't they. And it would be the first interpretation of them that had.

This might explain why MI5 had been tailing me from the off; why we'd been targeted twice at Heathrow, and why our baggage had been tampered with. It could even explain the cold-blooded murder of a businesswoman in a London Street. Maybe the tabloids weren't so far off the mark with their 'similarities' to the Jill Dando case. International espionage too? Why not?

Oh well, I guess I'd never know now. I was well and truly off the case now. Even contact with Stephanie was off limits.

Job finished, but not done. And a very, very unsatisfactory ending.

CHAPTER THIRTY-EIGHT

Anna was shocked. And very, very cross. 'Anything could've happened, Mum,' she said. Yes, I told her, and it pretty much had. And implicit in her criticism was: *think of me.* After all, that's exactly what I would've said, or implied, or thought, if she'd done something that daft. She was right to be angry. I'd been irresponsible.

A coffee, a catch up, and a spot of confession: my confessional box of choice being a window seat in a Wardour Street café.

Outside, the first spits and spats of rain were dampening pavements, wetting windscreens and hurrying people on.

I'd probably been tailed to Anna, but I didn't care. According to Fisher I wasn't supposed to tell anyone. Part of the deal. But for me, there was no deal. Anyway, I needed someone to confide in, and Anna, as ever, would be that someone.

Fisher had given the impression he was doing me some great favour by keeping it all under wraps. He'd implied, strongly, that if it all came out my career would be over. What career? I'd had enough. And anyway, he wasn't keeping it a secret for my benefit. As soon as it suited him, he'd be shouting from the rooftops. So I owed him nothing – and Anna everything.

'I just don't know why you bloody do it, Mum,' she said, shaking her head. 'You hardly need the money.'

She was right, of course – no mortgage, a decent pension. What I didn't dare tell her was what I'd told Fisher. No money had changed hands. Well, not *my* hands anyway. I simply told her what I'd told her before: it wasn't a financial thing. But in that case, what thing was it? An adrenalin thing? A do-gooding thing? Whatever it was, it was a thing I was doing no more. I was getting out. I was way too old for it.

Once she'd got over the initial shock and the delayed concern for me, she asked about Stephanie.

'Well,' I said. 'If I'm truthful, I'm surprised how she took it. When we were coming home, I mean.'

'In what way?'

'Well, maybe it was the shock or something, but she honestly didn't seem that bad. Not in floods of tears or anything, anyway.'

'I suppose these things affect different people in different ways,' shrugged Anna, cooling down a bit.

'Maybe,' I said. 'Maybe.'

But it was slightly strange. After all, it was probably her last chance. Not only had the deadline passed, but so had the money. I suppose there was an outside chance, a *tiny* possibility, that Paul would turn up alive somewhere. If those guys really were his kidnappers, they now had their money. Maybe, just maybe, they would now release him on their terms, in their way, somewhere else. It seemed unlikely though.

The other possibility was that they weren't the kidnappers at all. If that was the case, the real kidnappers could still be holding him in the forlorn hope that the bank would cough up a second time.

Suddenly, I found the term 'second time' going round my head.

Of course! That's why Fisher was keeping it quiet. If these guys were phoney, as far as the real kidnappers were concerned, there'd be no 'second time.' Just a first time.

Did Fisher still have some inside information about another, more genuine group? Did he know, for sure, that the guys who ripped us off didn't have Paul? Was Paul now in Syria or Iraq rather than Pakistan? Is that why he was keeping it out of the headlines: to keep the whole case ongoing and keep Paul alive?

I didn't raise these thoughts with Anna. I don't think she would've been too receptive to even more in-depth analysis.

So I kept it as brief as she would permit, and eventually the conversation came back round to her life. Quite right too, that's how it should be. I was there for her. One day I wouldn't be, of course. She would have a life without me, whereas I, hopefully, would never have a life without her. And that was why my actions had been so bloody stupid. I had no right to make that day come any earlier than was necessary.

So I was just happy to be back in the old routine, Anna's occasional sounding board: a phone call, a text, perhaps a bite to eat during one of my Bernard visits.

And talking of Bernard, he too was good to get back to. Not in the same way, of course. My love for Anna was nature talking: genes. Having Anna had made me immortal. Bernard could never help repeat that trick. Not at my age, anyway.

When I told him what I'd been up to, he, too, was shocked, if less censorious. I suppose, when someone keeps a secret from you, even if they tell you later, it changes their perception of you. That can go both ways, but in this case I think it gave him more respect for me. Not just the derring-do nature of what I'd done, but the silence. When you don't confide in someone, it makes *them* wonder and gives *you* an independence.

We were sitting opposite each other, at a corner table, in a Soho boozer, later that night.

'It sounds to me like you did everything you possibly could,' he said.

'Wasn't good enough though, was it?' I replied, sipping at my wine. 'Overall, I mean. I didn't deliver, did I?'

'Paul, you mean?'

'Yes.'

'Neither did two entire police forces,' he said, shrugging. *'And* you gave Stephanie a load of support along the way.'

I said nothing to this. I didn't feel I'd been especially successful at that either.

'Don't worry,' he added, touching my arm. 'You've done a terrific job, just move on.'

And I suppose that was what I did. And as the days and weeks passed, even my lesser worry: the loss of my oh-so-precious reputation, diminished too. Delayed news, in this case, would be good news. After all, if at any time in the future Paul was found alive my actions would be distanced from it. I'd come over as heroic, if failed, rather than stupid. And if he was found dead, those same actions wouldn't have been the cause. Distance and time, plus having the media on your side, can heal many a mental scar.

And talking of which, there was one event during those weeks that did begin to heal one old wound. A problem I'd almost given up on.

It was Friday lunchtime and he'd finished work early. And for once, instead of Soho, he'd met me at the South Bank, for bit of contemporary culture.

The Tate Modern is an odd place. I couldn't work out where the cloakrooms ended and the gallery began. Was I sitting on a toilet or an installation? At least Bernard was similarly bemused. Traipsing around blank canvases and empty rooms. It did nothing for either of us. Apart from showing compatibility, I suppose: philistines, both.

Eventually, full of confusion, if not inspiration, we waived the white flag, or perhaps the blank canvas, and left for a nearby pub.

Bernard got the drinks in and I bagged a spectacular riverside view: St Paul's, Tower Bridge, plus full, silhouetted, supporting cast. Being November, the old river was turning swiftly from afternoon gold, to evening treacle. We had already made our minds up to go back to Soho for the night, but Bernard had this sudden idea.

'I'm going to make a new woman of you,' he said, with a slight twinkle in his eye.

'I thought you already had,' I said.

'*Another* new woman, then. Your phobia, I mean.'

'Phobia?'

'Yes, your *claustro*phobia. Remember? We'll take the Jubilee Line.'

Perhaps it was the alcohol. Or perhaps it was the knowing he'd be there with me. Either way, I said yes. So we drank up, left the pub, walked beside the evening river: through darkened arches and cobblestone alleys, crossed the closing Borough Market, and finally found London Bridge Underground.

Down the steps, across the ticket hall, zap Oysters and, with hordes of others, we made it to the edge of the elevators. Descending below us, via moving steel steps, was hell.

Bernard, parachutist style, stepped first. Scared of being left behind, and holding tightly onto the belt of his coat, I followed. And down we rumbled.

One step above him, and now hugging his back, we were now roughly the same height. Just the smell of his hair was keeping panic at bay.

'Now, open your eyes, Pamela' he said.

How did he know they were closed? Do men have six senses too? I wasn't aware they had any.

'Open your eyes,' he repeated: 'Take it all in, you're a detective.'

Some detective! I was petrified.

We got to the bottom and, taking a deep breath, made it to the platform edge. Or not quite. Jubilee Line platforms are partitioned off from the trains by glass doors. Only when the train fully stops do they open. Of course, because of this, the commuters know where the carriage doors will be, so they stand in clumps, ready for the charge. We didn't, we stood away from the clump, staring out into the black void ahead of us: a dark, sinister aquarium.

The train came and everyone moved in for the kill, with us just about bringing up the rear. Bernard was just able to get one foot on the train and one hand on the bar above. I clung onto his back, my only hope of survival. The doors forced themselves closed behind me, squeezing me in like a zip fastener on a bulging bag.

Optimistically, I'd had visions of getting through this ordeal face-to-face, loving eyes to loving eyes, with my gallant, phobia-free hero. But sardined in, I was merely nose-to-back. Until the next station, that is.

It's sod's law of the Tube, that whoever's nearest the door doesn't want to get off, and whoever isn't, does. We were soon regurgitated back out by a wave of spent commuters, and pushed back in by the return wave of fresh ones.

I was now on my own, somehow managing to end up squeezed against the doors facing outward. I spent the remainder of the journey, nose-to-glass, watching endless streams of sooty cabling slither past.

I followed Bernard's instructions though: *not* closing my eyes and *not* reciting endless Hail Marys. I also tried *not* to think of the miles of dark tunnelling ahead and the tons of damp earth above.

Finally, we piled out with a hundred others, re-linked, shuffled forward, through windy, foul-smelling tunnels, then slowly reversed the original process: rising slowly back up to the Earth's crust – and the relatively fresh air of Green Park Tube. We paused on the pavement, breathed in, and let everyone pass.

'Made it,' I said.

'Well done,' he said.

Walking our way down Piccadilly towards Soho, we made a pact. In future, like it or not, this would be part of our dating. We'd take Tubes together until I was confident enough to do it by myself. Then I'd do the same for Anna. New beginnings all round.

CHAPTER THIRTY-NINE

That night, lying in his bed, propped up on my pillow and flicking through a magazine, I told him about this idea I'd been mulling over.

'You know, I've been thinking about moving,' I said.

'Where to?' he answered.

'Somewhere more central. Round here, maybe.'

I realise this was getting into slightly dangerous territory. I honestly wasn't angling to move in or anything. I really wasn't. Quite apart from everything else, it wouldn't be practical. We had our own lives. And anyway, he already had one live-in lover: his work. And when he wasn't working away downstairs, we'd be cramped into a one-bedroom flat upstairs. Except for weekends when he'd be off to Watford or wherever to see his sons. Worst of all worlds. So even if he *had* floated the idea of cohabiting, I would've said thanks, but no thanks. But the point is, he hadn't.

However, he did ask me, more generally, why I'd want to give up a three bedroom, big gardened house for a poky little West End flat. Simple answer? Gardening and housework. I wasn't getting any younger. Anyway, a Soho address would work for a detective, wouldn't it? And in a

218

way it would feel like coming back home. Like a long lost friend. Like Bernard, I suppose.

So he got out of bed, found his laptop, and we spent what remained of the evening on the internet, looking at what I could buy if I sold, or rent if I let. And it was all quite exciting. Cosy little flats in Soho, slightly bigger ones in Fitzrovia, the possibilities were endless.

The next morning, he was up first, bringing me a cup of tea in bed, asking me if I'd slept well, which I had, and getting ready for work.

He did all those man things: pulling a face in the mirror as he shaved, buttoning up his shirt with stubby fingers; even the way he scraped his change off the sideboard and into the palm of his hand. And that was without all the more clichéd abrasives: upright toilet seat from him, nail varnish in the fridge from me, pubes on the soap from both of us. So, no; propped up there observing him, even if he'd suggested living together, I'd definitely have said no. I wasn't quite ready for that. But like I said, he never did.

I think I was irritating him a bit. Just lying there, drinking his tea, coming up with stupid questions. He needed to get working and I didn't. The price he had to pay for having me stay – or simply having me, I suppose. But I still think he was a bit irritated by something.

As he was looking for something or other I asked him about his company. I'd never thought about it before, but I was wondering if there were any other directors.

'Yes,' he said, finding whatever it was he'd lost. 'A sleeping partner, not involved.'

He didn't seem to want to elaborate on it, going out to the kitchen for something. So I left it at that. Eventually he went downstairs, leaving me to take my time: lie in bed, read a magazine and drink tea. Then I got up, had a leisurely shower, dressed and made up.

Trying to prop up my little magnifying mirror on his kitchen table: a cruel necessity: the devil being in the wrinkly detail, I caught sight of that old school photo again. It looked slightly askew. Maybe that was the problem. Maybe that's what had always irritated me about it. On the other hand I couldn't remember it being skewed before.

I got up from the table, walked over to it, looked at it again – squaring it up a little – stood back and looked at it yet again. Was that better? Did it now fit in? No, it honestly didn't. It still looked very, very out of place in this flat. But I just couldn't say why.

So I mentally shrugged and sat down again. Perhaps it was just me that was out of place. In this flat, I mean.

CHAPTER FORTY

Early December. Six weeks after that second Karachi trip, and well past the stage when it was the first thing on my mind when I woke up in the morning. And that's when it finally happened. The inevitable.

I was in the kitchen, the toaster had just set the smoke alarm off, and I was still in my dressing gown. I'd opened the back door into the garden and was frantically wafting it. My mobile rang. I left the door, walked over to the table, picked up my phone and looked at it: *Anna*. At that point, had it been any other name, I probably wouldn't have taken it.

'Hi Babes,' I said, walking back to the door and closing it. 'How's things?'

'You haven't heard?'

'Heard?'

There was a silence on the end of the line. A bad news silence.

'Paul's dead,' she said.

I pulled up a chair, said nothing, sat down.

'You still there, Mum?'

'Yes, I, er ...'

'It's all over the news.'

'Where ... I mean, how did it ...?

'Another video.'

'On the TV?'

'No, they're sparing us that. I'm sure the whole thing's out there somewhere, but I wouldn't suggest searching for it.'

This was beyond horrible. It was disgusting.

After a pause, I said: 'Did they say anything about Stephanie?'

'Yes,' she said, 'That's the other thing … on the news, I mean. She's gone missing.'

'Since this news broke, you mean?'

'They didn't say exactly when.'

'So what're they saying's happened? To her, I mean?'

'They don't know, but the assumption is she's …'

'Done something …' I was about to say 'stupid,' but I checked myself. Somehow it felt wrong. Given what she'd presumably just witnessed, taking your own life certainly wouldn't be that stupid.

'But there's no evidence – no note, or anything?'

'If there is, it wasn't mentioned.'

There was another long silence. I didn't ask if my name came up. Worrying about my reputation, by comparison, would've been crass. Possibly Anna picked up on this because the next thing she said was: 'It mentions you, Mum.'

'Right,' I sighed.

'Look, I'll check it myself. Thanks for the warning. Is everything else Okay?'

What a stupid bloody question. My daughter tells me that a close friend has gone missing, possibly suicide, and that her husband has just been executed on prime time TV. And I sign off with: *'Is everything else Okay?'*

Anna simply said yes, and I said I'd phone her back when I'd seen the news.

I walked to the lounge, put down my mobile, picked up the remote, bit my lip and zapped.

Breakfast TV. Halfway through the weather. I considered flicking to News 24 but didn't. Something to do with seeing what everyone else was seeing. To do with checking just where this story stood in today's good news charts. I didn't have to wait long, it cut straight back to the studio:

'British Hostage, Paul Hutchinson has been executed,' said a stern-faced Bill Turnbull. *'A video was posted on the Internet, but has now been removed.*

Cut to a mercifully pre-kidnap photo of Paul wearing a suit and tie.

'No further demands were made. The execution appears to be the work of radical extremist Pervez Zaqqi (cut to close up photo of well-known terrorist) *whose face can clearly be seen in the video. This is the first time an actual abductor has been identified.* Cut back to Turnbull: *It has also just come to light that money was handed over some weeks ago – though no further details are available at present.'*

Cut to Susanna Reid: *'His wife, Stephanie Hutchinson, and British Detective, Pamela Andrews apparently travelled to Karachi in October in a failed attempt to secure his release.'*

Cut back to video footage. In the distance, a few Pakistani military vehicles are straggled across open scrubland. *'It is believed he was murdered in a remote area of the Khirthar National Park, just north of Karachi.'*

Cut to different footage: telephoto lens, long distance. Army personnel are standing by a taped-off area of rocky outcrop. *'At least one of the hostage videos was also filmed in this area,* continued Susanna. *As yet, there has been no comment from the Pakistani Authorities.'*

Cut to a full screen photo of Stephanie. Cut to some recycled footage of her house in Brighton.

'Meanwhile, back in Britain,' Cut to close up of Turnbull *'Stephanie Hutchinson, his wife, is reported to have gone missing.'*

Cut back to the studio.

Between them, Bill and Susanna completed the bulletin by simply running through the events of the original story. Some of the material was old and everything about the report – hasty and cobbled together – suggested it was still breaking, unconfirmed news.

Cut to new story: Flooding in the West Country.

I switched off the TV and, feeling sick, sat down. Stunned.

CHAPTER FORTY-ONE

'So you've had no contact with her?' asked DCI Ben Crawley, a deadpan, dandruff-shouldered detective, who'd travelled all the way up from Brighton just to grace my little office. 'Since you and Stephanie got back, I mean.'

He was sitting on my sofa between the friendly face of Andy McCullough and the not so friendly face of Mr Fish. Three wise monkeys, all in a row. Joined up policing, I suppose.

'I did exactly as I was told,' I said

'*Exactly*?' questioned Fish. 'Haven't you been, well … spreading the word a little?'

I presumed he was referring to Anna and Bernard. I doubt he knew for sure that I'd told them, but he probably knew I'd met them soon after and guessed the rest.

'Look, Pamela,' said Andy, 'We really all need to help each other here.'

'I've told you everything I know,' I said.

'Then tell us again,' said Crawley.

And that, leaning back in my chair, folding my arms and taking my time, is precisely what I did. Every last tiny detail. From the point when Stephanie had first called my mobile, to the point when they just walked in my door. I included the 'baggaging' call, mainly to catch their reaction to it – they looked genuinely clueless – and even the strange incident of the pig's liver and the note. Crawley asked me why I'd never mentioned this before and I said I hadn't thought it relevant.

'Everything's relevant,' he said.

I suppose it took about an hour in all. I then turned the tables and asked them a few questions:

'So what makes you think Stephanie's taken her life?'

They looked at each other. Two DCIs and an MI5/GCHQ. Her Majesty's alphabet soup. It was almost laughable. I mean, who was boss here? Between them, they hadn't even decided what they could and couldn't tell me.

'Bank account,' said Fish, deciding finally that he was the decision-maker. 'Nothing's gone in, nothing's gone out. Her handbag and purse were still on the table. Even her mobile phone and house keys. The only thing missing is her car.

'Passport?' I asked.

'In the bureau,' he answered.

'And no suicide note?'

'No, but you don't always get one,' he said.

He was right, you don't.

'Anyway,' added Fish, 'Who would she leave it to? She had no one.'

Was that a subtle dig? Was he implying that Stephanie had no one, i.e. no partner because *I* had poked my nose in? Because *I* had screwed up?

'But you've found no body?' I asked.

'Not yet. Nor her car.

'And nothing on CCTV?'

'No, not yet.'

I thought for a second.

'And you're no closer to finding Paul's murderers?'

There was a long silence. We were back on Paul's case. Were they permitted to open up a little on that, too?

'We know who it is, yes.'

'Yes, but do you know *where* he is?'

'Well, Pamela,' said Fish, 'If we had the answer to that, we wouldn't be here, would we.'

'I thought you were here for Stephanie,' I said.

'We're here to help everybody,' he said, 'including you, Pamela.

'I can look after myself,' is all I said.

'It doesn't seem like it,' is all Crawley replied.

CHAPTER FORTY-TWO

The next few weeks weren't the best. Outside my house was an amorphous huddle of hacks, sometimes one or two, sometimes more. It was raining most of the time and I'm not sure who was the worst off – them, with their soggy coats and cardboards cups – or me under siege and feeling like a failure.

As for keeping them at arm's length, my little office, being on a main road, offered a slightly better option. Above a shop, I couldn't see them. And they, by and large, couldn't see me. Plus I didn't feel guilty about the neighbours. Quite the opposite, in a way. The Shortlands Café was doing a roaring trade in the bacon sarnies, and Martin's News had never sold so many packets of fags and chewing gum.

I had a couple more meetings with the police, though they weren't that helpful. Bromley police station, like the rest of suburbia, was gearing up for Christmas: one of their busiest times of year. Office parties and family piss-ups: the tinsel soon turns to tears.

Drip-by-drip, I did learn a few more details though. Suicide was looking more and more likely. Stephanie's car had been found in a Gravesend side street smothered in two-week's worth of parking tickets. And Gravesend is on the tidal Thames, so even though there was no body yet, it didn't mean too much. On that stretch of the river they can take ages to bob up. Very often in a completely different place.

Once her car was located, her movements, on the night of Paul's execution, were easy to trace. Working backwards from the Gravesend and Dartford areas, she was picked up by cameras on the M25, the M23 – then right back to Brighton.

No one seemed to know why she'd chosen the Dartford area. There were plenty of nearer suicide spots: big white cliffs and crashing seas surrounded her Brighton home.

'Maybe the answer's in the name,' I suggested to Andy, ruefully: 'Gravesend?'

That was about a month on, and I suppose, the fact that I could display darkish humour was proof that I was beginning to get over it.

Stephanie was a lovely girl, and a good friend, but when all was said and done, she was a client. I might add that, as a copper, I'd learned to distance myself from death and disaster. And to that end, black humour can be a useful tool.

I well remember, back in my Met years, being the first on the scene of another suicide. In this case the body *was* found in the car, and it, too, had been smothered in parking tickets – the car not the corpse. 'A fine way to go,' was how I'd described the scene.

Of course, it's not the suicid*er*, but the suicid*ee,* you really feel for. Those left behind. But in Stephanie's case I'm not sure that really applied. Her father was long dead, and her mother, by all accounts, was too selfish to care. It's true that her brother had come over from Australia, but that was out of duty rather than dedication. Stephanie once told me that, as children, they hadn't got on. And by the way, when her brother was over here, he'd only visited his mother once, *and* the three of them had never even met up. Imagine it! All the way, from one side of the world to the

229

other, and mother, daughter and son never even sit in the same room together. So, given Paul's fate, maybe she'd chosen the best option. I'd certainly come across lesser motives.

And slowly, as the nights drew in, it faded from the headlines. And the run up to Christmas, with its bits to buy and cards to send provided the perfect distraction.

Since my divorce, swiftly followed by my mother's death, Christmases had fallen into a limited number of permutations based around Anna and/or my sister's family. This year I would be slightly different: Anna, me, and Zack makes three. A whole new order. Daughter plus partner, all close enough to spend Christmas together.

Ideally it would've been four, but December 25th was apparently a day of wary armistice in the Simmonds family. Bernard put up with his ex and she put up with Bernard for the sake of the boys. '*Ex*-mas,' he'd called it.

So for me it would be the whole shebang: the turkey and the trimmings and the crackers and the jokes. I even bought a real Christmas tree: the first in my house since my divorce. Given the big deal my ex used to make of dressing the bloody thing I expected it to be difficult. It wasn't.

In the end I went for the tiny blue flashing lights option. As an ex-cop, it seemed apt.

The big day went well, with Zack the perfect guest. A male that that can multi-task (talk *and* listen) is worth hanging on to. He was helpful, too: confident enough to volunteer for cork-popping, unpretentious enough to get it wrong, and then laugh at himself when he got soaked. Oh yes, and tall enough for those top cupboards, too. If Anna was in this for the long haul, I couldn't think of a better partner.

They left on the 27th and Bernard came on the 28th. We no longer had to meet at the station, he knew the way by now, and when he arrived, he offered the normal seasonal greetings and kissed me under the mistletoe. Now if you know nothing of the terrible Su A case, this won't seem like much of a deal. But if you do, you'll know the significance of even having the stuff in the house.

That afternoon we went round to Liz's. She's my big sister. It was a full house: hubby Terry, their grown-up daughter, Sarah, her husband, Brendan, plus twin girls Kirsten and Charlotte, so she had her hands full.

Bernard did what men do best in such situations: looking awkward around babies and keeping well away from the messy bits. Mind you, he did have a talent for palming things, so he could make salted peanuts vanish from his hand and reappear behind the twins' ears.

They loved this of course. He shouldn't have allowed them to eat them afterwards though. And unbeknown to me he'd even bought them Christmas presents: two sets of Lego bricks. This was sweet of him, but they were way too young, of course. Like the peanuts, they ended up in their mouths, which meant confiscation, tears and a second telling off for Bernard. Worse still, he stood on a stray one (brick, not twin) and said the 'f' word. So things could've gone better, I suppose. I think he found it all a bit of an ordeal.

Men are strange creatures. They can go through the most primal of sex sessions with you, yet meeting your sister's family is death-by-embarrassment. I suppose they're programmed to get into women's bodies rather than their minds – or their families, come to think about it.

But he got through it. *We* got through it. And who would have thought it? After all that slightly sordid Soho stuff, here we were: two civilised, suburban fifty-somethings, amongst family and friends.

So, all things considered, the end of the year wasn't too bad. Anna had Zack and I had Bernard. And the Stephanie thing was over.

Or so I thought.

CHAPTER FORTY-THREE

It was only a tiny point. A throwaway line overheard by Anna. Innocent, but changing everything.

She'd heard it at the beginning of the week but I wouldn't find out about it until the end. That's because, overnight, the world froze. Or at least, Britain did. And I was stuck at home. We'd had our warnings: solemn weather forecasters, gathering isobars, and flashing gritter trucks. But it made no difference – in no time the whole country slithered to a halt.

It started with just a few flakes, gently falling against grey-white skies. By dusk it had become steady, and by night, a blizzard. Swirling and blanketing: covering hedges, paths and cars. Even streetlights had snowy hats.

The next morning I opened my curtains to a different world: sugar-coated and silent; a sparkling winter's day. Everything newly softened, evenly whitened and smoothly joined.

I went downstairs and, still in my dressing gown, crumbled up some bread, mixed it with some wild bird food, put on my coat and wellies, forced open the back door and made my way, crunching and sinking, across my garden. After clearing a patch and scattering my offerings, I retraced the holes I'd made in the snow. This almost required a Ministry of Silly Walks sketch. Why are re-traced steps so different?

Reaching the back door, I kicked the snow off my boots, hopped back inside and gave a little shiver. I then took off my coat, switched on the kettle, sat on a stool and looked out. The scene outside was impossibly beautiful. Sunny and sparkly, who says nature doesn't do artificial? It was pure, natural bling.

Birds were already gathering: robins and blackbirds, magpies and crows. All vying and quarrelling, but few actually eating. All desperate for food, but pecking orders must be maintained.

I switched on Radio 4. The news was about snow and snow and snow. God knows, don't we wallow in it. Not the snow, obviously, the weather.

Oh well, what to do now? You see, I was supposed to be going to go to London. The sales were on and Bernard's would have been a perfect base. But there were no trains.

So I showered, dressed and put on some make up. From upstairs, I rechecked the garden: birds still hopping, but now less food and more tiny footprints, and then I phoned Bernard. He was hardly surprised I wasn't going. London, apparently, was empty. Mind you, it worked for him. No clients and loads to catch up on. So I kiss-kissed him a goodbye and put the phone down.

Back where I started: what to do? My little office was walkable, or perhaps slitherable, but I had no pressing cases. Even adultery stops in the snow. So I decided to bake a cake.

I don't know why, they seldom work. All tied up with being a proper mum or some kind of domestic goddess, I suppose. I blame *Bake Offs* etcetera. They make women feel inadequate. Me, anyway.

Within sixty curse-punctuated minutes, I was regretting it. Peering back at me, through my oven door, was a concave, damp, soggy splodge. Oh well, at least it was an appropriately named cake. Is there a duller word in the

English language, when applied to cooking or weather, than drizzle?

I was just opening the oven door when my mobile rang. Phones and oven gloves are not, like my cake, a very good mix. Flustered, I just got the call before it rang off.

It was Anna.

'Sorry Love. Phew, I'm baking!'

'Hot flushes?'

'No, Anna. I mean *I actually am baking,* as in a cake.'

'You ... a cake?'

'Yes me, a cake.'

Long silence.

'Right. Well anyway. Snowy, isn't it?'

Good God, Anna. Is that why you've rung me? To tell me that? Clearly she, too, was bored. There again, whatever she had to say, I would just listen. It's my role: offer support and wreck cakes. So while my kitchen cleared of smoke, I just sat down and let her talk.

She mentioned the weekend's bad news on the Stephanie case, of course. An article of her clothing had been washed up on The Isle of Sheppey, just downstream from where her car had been found.

'Poor woman,' is all I could think to say. It was all anyone could say, really.

We moved away from the subject a little, just lightening things a little, then Anna cut back with: 'Oh yes that reminds me. That line that she said she'd heard – the one about help with the baggage?'

'Oh yes,' I said.

'Well I heard almost exactly the same line yesterday. But it wasn't baggage, it was garbage.'

'How do you mean?'

'Well, I was in this post production house – not Effigy Post, another company – when someone said "I'll need some help with the garbaging."'

'Garbaging?'

'Yes.'

'What's that?'

'Well, I thought it was something to do with putting the bins out, but apparently it's kind of like cleaning up the rubbish on the picture. You know, with blue screen and stuff. Getting rid of the patches that don't work properly. It's called garbage matting. Really boring work.'

Frankly, it didn't sound any more fun than baking.

'Are you saying that's what Stephanie could have overheard?'

'Well, it's possible. We did wonder whether that conversation could've been between Paul and Poppy, didn't we. And the person I heard using that expression did exactly the same job.'

'As Poppy Foster, you mean? An assistant?'

'Yes.'

We both kind of left it at that, moving back off the subject, with Anna saying she might even try walking to her nearest Underground, Elephant & Castle, as some of the Tube trains were still running. I told her to be careful on the pavement, gave her my love and rang off.

About an hour later I got a text from her saying she'd got to work safely. Bless her.

The next day was dull, snowy, but dry. I decided to put on my walking boots and hazard a hike. Once I got going, wrapped up warm and misty-breathed, the going wasn't too bad. The path across my local rec was all the better for being semi-trodden and compacted. So my grip was okay.

That part of the park is flat, but once I'd crossed the little river, with puzzled ducks shivering and slithering on solid, opaque air bubbles, the path soon climbed.

Getting to the top is tough at the best of times, so I'm not sure why I did it. But I suppose Martin's Hill is my little mountain. Because it's there: to be conquered in all seasons. And once I put my back into it, it wasn't too bad.

I finally made it to the top and, bent semi-double, put my hands on my knees. Clearly not as fit as I once was. I breathed in deeply. Then I straightened up, and looked outward.

My suburban valley. White and beautiful. In the distance, diffuse and frozen, the pale skeleton of the Crystal Palace mast. With her A-line, latticework skirt draped into the mist, she looked even more feminine.

This spot has always been important to me. A sort of thinking post. Many a big crossroad in my life: quitting the Met, leaving my ex, solving cases, have been pondered here.

The seat was snow covered, so I just stood, looked, and got my breath back.

I found myself thinking about that old mast. Redundant, she was. The world gone digital. A shame, really. I could just about cope with that old-fashioned analogue stuff. The way I would imagine it, was that there was this very big mummy aerial and all the houses had little baby aerials on their heads. And the mummy aerial sent all the baby aerials her pictures. Yes, I could just about cope with that.

Now the mother was past it. Paler, greyer, older. We don't need aerials now, don't even need televisions. Movies on pads, films on phones, everything on demand. That term defines a whole new generation, doesn't it? On Demand.

Oh well, that stuff's for Anna. Me? Like that old skeleton on the hill, I suppose, I was past it. Then a thought came into my mind. To do with television, to do with digital, to do with what Anna had mentioned the day before. It was a really crazy, off-the-wall thought, but it hit me like a flash. And it put Poppy Foster right back in the frame.

When I got back home, I took off my coat, gloves and scarf, switched on the kettle, sat down and thawed out – thinking about it again. Yes, an absolutely crazy thought. But possible?

As it turned out, I had plenty of time to mull it over. Two days, holed up in snowbound suburbia, waiting for the snow to stop and the trains to start.

It wasn't just my crazy theory I was pondering upon though, it was bigger than that. Way, way bigger than that. If I was right, it would open the whole damned thing right back up again.

The question was: did I want all that again? I'd promised Anna, absolutely cross-my-heart-and-hope-to … well, not quite die: I'd come close enough to that already. But you know what I mean. I'd *really* promised.

But if I was right, no one had ever pulled off anything quite like it. A sting worthy of a Hollywood script. But I didn't need to travel that far to check it out. I didn't even need to go to Karachi. Just as so many people had said at the beginning of this case, it was far, far closer to home. It was in Soho.

CHAPTER FORTY-FOUR

New Year's Eve came and went. Anna was partying, Bernard, unbelievably, working, and I had little to celebrate. In the end, bored rigid by the TV, I went to bed early. I must say that I find the whole Hogmanay thing a bit overblown anyway, so it was no big loss. And the next day was like any other, too, apart from the fact the temperature had plummeted again. With trains and roads still iced up, I couldn't get to Anna and she, plus added hangover, certainly wasn't coming to me.

By the Thursday, I'd had enough. I decided to weather the weather and find a train. So through biting winds and salted streets I wheeled my little overnight bag, and, once at Shortlands Station, stood and froze. Eventually a train dawdled in, and, with a few hardy others, I crammed into an already packed carriage – which then refused to budge.

With arms outstretched and bag crammed between feet, we eventually crawled, inch-by-inch, forward. We got as far as Beckenham Junction and it just gave up, or perhaps froze up. So we all alighted and, after another glacial ten minutes, a muffled announcement told us to cross the footbridge and join a train to London Bridge.

We crossed over, piled on, and slowly, very slowly, we inched our way via a scenic route across snowy South London – ending up, surprisingly, at London Bridge Then we alighted again, and changed platforms again. And froze again.

Another snail-train chugged us slowly onward and, after a journey lasting almost two hours, with no feelings left in my limbs, we finally pulled into Charing Cross.

Spewed back out, to echoed announcements of further delays, I trundled my trolley out through the frozen, dejected masses. Why was I doing this? Bernard, I suppose.

It was to be his last night in Town before going away on business. Anna, too, though she only had time for a coffee. But there was yet another reason to put myself through all this. You see, I did have half a mind to fit in another meeting.

I thought, by the time I'd got to London, I would have made up my mind about it – especially given the time it had taken – but I hadn't. So it would be Anna first, then Bernard, and by then I might have come up with a decision.

I walked up through an almost empty Leicester Square, still recovering from New Year, via a bustling Chinatown, still preparing for it, and finally onto Soho: and a warm, welcoming Patisserie Valerie. I ordered two coffees, walked them to a window table and, whilst still de-layering, Anna arrived. We kissed, sat down and just yapped.

It was good. Talking, I mean. I didn't mention my crazy theory. She'd have gone absolutely nuts if I'd even hinted at getting involved in all that again. Anyway, she only had about half-an-hour to spare. It sounds ridiculous, but even for that short time, the awful journey was almost worth it.

After she'd left, I decided to just go for it and test out my idea. If I got lucky, it wouldn't take long. Anyway, Bernard would be tied up for ages. His office was in that direction so it wouldn't delay things much.

So I trundled my bag up to Bernard's, where the Receptionist, Kirsty, wished me Happy New Year, and parked my stuff there. I then carried on towards Great Marlborough with every intention of just going in there and taking pot luck with whomever I could have a word with. But in the end, I didn't. I briefly paused outside, decided it needed better planning, and continued on my way to Liberty's, a shop in which I could spend many a happy hour.

Then I window shopped along Oxford Street, which was affordable but frantic, cut through South Moulton, which was neither, and ended up back in Regents. After much changing of mind, I treated myself to a single, overpriced, Hermes scarf. Not the old-fashioned stirrups-and-saddles type though. I never did get the connection between headscarves and horse accessories.

It was only half past five, yet fully dark, by the time I got back to Bernard's. Kirsty, after asking how things were, wheeled out the bag she'd been safekeeping for me. She then said how sad it was the way the Stephanie case had ended, and, apart from simply agreeing, there was little I could add. I couldn't help wondering if perhaps it hadn't, though – ended, I mean.

Despite the hour, Bernard's was still buzzing: phones ringing, people toing and froing, and the sound of advertising jingles and voiceovers from behind closed doors. Unsurprisingly, Bernard was tied up, but Kirsty simply fished out the keys and told me I could take myself up. She was busy, but I don't think that was the only reason. I was becoming more part of the furniture – more accepted. And walking up those stairs, jangling those keys and letting myself in, everything was becoming more familiar. No groping on the wrong side for light switches, or going through bathroom doors only to find bedrooms. No opening fridges and finding dishwashers.

It was a good feeling. Me, coat off, kettle on, padding around in my slippers – comfortable and confident, in 'my' little West End world.

Having made myself a cuppa, I took it to the kitchen table and sat down. Nothing much to do, so I texted Anna to tell her where I was – which was unnecessary. Then I put my phone down, looked around. No changes. Which meant that picture was still looking at me. I thought about it for a while, sized it up. Then a ridiculous thought struck me. Could it be linked to my crazy notion?

I got up and walked over to it. No, surely not. If it were, it would make the whole thing even weirder.

'Hi,' said Bernard.

I turned, smiled and walked over.

It's funny, but as a couple, we'd never quite got to 'darlings' and 'honey' and stuff. Just the 'Hi.' And like the welcoming wife, greeting the returning hubby, I kissed him. More and more, it was becoming our, rather than just his, domain.

It took him a few minutes to switch modes: that work / life overlap thing. He told me about the day he'd had, and some difficult client or other. It must be that much more full-on when your work's downstairs. I used to absolutely hate commuting, but it did serve a purpose. A sort of decompression zone between two worlds.

I'd kind of imagined we'd go out to eat, but we didn't. That was OK, too. A bottle of New Year Clicquot and a takeaway from Chinatown? What could be better?

We talked about most things: my day, his imminent business trip, and I did think about bringing up my crazy theory. You see, in many ways, he'd have been the perfect person to ask. But as we talked, it all seemed less and less right.

I could see he was getting tired: he had a long day coming up tomorrow, too. So I got up from the sofa and got myself ready for bed.

When I got back in he was snoring on the sofa. So I left it as long as I could then woke him up and, like an old married couple, we went to bed. And simply slept. Which was fine by me. Yet over our last few meetings I'd felt there'd been something troubling him: something he wanted to tell me.

The next morning we were up horribly early. He was catching a first flight out from Heathrow and I'd be returning to Bromley. Staying in his flat wasn't on offer. Anyway, I felt I should see him off, at least.

It was still dark when we left. Pulling our bags, it must have looked as if we were off together. The difference between men and women, I suppose. My overnight case and shopping was bigger than his two-week suitcase.

We walked through a pre-dawn Soho with almost no vehicles about – a munching garbage truck in Berwick Street, a watching police car in Wardour – and even fewer people: sleeping rags in one doorway, a cursing couple in another. As we neared Leicester Square the first workers, mobiles to ear, takeaway coffees to hand, were emerging from the Underground.

Almost opposite, just into Cranbourne Street, we breakfasted. Small café, face-to-face. Just like our first date. You know, six months had passed since then. What changes I'd been through.

Having dregged our coffees and fingertipped our final crumbs, we buttoned up again and left. The streets were lighter and busier.

We trundled our bags back across the road to Leicester Square. He'd be taking the Piccadilly Line to Heathrow, I'd be walking back down to Charing Cross, and then home.

I pulled up the lapels of his raincoat, kissed him goodbye and told him to be good: cracking some weak joke about loose Italian women. He responded with an even weaker joke about loose London men, gave me one last peck, turned and walked to the escalator. I waited a second, watching him descend. You know, I really wanted him to turn around just one last time. But he didn't.

It had been some time since I'd experienced such bittersweet goodbyes. Call it intuition if you like, but there was something he just wasn't telling me.

Was this to be a final farewell?

CHAPTER FORTY-FIVE

'Do you like really post production work?' I asked Poppy.

She thought for a second, curling a napkin around her pretty little finger.

'Yes, of course,' she said, looking up.

Should I cut to the chase, or should I skirt around it a bit?

We were sitting in the spacious atrium-cum-chill-out area suspended high up above Effigy Post's main reception area. A few other people were lounging about, sipping coffees, engrossed in their iPads. Below us, people milled and met. Clients or staff, it was difficult to tell. Either way, all were young, all were media.

It had been an off-the-cuff decision. After saying goodbye to Bernard I'd had every intention of going home: turning from Bernard, taking the little alleyways that criss-crossed between theatre doors, emerging into St Martin's and turning right to Charing Cross.

But then I'd thought about my theory. I could check it out. Well, sort of. I could walk back into Soho and call in on Effigy Post.

So I'd done just that, getting through to Nick Summers. With Rose Denton now dead and buried, Head of Production seemed a logical place to start. I asked him if I could have a brief chat with one of his staff and he said yes.

And that's exactly why Poppy Foster was sitting in front of me.

'You were a film student weren't you?' I asked.

'Yes, that's right,' she said.

'Camerawork?'

'Yes,' she shrugged, 'But not only.'

'Mainly, though.'

'Yes, that's what I always wanted to do.'

'And now you're in post-production.'

She didn't reply. Obviously she was.

'And it can be boring?'

'Sometimes,' she said. 'All jobs are.'

'True,' I conceded. 'But garbage matting, for example.'

She looked at me. I was pretty sure what she was thinking: *'Where did I pick up that bloody term?'* And the other question in those pretty blue eyes was: *'And what's it got to do with you, Mrs Middle-Aged Smartarse?'*

'Why are you asking me this?' she said, reading my mind, just as I was reading hers.

'Well,' I said, flipping through my notebook, 'The night before Paul's disappearance, he took a phone call. I looked down at the words I'd written: 'She'll need some help with the garbaging.'

I looked back up at her.

'I thought we were past all that,' she said.

'Past all what?'

'Paul's dead now, and Stephanie.'

I looked directly at her: 'And Rose Denton?' I said. 'She's dead now, too, isn't she?'

And with that, Poppy just got up and left.

You know, I'm used to people just upping and leaving. Goes with the territory, I suppose. Unfortunately, also with that territory, though not with the police's, is my lack of any recourse to any kind of follow up.

I'd come as close as I dared to showing my hand. But it was a one-sided game. She could simply pass that information on. And if my guess was right, she would.

I was getting very close to the stage where I'd simply have to tell the police, but I needed more than just a hunch. I was getting close though. Very, very close indeed.

When I got back to Bromley, rather than go home, I went straight to my office. I boiled a kettle, dunked a tea bag, and switched on my computer. Then I did something I pretty much always do when I work on a case involving a company, rather than just an individual. I checked Companies House website.

I noted that Rose Denton was still named as both a shareholder and Managing Director of Effigy Post, so clearly, changes to that aspect of the company hadn't yet been decided or updated. There were four other shareholders named, none of whom I recognised.

I then did a similar thing with both the advertising agency and the bank, but there wasn't any crossover between any of the parties. You see, given my little hunch, I'd been wondering if there was any kind of collusion going on. But nothing in front of me suggested there was.

Then, completely off-the-cuff, an idea came to me. It wasn't directly related to the case, but it was related to the industry I'd been looking into. While I was in the Companies House register I decided to check out Simmonds Editing Limited. And, as it turned out, I was just a mouse click away from changing everything.

First up was the company's Registered Office. This was given as *7, Morrison Court, London EC1A.* No surprises there, it was almost certainly the company accountant's address. Then I got to the company directors. The Managing Director was given as Bernard Anthony Simmonds, which again, was no surprise.

But the company's Service Address, which in his case should be his *actual* address, wasn't in Brewer Street. It was in Burnstone Close, Watford. Now, from the little I knew of his past, Watford was where he lived when he was still married. Perhaps it wasn't such a big deal, though. Maybe he originally ran his business from his home and it hadn't been changed on the register. After all, according to the entry for Effigy Postproductions' their Managing Director was now deceased!

But the real shock came when I got to the only other director: *Cynthia Amelia Simmonds.*

Was this right? Yes, definitely. The two directors were Bernard Simmonds and Cynthia Simmonds.

Now stay calm, and don't jump to conclusions, Pamela. It could mean lots, but it could mean nothing. Plenty of people have estranged business partners. Nowadays, divorcing is easier than sacking. Especially if it's someone you've already divorced. Already divorced?

Just to check, I look up her address. *Burnstone Close, Watford.*

My heart sank just a little bit more.

So I quit the page, leant back, and thought. Not conclusive. Like I said, perhaps he never got round to changing his address on the register.

I bit my lip and thought a bit more.

Was that why Bernard was so cagey about his fellow director? Almost certainly. There again, he would be. It's natural. Your ex-wife is still an unwanted director and your significant other (I hope that would be my description) happens to bring up the subject. You'd be evasive, wouldn't you?

I got up, walked to the window. The garden looked barren. In the half-melted, re-frozen snow, a single blackbird was pecking at the lawn. Another blackbird came out from a bush. They kind of challenged each other: hopped about a bit, postured. Then one left.

Suddenly I remembered his words: *'Sleeping partner.'* That was how he'd described his other director. Sleeping partner? Oh, Bernard, I do hope you're not trying to be clever with me.

How could I find out? Simple, I'd put it to him straight. There again, he could say he hadn't wanted to hurt my feelings. Say he'd been trying to get her out of the company for years. He could even claim her solicitor had insisted: *'For the sake of your children, Mrs Simmonds,'* he'd claim her solicitor said, *'You must stay involved. You need to keep check of your ex-husband's finances and stay on board. Stay on* the *board, in fact.'*

Yes, I could hear a lawyer saying exactly that. Trouble is, I could hear Bernard saying exactly that, too. Plausible isn't necessarily truthful.

CHAPTER FORTY-SIX

'I'm missing you, Pam,' said Bernard.

'Oh come on, all that wining and dining?' I said, phone to ear, settling into the sofa.

He told me it was all pretty tedious – which I could kind of relate to. Kind of. Two weeks of working days and networking nights can be hard, I suppose – even in a place like Milan. Still, at least there was the shopping. I know what *I'd* be doing in my lunch break!

'I expect more than a pre-packed Panettone, you know,' I joked.

'I'll do my best,' he replied.

In truth, I wasn't anticipating haute couture. Men can hardly get their own wardrobe right, let alone women's. No, Chanel would do. In a bottle.

There were more pressing issues than duty free anyway. Twenty-four hours earlier I'd been up for going in with all guns blazing. The whole business partner thing, you see. But I'd cooled on it. And now he was actually phoning me, I'd completely changed my mind and decided against it. If he had an explanation and I'm sure he would, it could wait. Face-to-face would be better. Anyway, he hadn't told me in six months so another couple of days weren't going to hurt, were they.

Anyway, there was something else I wanted to run past him first.

'Look, Bernard,' I said. 'There's something I've been thinking about. Something I've been meaning to ask you.'

I sat forwards a little and put my coffee down. For what I was about to suggest, I needed all my wits.

'I'm sure you'll think I'm daft.'

'No,' he said, 'I'm sure I won't. Go ahead.'

'Well, in your business, can someone completely falsify pictures?'

'How do you mean?'

'Well, I've seen it done in advertisements. You know, making babies talk, adding dinosaurs and stuff.'

'Oh yes, right. Well of course, why do you ask?'

I paused for a second. Thought about what I was about to say. The sheer absurdity of it. But then I just went for it.

'Would it have been possible to put Paul Hutchinson somewhere he wasn't?'

There was a slightly tinny silence on the phone.

'Well,' I repeated. 'Would it?'

I was expecting a laugh. Maybe even total ridicule. In many ways, the last word I was expecting was his next.

'Yes … it would.'

'So you think it's possible?'

'You're suggesting that the videos of Paul were false.'

I didn't answer, but yes, that was exactly what I was thinking.

'Well,' he said, after a long pause, 'I suppose if there's anywhere it could be done …'

'Are they the best? Effigy Post, I mean?'

'One of them. But Soho's packed with them. If you've seen it done, it's probably been done round there.'

'But couldn't you tell. If it was false, I mean?'

'*I* probably couldn't, even as film editor. But I suppose absolute experts could. If it was put under a microscope, I mean. Magnify the pixels and stuff.'

'How about the lighting, could that give it away?'

'Yes, if it wasn't matched perfectly.'

'So the filming would have to have been done really carefully too.'

'Yes.'

'So,' I said, thinking aloud 'Could someone who's studied lighting at university do it?'

'I suppose so. With the right advice from whoever's doing the post.'

'And what about if that person was *actually in* post-production too?'

'All the better, I suppose. But who are you thinking of?'

'Poppy Foster. When they shared that hotel suite. Maybe she was filming him.'

He gave a slight laugh, then added: 'Filming rather than the other 'f-ing'

'Exactly,' I said. 'But don't they have to film against a blue screen or something? I can't imagine them setting that up in a hotel room!'

Bernard didn't reply immediately, but then said: 'Difference matting, maybe.'

'What's that?'

You shoot two identical shots. One has the person in it, and one's empty. The computer spots the difference between the two and produces a matte – like a cut-out.'

'Why's that better than using blue or whatever?'

'Well, as you say, you don't even have to set a screen up. You film it in situ. Same lighting, same feel.'

'You mean in that actual desert?'

'Yes. Then you shoot the two guys later, in the same setting. The look's identical'

I had this mental picture. Paul and Poppy travel out to the locations where the videos will be made, possibly using the same driver that took us. She then films him standing there alone, then moves him out and films it blank. Then, weeks later, once he's in hiding, she films the two 'kidnappers' there. She could do that much nearer the date – enabling one of them, for instance, to hold up a newspaper to 'prove' it's been filmed later.

'But how would they get that terrorist into the shot?'

'That would be existing material, heavily treated. They would have to line the new shots up carefully to it. Mind you, it would be difficult to do well. I can't imagine an assistant posting that,' said Bernard.

'Poppy, you mean?'

'Yes, she could never do that type of work.'

'How about Sam Palmer?' I said, picturing the Aussie I'd interviewed all those months earlier.

'So you're saying she films it, and he puts it all together, assisted by her,' said Bernard.

'Why not? And this difference matting: could it involve more work? Than blue screen, I mean?'

'How do you mean?'

'Garbage matting, for instance,' I said.

'Blimey! You've been doing your homework. Where did you get that from?'

'It's a long story, Bernard, a very long story.'

I thought for a second. There was still one thing that just didn't add up.

'Didn't you say that a real expert could tell?'

'I would imagine so, if you magnified it up.'

I found myself wondering about MI5, GCHQ and Scotland Yard. Even the CIA and the Pentagon. Are we expected to believe that no one thought to check this stuff out?

We kind of left it at that – with him asking what I was going to do about it and me saying I wasn't sure. Report it to the police, maybe – *if* they'd believe me.

'I think I'm going to sleep on it for now, but if I do, would you mind being there. For the technical stuff, I mean – when you get back.'

'Um, yes, I suppose I could.'

He didn't sound too sure, but then neither did I. OK, it certainly fitted together: why Poppy was in Karachi with Paul; why Rose was murdered; why our handover was so expertly botched up. But if it *is* what happened, assuming it's even possible, it would mean Stephanie had been deceiving me all along. I found this hard to believe. And talking of deceiving, was it really possible to produce fake videos that are so undetectable that they can pass forensic analysis? Unlikely.

So would I go to the police? Not yet. Like the issue of Bernard's business partner, it could wait. For now.

You see, as ever, there was one other person I wanted to run all these issues past. The person who's opinion I respected more than anyone in the world.

CHAPTER FORTY-SEVEN

Silence can tell you many things. There's the silence that says yes, and the silence that says no. There's the silence that doesn't believe a word you're saying, and the silence that does. Now Anna's silence, when I told her about my crazy theory, was the final type.

'I've had this thought,' I'd said to her, after finally plucking up courage and picking up the phone.

'About the kidnapping, I mean. You see, I think it may never have happened. Or the execution. It was all done in post.'

Then that silence.

'It all matches up,' I'd said. 'Poppy did the filming, Sam did the clever stuff.

Again, silence.

'Oh yes,' I added, 'And I was stupid enough to be the mule.'

'Sorry, Mum. Let me get this right. You're saying they're still alive?'

'Yes, except for Rose. She was unlucky – stumbled across what was happening.'

More silence, and an even longer pause.

'I've run it past Bernard. He's pretty up on this sort of stuff and I thought he'd poo-poo it, but he didn't. He even came up with a few more thoughts about it.

Still Anna said nothing.

'So what do you think?'

'I think, Mum, you should tell the police.'

Good answer, I suppose, but…

'I'm not sure they're going to believe me, Anna,' I said. 'Would you? In their position, I mean?'

After a bit she said: 'Tell you what, Mum. I've got nothing on tonight. Why don't I come round? Perhaps we can do some research.'

Great idea. The snow was thawing, the trains were running, and I might even try my luck in the kitchen again. She hadn't been round for some time, so two birds with one stone.

'There's something else I wanted to run past you.'

'What's that, Mum?'

'Well, what would you think if your partner's ex-partner was still their partner?'

'Pardon?'

'Simmonds Editing. The other director is Cynthia Simmonds.'

There was another one of Anna's long silences. Finally she said: 'Well, thinking about it, I do know other situations like that. One of the production companies I work for. His ex is still a director. It happens. *Shit* happens.'

Then she added: 'It's not so easy losing a business partner. If they really don't want to go, I mean.'

'Yes,' I said. 'That's what I was thinking. But would you tell your new partner. Friend, I mean.'

'You mean lover, Mum.'

'Okay, Anna. Lover, then.'

'Well, if I thought it could scare them away, probably no. Not immediately. But eventually, yes. I'd have to.

She was right, of course. The trouble was the word 'eventually.' Six months? Wasn't that 'eventually' enough?

CHAPTER FORTY-EIGHT

Anna arrived at about eight, taking off her coat, unwinding her scarf and pressing her cold cheek against mine. I offered her a drink and she went for hot chocolate. Somehow, it was always going to be a booze-free night.

I got the drinks in, she got the laptop out and we had a kind of re-catch up between the two rooms. Finally, settling down together at the lounge table, we started our research – or perhaps I should say Anna did.

'I need to warn you of something, Mum,' she said, before we'd even kicked off. 'You see, I want to start with the kidnap videos. And that includes the execution. Have you already seen it?'

Another first. Daughter warning mother about explicit online content. But I could see her point. It was indeed horrible. But it was a logical place to start, too. Whether we'd learn anything from it was doubtful. Far better eyes would have scrutinized it than ours.

'Yes,' I said, 'I have. But only up to the point when ...'

'Well,' she said, saving me from describing anything too grisly, 'If it's any comfort, that's probably all we'll find. The full version, if it ever existed, seems to have disappeared.'

And with that, she set about finding the videos, lining them up in sequence at the bottom of the screen, then pulling them up one-by-one.

They were shocking, of course, and I did have to kind of detach myself, but whilst it was distasteful, it certainly didn't look fake.

Next, she decided to check out Effigy Post's showreel. Again, that was logical. After all, if an image has been played with by someone, why not check *other* images they've played with – see if there are any similarities. Talking of which, within Effigy's home page were separate showreels for all their key staff, including, interestingly, Sam Palmer.

As expected, there were plenty of similar shots: dead movie stars sharing the screen with living movie stars, several generations of Dr Whos within the same clip, and an entire football team made up of players from different eras.

'OK,' said Anna, sitting back. 'Are any of these more or less believable than the hostage videos?'

'Not really, I said. 'They all look real to me. There again, I'm no expert. It doesn't necessarily mean they're done by the same person.'

'Of course,' she said, 'but at least we've established that it's definitely possible – technically. Tell you what – let's look at a few other post houses.'

She then pulled up material from about half-a-dozen others. Not just commercials, but pop videos, movies and TV programs. And all of them were littered with visually believable, yet physically impossible images: The Beatles performing with Elvis, an *Easy Rider* Dennis Hopper sharing the screen with his middle aged self, and a *Breakfast at Tiffany's* Audrey Hepburn in a modern day chocolate bar ad. Some weren't even that recent: dancing babies, swimming hippos, even a living Stephen Fry chatting up a dead Marilyn Monroe.

'If anything,' said Anna, 'this older stuff supports your theory more. If you could do this ten years ago, given today's technology ...'

I simply nodded. Again, I could see her point.

'And,' she continued, with her finger on the screen, 'look how wobbly the camera is in this one:'

She was running an old commercial where a dead Steve McQueen was driving a modern-day car.

'Is that a factor: wobbliness?'

'For sure,' she said. 'It's a whole load more difficult faking a man driving round hairpin bends, than side-by-side in a desert with a locked-off camera.'

I hadn't heard that term before, but understood implicitly what it meant – and again I could see her point. After all, if the angles don't change, it's obviously easier to work on.

Not that it really proved much because the next clips she pulled up, of other terrorist videos, all had 'locked off' cameras, too. So it might be easier for post-production work, but it didn't prove it was faked.

Finally, we went back to where we'd started and ran the kidnap videos again. And it was all very interesting and convincing, real or otherwise, but it proved nothing.

So we took a break. Or at least, I did. Anna, like the rain now on my windows, seemed set in for the night. Once my daughter gets her head into a computer screen she just goes on and on. A generational thing, I suppose.

So I went into the kitchen, brewed up some coffee and stuck an M&S lasagna in the oven. My Nigella afternoon had, well, just baked off, I suppose.

Waiting for the kettle to boil and oven to pre-heat, I found myself looking at the raindrops: sodium orange from the streetlights, against the pitch black of the night. You know, I love watching them. On windows, I mean.

Sometimes they pause, sometimes they meet, almost like finding a friend, and sometimes they change direction. And after they've paused, met up, they suddenly hurry off faster: get to the bottom of things a whole load quicker.

When I got back to the lounge, with two coffees in hand, Anna had some pictures of the Cottingly Fairies on the screen. Now I was quite familiar with these images: a world famous Victorian fake case that had re-emerged strongly in the 80s or 90s.

'Aha,' I said, putting down the coffee, 'Talking of fakes.'

'Yes,' said Anna, 'But the interesting thing is that one of them, apparently, still can't be disproved.'

'Really?'

'Yes,' she said, 'According to this.'

I sat down next to her and read what was on the screen – most of which I already knew.

The five pictures had been 'photographed' by two 16 year-old school girls, Elsie Wright and Francis Griffiths just after the First World War. They fooled everyone at the time, from Kodak to Sir Arthur Conan Doyle. Yet to modern-day eyes they looked cutesy, posed and ridiculously phony.

'But here's the real surprise, Mum,' said Anna, pointing further down the screen. 'The only reason Elsie confessed was because she had to. You see, a children's book with the same illustrations was discovered, in 1979.'

'Really,' I said, not especially amazed.

'Yes, and even then, the fifth photograph, which *wasn't* like the book, can't be disproved to this day.'

'So you're saying they still can't be scientifically disproved?'

'Yes, according to this.'

'But they're obviously fake.'

'To our eyes, yes. But not according to modern-day analysis.'

'But why ... I mean, how?'

'That's what we need to find out, Mum.'

To me this was ridiculous. What's the point of technology if it's no better than the naked eye?

Anna went back into Google and kicked off by putting up *trick photography*. This seemed to lead her to *fake photography*, which in turn took her to *multi exposure photography*, then *forensic photography*.

Frankly, I was getting bored. I suppose, as a detective, I shouldn't have been. Especially the forensics bit. But I'm a standing-up-and-doing person, not a sitting-down-and-checking person.

So as she got stuck in: trawling websites, reading and rejecting, I went back out to the kitchen, took the pasta out of the oven, ran water over some lettuce, sawed a baguette in half and tra-la ... a gourmet meal for two!

I was walking back in, balancing two trays, when she said: 'You know, Mum, I think I might've got it,' then absent-mindedly added: 'Oh food, well done.'

As I put the trays down she said: 'Get this, Mum. It's from a company that analyses images: *"If the picture quality's low, results will be affected. Adding noise or grain to images, intentionally or otherwise, can badly affect results."*

I must admit that it didn't strike me as especially earth-shattering, so I didn't really comment – just sat down next to her.

'And this one,' she said, bringing up another web page: *'Old, badly damaged and heavily duplicated material may defy analysis. Furthermore, duplicating an image may render any results inconclusive.'*

'Think of those pictures, Mum. What were they like? Sharp focus or old and grainy?'

I was beginning to see her point. They were the latter.

'The quality's poor for a reason, Mum. It wasn't even digital, it was analogue. Probably duplicated half-a-dozen times.'

'You're saying it could have been degraded on purpose?'

'Yes. It's like standing next to a photocopier, copying and recopying time and again. In the end the quality's …'

'Unanalyzable,' I said, completing her sentence.

'Exactly. According to what's written here, anyway. And think about it, Mum: if those old photos of fairies, taken by 16 year-olds, *still* can't be disproved …'

On an evening of many good points, Anna had yet another.

'Okay,' I said, 'So why hasn't anyone else spotted it?'

'Why would they? Everyone assumes it's recorded on clapped-out old equipment because that's what most terrorists *do*. We're all so bloody used to Bin Laden-in-a-cave, Mum. No one questions it.'

Again, she was right. I found myself thinking back to when I first saw it. What was my reaction? Shock, of course. But did I question the poor quality? Of course I didn't. Like everyone else, I'd *expected* it to be poor. Firstly, there's the You Tube factor, but secondly, it's what criminals *do*. Photos, films, ransom notes: they're *always* duplicates because they're *always* covering their tracks. The police just wouldn't question it.

So the images were put together digitally, painstakingly, to produce absolute perfection. But then duplicated poorly, probably time and again until all the joins, all the seams, were gone.

I looked at Anna and smiled, and she looked back at me … and smiled.

'You know, Anna,' I said. 'I do think you might be onto something.

'*We*, Mum,' she said, smiling, *'We.'*

'So, um, who do you think did it?' she said, forking her lasagne.

'Sam,' I said. 'It just has to be.'

CHAPTER FORTY-NINE

As we boarded the train at Bromley North, Anna was still telling me to go directly to the police rather than Effigy Post. My argument against this, just as it had been the night before, was that they simply wouldn't believe me. But was that the only reason? Or was it just me being me? I can still hear that description of me from my Mum: *'Like a Dog with a bone once you get going, Pamela,'* she'd say, *'Like a dog with a bone.'*

And that's why I'd rung up Nick Summers, Effigy's Head of Production, and requested, yet again, a meeting with one of his team, namely Sam Palmer, where I'd put it to him straight, or as straight as I dared.

If my crazy theory was rubbish, I'd know. Words can lie, but eyes can't. Nor body language. And if it wasn't rubbish, then I'd hand it over to the police.

And that's why I was going up to Town, though not why Anna was. She'd be getting off at London Bridge for some meeting in The City, and I'd carry on to Charing Cross.

We managed to find seats opposite each other, but were very soon restricted in our chitchat by the poor seat-less souls who boarded the train at Hither Green and beyond. Anna was fine though: she had her mobile for company, but I found myself just looking out of the window and wondering.

Had I really been that taken in? By Stephanie, I mean. Had she really been a party to all this from the off? Surely not. After all, if she had, the one thing she wouldn't need, wouldn't even want, is a private investigator poking her nose in. So the fact that she *had* contacted me suggests innocence alone.

On the other hand, you could argue that she, together with Paul and Sam and Poppy – and maybe even Farooki – had got me involved because A) they wanted a stooge to make Stephanie's situation look all the more authentic, and B) a mule to drop off the money. Personally, I wouldn't buy that, but it is an argument.

However, there was one aspect of my early meetings with Stephanie that really would suggest she was an innocent party, at that stage, anyway. The whole 'luggage / baggage' conversation.

If Stephanie was involved in the scam when I first interviewed her, why would she volunteer that information? After all, that line, albeit misheard, was one of the things that led Anna and I to crack the entire case, assuming we *had* cracked the entire case.

So no, I don't think she was involved at that time. The plan, I believe, was to keep Stephanie in the dark in the very early stages and then, when it got to the 'kidnapping' stage, Paul would make contact. Prior to that, he really *was* a missing person and she *was* a missing person's wife, making it all the more believable.

And that would explain why, when she first contacted me, she was so distraught, yet when the actual kidnap videos came out she was strangely laid back about it – even after the horrific 'execution' of her husband.

I'd taken her lack of emotion as detachment. A way of coping with the awfulness of it all. But in hindsight, I don't think it was. She was well aware of what was going on by the time that final video came through.

Then there's another point that suggested Stephanie was only aware later on, too. Something that had been bugging me for months. Why was Stephanie so adamant about attending Rose's funeral: a woman she'd never even met? The answer? Guilt. She'd never expected this to cost anyone's life. That goes for Poppy, too, another person whose demeanour changed after the shooting. After all, at one stage she even rang up Anna and nearly confessed, only to clam up again later.

So who did kill Rose? Stephanie was out, for sure. As for Paul, he was in hiding, possibly in Pakistan, so he'd hardly be walking around the streets of London streets with a gun in his hand, would he? Poppy, I believe would be incapable of shooting a woman in the head, and anyway, the assailant was identified as a man. Which yet again pointed to Sam Palmer. He, for my money, was the man.

Quite apart from the fact that Rose probably opened the door to someone she knew, he also had the strongest motive. Let's get this straight: murdering someone is never easy, and in this case it wasn't on anyone's original agenda. This was *supposed to be* a victimless crime. But I'd guess Rose simply walked into Sam's suite one night when she, and he, was burning the midnight oil. That would very much fit her character: company woman through-and-through: working late, and into everything.

So he was the man in the hot seat, so to speak. Oh, and one other point. He clearly had a chip on his shoulder about authority, and women, I would guess. And generally, there's no greater authority figure than your boss, is there? So why not just shut her up for good?

And what of Farooki? If he was the Mr. Big behind all this, and I believe he was, why even do it? Why give away £30m of your own bank's money to simply get it back later? The answer to that, is in the question: *bank's* money, not *his* money.

He seemed to live a pretty lavish lifestyle and, who knows, there could even have been gambling debts. As for Paul and Sam, they were both ambitious, money-oriented young men – with the latter, I would guess, harbouring a coke habit. So they all had motives.

There would have been other players in this scam, of course. The masked 'kidnappers' in the videos, the taxi driver with the money in his boot, people at airports and hotels too. But they would only be bit-part players. A few thousand to each would have kept them happy. They wouldn't even have necessarily have known how the scam was going to work. And I can't imagine Poppy Foster got that much money either. Whereas Farooki, together with Sam Palmer and the Hutchinsons, would probably be pocketing the best part of £10m each. So I was pretty sure it was Farooki who was calling the shots. Mind you, I was also pretty sure it was Palmer who actually fired them.

London Bridge: thousands piled off, thousands piled on – making it pretty much impossible for Anna to do much more than mime me a kiss and a 'Goodbye, Mum' – and wish me good luck.

I returned the compliment with a 'Thanks for last night, I'll ring you later.'

As the train pulled out, it was spitting outside again. Raindrops on windows again, – slightly more swept, slightly more horizontal, but still they paused, thought, and moved on. Not unlike solving a crime, I suppose.

Slowly, the train clickety-clacked its way over Borough Market, through Waterloo East, over the swirling Thames, into the caged-in ironwork of Hungerford Bridge and finally, arrived at Charing Cross Station.

Very soon, I'd know.

CHAPTER FIFTY

Hood up against the drizzle, I left the touting tour buses and shouting paper sellers of Charing Cross, then walked up past Oscar Wilde's coffin and Edith Cavell's statue, crossed a damp Leicester Square and entered Soho: daytime neon, soggy streets.

On the corner of Compton and Wardour, my phone rang. I pulled it out: *Bernard,* it said. I hit the green.

'Ciao, lover boy,' I said.

'Ciao, Pammi,' he replied. 'How's things?'

'Okay, a bit wet,' I said. 'And you?'

'Fine,' he said, 'Weather okay, too. On my way to the airport. How about you?'

'On my way to Effigy Post.'

'Oh yes, right,' he said. 'Good luck.'

He then gave me a few technical pointers as to what to ask and warned me to tread carefully. Then, pretty much out of the blue, he said: 'You know, I've been thinking about what you said.'

'What's that?'

'About us talking to the police. Together, I mean.'

'Oh yes,' I said.

'Well, if it's OK I'd rather not.'

I was flabbergasted, utterly shocked. All I'd been asking for was a bit of moral support.

'Oh,' I said 'That's OK.' Which it certainly wasn't.

I suppose I shouldn't have been surprised. He was less than keen when I'd mentioned it before. Mind you, I hadn't expected an outright refusal either. So I paused, moved under a restaurant's dripping awning and listened to his overlong explanation. And how would I describe it? Stuttering, fabricated, and, sorry to be so vulgar, full of bullshit.

'I'm not the best man for the job,' he said. 'If you want technical backup, there are better people than me,' he said. 'I can put you in touch with some of them,' he said.

Eventually, tired of talking to my silence, he rang off – telling me he'd ring me when he landed.

You know, I just didn't get it. There was something he wasn't telling me. Something missing. So I just stood there, underneath the wet canvas, thinking.

Why *wouldn't* somebody want to be present when the police were there? Especially a friendly cop like Andy? I mean, all it would be is a chat, at either Bernard's place or mine, a bit of tea, a bit of sympathy and some technical support. Any formal statements could wait.

I could only come up with two or three reasons. First up was the possibility that he was in some way involved in Paul Hutchinson's disappearance. But that would have been very coincidental. After all, I'd bumped into Bernard, an old school friend, by pure chance, hadn't I? He'd been so helpful on the case, too. Up until now, anyway.

Option number two was that he had some kind of criminal record. But so what? That wouldn't come up during a friendly chat, would it? Anyway, I didn't give a damn about criminal records. I'd spent twenty-five-years in the police. Criminal records was what I did!

This left perhaps one other possibility. Exposure. You see, I'd already featured on one brief clip: me walking down a Soho street in a local news roundup, with a voiceover going on about my involvement, dragging up my previous big case. So was that the problem? Publicity? After all, it was only going to grow as the case built up.

Then it struck me. Like a bolt out of the blue. I suppose I must have realized, or started to realize, a long, long time ago. Subconsciously, I mean. After all, those dreams were tied up with it. That picture on his wall. *I'm in the wrong place,* it had said.

Now I had a choice. I could carry on up Wardour Street, throw a left into Great Marlborough and go straight to Effigy. That way I'd probably be about 15 minutes early. Or I could turn immediately left into Brewer Street and go to Bernard's. It was only about a minute away, so the choice, to me, was no choice at all. Simmonds Editing it would be.

'Hi,' said Kirsty, looking up and smiling at me as I pushed through the glass doors. 'What, brings you here?'

'Well, I was in the area and I was wondering if you could help me. You see, I've left something upstairs and—'

'No problem,' she said, already fishing for the keys in her drawer, 'I'm sure he wouldn't mind you going up.'

While still rummaging, she added: 'While-the-cat's-away, eh?' and gave a little laugh. It was a joke, of course, but an interesting one. Then she said: 'Ahaa,' and held up the keys.

'Do you mind going by yourself?'

'No,' I said, 'No problem. I'll only be a second anyway.'

I thanked her, made my way across reception and went up the stairs to Bernard's door. I unlocked it, pushed it open, put my hand round the door, and found the switch. Lights on: I walked in.

The lounge was exactly as we'd left it. Well, it would be. I made straight for the kitchen and switched on the light. Again, as we left it. I walked up to the picture and looked at it. Illogical as ever. Size and positioning: totally wrong. Between room corner and door jam, it was almost touching on both sides, and way too big for its confined space. It should have been narrower and portrait shape, not landscape. Everything else in this flat was faultless: a perfect, professional, bachelor pad. Thought-out, yes, but homely, no. This was the opposite. It was homely: Bernard as a kid. But *not* thought-out: wrong place and dimensions. Photo apart, everything else in the room was graphically balanced.

I took a step forward, clasped the picture and lifted it off the wall.

My heart sunk, just slightly. What I'd feared, but sadly, what I'd expected too.

On the wall, just visible, was a smaller, faded, square. There was still a chance it was just the imprint of a previous resident's picture. Or perhaps one of Bernard's. An outside chance, but still a chance.

I took the picture to the table and placed it there. Then I walked over to the small mirror on the opposite wall and looked at it. Me, reflected back. I looked old. You know, I'd done many a spruce up and final check in this little space.

I lifted it off and stood back. I then switched my gaze back and forth between the two blank gaps. The same degree of fading, yes. But one gap was mirror shaped and the other *wasn't* picture shaped. Or *this* picture shaped. Slowly, my worst fears were being realised.

I put the mirror back on the wall, turned and walked to the units.

Opening doors and cupboards, then more doors, more cupboards, I started ransacking. More and more frenetic. Nothing. Or at least, nothing I wouldn't expect.

OK, let's get logical.

I walked back to the centre of the room and looked around. Now, imagine. You're 6ft tall. You also have a long, male reach. Where would you hide something if you wanted easy access, but *didn't* want a 5ft 4 female to have easy access?

I pulled a chair out from under the table and took it to the kitchen cabinets. I then got up on it and balanced myself. Hands on cabinets, I pulled myself onto tiptoes and peered above them. It was dark and dusty. My eyes slowly adjusted. Yes, there *is* something. It could be a picture but could also be an old magazine. Perhaps even assembly instructions for the original units.

I tried to reach it. Not quite. I got down again, moved the chair along, got back up, stretched my right arm in and located it by touch.

I pulled it out. A picture, but upside down. Tellingly, it wasn't dusty. Slowly, I turned it.

My heart sunk.

Holding the picture, I got back down and looked at it again.

At that instant in my life, during that tiny millisecond, how did I feel? Was I happy at being right, or angry at being wronged? Perhaps the tiniest bit of the former. But a *huge* amount of the latter!

I'm shaking with fury. Or is it tears? No, it's fury. For me *and* for her. Fury *for* her, not *at* her. This poor woman's been wronged, too.

I look at her. Not unlike me, really. Similar colouring, similar age, perhaps a year or so younger.

I get back down, sit on the chair and think. Was there another explanation? Surely there has to be? But no. If I were clutching at straws I'd say it might *just*, but only just, be understandable if his sons were in this picture too. The boys with their mum. *Just about* explainable for when I'm not here. But that really would be clutching at straws, wouldn't it? Anyway, the boys aren't in the picture. Just her. Then there's the other point. If it were a very old picture of her. Maybe then I could buy it. Just. But it's not. Then there's the hiding of it. Not permanently, not forever, but temporarily, accessibly. So she obviously still comes here. So up and down the picture goes. Up and down, up and down, like...

More fury, like a wave: rising again, hitting me again. Sleeping partner. Very clever, Bernard. Very bloody clever.

And *that's* why he didn't want to get involved with the police. You know, that brief clip I told you about? Me walking down a Soho street? Well, it wasn't just *any* Soho street. It was *this* Soho street.

I can almost imagine Cynthia pointing it out: *"Look, Bernard, there's that woman detective – and she's in your street."*

You see, it was all getting just a bit too close for comfort.

The things we bloody did! How could he! I'm embarrassed to even think about it. I'm an old woman, for God sake. Well, past middle age, anyway. Why didn't he get some young thing? They're built for that sort of stuff, aren't they? Why not Kirsty, downstairs, for instance? That's what men do, isn't it. Go off with some younger model. There again, maybe he's got dozens of bloody school pictures hidden around the place! Like bloody Happy Snaps.

I sit down again, almost in tears. We were so close, weren't we? Not the sex, I mean. The days in the park, the

274

walking? The day at Liz's. The children, the grandchildren, the family stuff.

I suppose it was a final conquest. The girl he always fancied from way back when. Like shaking hands with Bobby bloody Charlton or something. Fury rises again. Men! Bloody, sodding men!

I stand up, lift up the picture and look at it. Shaking, I am. I lift it higher, ready to throw it, to smash it on the floor. But I don't. Why should I smash her? What's she done wrong?

I know, I'll smash the *other* picture!

I go to the table, pick it up and look at it. A group of school children. Innocent, young. A million years ago. Why smash this? Why smash anything? Everything's in pieces anyway.

I lay them back on the table side-by-side.

I go to a drawer, find a pencil and paper. Resting the paper on the worktop, I write THANKS. I then walk to the hook where the picture was and impale it on it. He can take it as he wants: ironic, hateful, genuine, whatever.

You can screw me, Bernard, but you can't screw *with* me. The meeting at Effigy could wait, I'm meeting you off that bloody plane!

I picture it. He comes out of arrivals with his work colleagues and walks through the roped-off area where friends and family meet, where taxi drivers stand with names aloft. I won't have names aloft. I'll have bloody pictures aloft!

I close the door behind me, descend the stairs and find my way back to Kirsty. She's sitting at reception talking to another girl: an editor, I think. I wonder if they know what's been going on. Yes, of course they know what's been going on. Must do. Probably everyone does. Then again, it's not their fault, is it? Their boss, cheating on his wife, upstairs, in their working premises.

Should I say something, scream something, throw something? No. Maintain a bit of decorum, Pamela.

'So Bernard's back tonight,' says the girl talking to Kirsty.

'Yes,' I say, smiling sweetly.

Then another penny drops. This is the girl Bernard told me about. The girl whose riposte: *'Why, is your nose longer than your dick?'* led to …

This very girl, without realising it, was responsible for …

I feel my face turning the same colour as my underwear that day.

'Are you alright?' asks Kirsty.

'Yes, yes, I say, flustered. 'It's just a bit warm in here, I suppose.'

I cough, collect myself: 'I was er, just thinking about Bernard flying back from Milan and …'

'Milan?' says Kirsty, 'He's coming from Corfu.'

Crash. Another bagful of pennies hits the floor. Business in Corfu? No way. *Holidays* in Corfu. *Family* holidays Corfu.

Suddenly my plan doesn't seem such a good one. Don't get me wrong, it would be utterly luscious: Bernard, together with wife and possibly boys, walks out of Heathrow arrivals to see me holding up two pictures. But what of Cynthia? What of the boys? They don't deserve that.

My mobile rings. It's Effigy.

'Hello, is that Pamela? It's Nick Summers here, I was wondering if …'

'Oh yes, sorry, Nick, I'm running late. I'm just around the corner now, and …'

I push back out through the door, and with mobile still to ear, nod a goodbye to the girls.

'I'll see you in a sec, Nick, if that's OK.'

'Yes,' he says. 'That's fine.'

I kill the call and start walking.

My hand is shaking. My whole bloody body is shaking. I feel physically sick.

CHAPTER FIFTY-ONE

I hurried across Golden Square, down Carnaby, and into Great Marlborough. Not so much because I was late but because I was furious. The clip-clop of a woman scorned. But I did need to get a grip. I'm a professional, or supposed to be. I shouldn't mix personal with professional. Compose yourself. You're just about to meet up with the Head of Production at a major London post house. And he, in turn, would be very kindly allowing you to interview a member of his team.

Outside Effigy Post, I took a deep breath, composed myself, taking a brief look at my reflection in their glass doors, and pushed my way through.

Nick was already standing at reception, waiting, making me feel just a little bit guilty. Compared to some of the other characters on this case, he'd remained a gentleman. Not only had he allowed me to interview members of his team individually, he'd done so during the distress and upheaval of losing his MD. Furthermore, during those interviews, Sam and Poppy had been sulky and unhelpful. Given that he'd sat in on some of them – or stood in – half the time he hadn't even been offered a chair. So it must have been pretty embarrassing for him.

'Sorry to hassle you about this, Pam,' he said, walking across the reception area and extending his hand, 'But Sam's got clients coming round soon, and ...'

'Oh, no,' I said 'It's me that should apologize. I got a bit tied up. It was good of you to fit me in.'

We then shook hands and whisked our way through reception, down corridors to find Sam's suite. Nick pushed the door open and, exactly as before, the room was is semi-darkness. Also as before, Sam was at his desk, silhouetted by his monitor.

It was then that I realised, stupidly, that this may not work out quite as well as I'd planned.

I'd somehow imagined a cosy one-to-one, putting my questions straight to him. But Nick had sat in on Sam's first interview and had even been around at the beginning of Poppy's. Now if this was indeed going to be my final meeting with Sam Palmer, I was going to have to put it to him straight. No beating about the bush. But I wasn't going to get away with that with someone else in the room.

'Um, I was wondering if I could speak to Sam alone,' I said.

Nick was looking straight at me, his back against the open door. Clearly he wasn't expecting this. Nor, when I glanced over to the desk, was Sam.

Of course, he could simply say no: not only to this request, but to the whole meeting thing. But I find that if you put things to people straight they tend to play ball.

'Er, Okay,' said Nick. 'If you've got no objections, Sam.'

Sam just shrugged.

'I'll leave you two together, then.'

Now the last time I'd interviewed Sam, Anna and I had sat on the sofa, six feet from his desk and two feet lower than his chair. This was mainly because Nick had led us there – plus the fact that there was only one spare chair anyway. This time it was going to be different. I didn't give a damn how sacrosanct his little desk, dials and keyboard were. Given what I'd just discovered back at Bernard's, I wasn't in the mood to pussyfoot around with anyone, least of all arrogant, selfish males. It was payback time. This particular male was going to get it with both barrels.

I walked straight over to him, pulled out the empty chair, swivelled it to him and sat down at his desk. Oh, I didn't bother with a handshake either – he hadn't last time.

'So,' I said. 'How's things?'

No answer.

'About six months now, isn't it?'

'What is?'

'Since our last meeting.'

'If it was down to me …' he said, with a sneer.

'If it was down to you, there wouldn't be *any* meetings. Am I right?'

Silence. Confirming it.

'Is that because you've got something to hide, Sam?'

He gave me a look, considered not answering, and then said: 'Like what?'

'You're good at your job, aren't you, Sam?' I said.

'Don't change the subject,' he said. 'What am I supposed to have to hide?'

'I'm not changing the subject. You being good at your job, and you having something to hide are exactly connected.'

Back into silence.

'Tell me, with your jiggery-pokery here,' I said, pointing at his keyboard and screen, 'Have you ever put someone in a place they aren't.'

'It's called Flame,' he said.

'Okay, with your *Flame* … Have you? Have you taken someone from one environment and put them in another?'

'Of course I have,' he said 'Check out my showreel.'

'Oh, I have,' I said. 'And it's very clever. And on that subject, I have another question.'

'Full of questions, aren't you?'

'It's my job, Sam.'

'And I,' he said turning, 'Need to get on with mine.'

'No problem, it'll only take a second.'

I then leaned back on my chair. By now I was speaking to the back of his head: 'You know all this stuff's high quality. When you start, I mean. Well, have you ever sort of, well, degraded anything purposely? You know, to disguise it?'

He turned back and I caught the briefest of looks in his eye. Then he swivelled the chair back round, picked up his desk phone and said: 'Are my next clients here yet?'

And that was it. I clearly wasn't going to get any more. But in a way, it was enough. I knew that look so well. Over the years I'd got more out of people who didn't speak than people who did.

And talking of getting out, that's exactly what I needed to do now. *Fast!*

CHAPTER FIFTY-TWO

Mobile to ear, I hurried back down those same corridors I'd originally walked down some six months earlier. Past Visual Effects and Animation, Grading and Graphics, and finally into Reception. I paused and tried to dial again. Specifically, it was Andy McCullough I was after. Police-wise, he'd be my best bet.

I still had no connection, so I pushed through the glass doors and out into the busy, traffic-clogged street.

I started walking: past Liberty, right into Argyll, past the Palladium. Still no connection. Without even needing to think about it, I was taking the most direct route: Oxford Circus to Victoria. From there I could get the fast train to Bromley South which was slap bang next to Bromley Police Station. This would mean using the Underground first, of course, but the time for phobias was long gone.

I got right up to the entrance to the Tube, but still couldn't get through. I decided to ring Anna instead. I really needed to tell someone, and anyway, I'd promised to tell her how it turned out.

So I stopped by the steps, piling up about twenty commuters behind me in the process, stepped to one side and tried her number. Again, nothing.

Still convinced I could go down the Tube alone: who needed bloody Bernard, I decided to forget the phone and descend.

The steps were packed and slippery, but at least they were one-way. Which is more than you can say of the ticket hall downstairs. Cram packed, pushing and shoving, a heaving morass. Presumably there was some kind of problem below, but it was already packed behind me, so there was no turning back. *And* I was beginning to feel ill. So much for bravado.

You know, on the journey up, Anna and I had been playing our kidding games again. We'd used Bromley North rather than Shortlands because it was 'more convenient.' Her destination was London Bridge, mine the West End, so why not? Nothing to do with avoiding the Tube, of course.

Inching forward, pushing ever nearer the barriers, I was in the middle of a thick soup of people: all shapes and sizes, all irritable and squeezing. But at least it was looking a little clearer past the barriers. I edged ever forward, the weight of people compressing me, suffocating me. I was beginning to feel faint, but I couldn't have collapsed even if I'd wanted to.

Right up to the barriers. I was next.

Suddenly, they stopped: *"Due to overcrowding on the platforms, for safety reasons the barriers are being temporarily closed,"* came the announcement. *"We apologise for the inconvenience. Normal service will be resumed as soon as possible"*

The one good thing, I suppose, was that at least I could now see ahead. I couldn't *get* to where I wanted to be, but at least I could *see* where I wanted to be. And with everyone else held up behind me, I had some elbow room too. It should be clearing on the platforms below me too.

A few minutes passed. I was beginning to feel better again. Then, suddenly, we were off again: barriers snapping, people pushing.

One of the first through, I crossed the hall, got to the escalators and paused. A woman behind swore and pushed past. Then others. It was a long, long way down, but again, there was no way back. Also, the more people that pushed ahead, the worse it would be when I got down there. I had no choice so I just held my breath, put my foot on the step and … started to move.

Descending, I quickly shuffled to the right. People were streaming past, almost running down. But at least I was moving.

Ever nearer the bottom, ever darker, I was beginning to feel sick again. I closed my eyes.

You know, without even realising it, I was getting that feeling again. Not just the claustrophobia, but the being watched. When did that start? In the hall upstairs? On the escalator?

MI5 are no longer tailing me, are they. *Are they?*

Nearing the bottom, I finally opened my eyes, took a deep breath, walked a few paces forward and paused.

Equilibrium back, I was beginning to feel less sick. I turned smartly and looked up at the escalator behind me. Was I being followed?

Glassy-eyed and impassive, all the commuters looked the same. In theory, any or all of them could have been watching me. It was impossible to say. So could it have been one of the people who have pushed past me? Was someone waiting ahead for me? I turned again. All I could see were the backs of hurrying raincoats. Again, impossible to say.

I needed to get moving because I didn't want to be packed in the middle of the platform, otherwise the one advantage I'd had when those gates reopened would be lost.

I turned right into another tunnel and walked straight ahead for the Victoria Line. I felt it again. Or was it just a touch of faintness? Was I just imagining things because I was a hundred foot down?

I decided it was just my imagination. I was enclosed, that's all. Out of the tunnel and onto the darkened platform. It wasn't too bad, mainly because I was still one of the first.

The indicator board said *'Next train: Brixton 2 minutes.'* Perfect, I should be able to get on it before the place gets too packed. I walked down the platform, found a space at the front and waited. And waited.

Two minutes came and went. Five minutes. Then six, seven, eight. Ten minutes went by before any kind of announcement. *'Sorry for the delay, which is due to technical difficulties at Euston.'* I looked up at the indicator board. The non-existent Brixton train was now, well, non-existent – replaced by a sign saying: *'Please listen for announcements.'* The other big change was the number of people. Now thousands, crammed in and around me. So I looked ahead. Just an empty track. Not a way out, but open, at least. Thinking about it, ruefully, that railway track was indeed a final way out – for some.

I noticed movement between sleepers and rails. I fixed on a spot. Nothing at first, then I saw it. A rat. Dirty grey. Sniffing amongst the oil and the filth. Good for you, little rat. Like the rest of us down here, surviving.

Then I got that feeling again. Someone watching. Unless it was just the stifling heat, the suffocation, the crammed in-ness. Do I turn? No, don't be ridiculous. I'd be nose-to-nose with the person behind.

A rumble. Could it be a train? I looked up at the indicator board. Still the same: *'Please listen for announcements.'*

But, I could definitely hear something. It was getting nearer. I could feel that putrid wind, the smell. It was a train. Just had to be.

I looked down the tunnel. Yes, lights. Whether I'd be near a door, whether I'd even be able to squeeze in, was something else. That thought, the pushing and the shoving, the rammed solid coach, made me feel even sicker. But there was no turning back.

Close and closer. I'm beginning to feel faint. Don't collapse now, Pamela. Not now. Keep yourself together. You can do it.

Closer and closer.

I breathe in hard. But it doesn't help. The air is cloying, treacly.

Closer and closer: just metres away. The roar, the lights, the stench.

I'm losing consciousness, my legs are …

I grab at a raincoat, falling.

Suddenly I'm pushed.

Clutching the coat, I manage to fall sideways. But the person behind me, the pusher, falls forward – head-first.

Body, train. Sickening thud.

I wake up, must have briefly blacked out.

I'm horizontal, lying on a woman, still clenching her raincoat.

Confused, disorientated, I still can't work out what's happened.

I get myself up, helping the woman, too. I'm still confused. So is she.

People all around are screaming. Some hysterical, crying, backing away from the train. It's squealed to a halt just short of the platform's end. It must have taken the body, the pusher, with it. Or part of it, anyway. Another part, a leg, joined to a piece of torso, is jammed between the train's running board and the platform.

Pointing upwards, the leg has a shoe on it. A man's shoe.

A couple of feet further down another group of people are backing away in horror, looking down at the platform. They've formed an arc around ... there's this ball ... an irregular ball. But it's not a ball. It has hair, half a face. It is a head.

The Head of Post Production.

Nick Summers.

CHAPTER FIFTY-THREE

So in the end, my phobia saved me. Or sort of saved me. Had I been standing properly upright, rigidly; had I not started to fall over as that train approached; had I not clung onto that raincoat, I would've been under its wheels.

Over a year has passed since that day and the trial is now over. I was right about the crime, but wrong about the culprit – or chief culprit. Mr Helpful, Mr Polite, Nick Summers. Sam Palmer was indeed involved, as the VFX man, but it was Summers who did the organising. Whether he did the killing of Rose Denton, we'll never know, but he probably did. He'd downloaded swathes of stuff and had a collection of lurid newspaper stories about it.

Palmer got just five years, for criminal deception, fraud and withholding evidence. Plea bargaining helped. Apart from confessing to the crime, he was also able to give police information which eventually led to the arrest of Paul and Stephanie, who were holed up in Brazil. It took a while for the extradition to come through, but Her Majesty got there in the end. She normally does.

Paul got eight years, Stephanie, just four. A bit of leniency was shown because she wasn't involved from the off, after which she just had to follow hubby, didn't she? That whole luggage / baggage conversation helped her cause.

Poppy, Sam's assistant, got off the lightest. One year suspended. According to her, when she first became involved, she had no idea what was going on. All she was asked to do was film a man in a desert. By the time she realised what was happening it was too late, or so she said, *and* was put under pressure by her two immediate bosses, Palmer and Summers. She was paid peanuts. Just £50K found its way into her account – and half of that after she'd wobbled, threatening to blow the whole thing wide open after Rose Denton's death. She'd been threatened at that time, or so she said. I believe that helped her cause, too.

So let's backtrack, starting from the period before I was even involved.

Summers and Palmer sent Poppy off to Karachi, where she filmed Paul Hutchinson, standing by himself, plus 'clean' backplates, in a desert setting. From these elements, difference mattes were extracted.

From the very off, absolutely nothing was ever sent electronically: no emails, texts or even phone calls. So she brought the material home by hand.

Once she was back in London, Sam Palmer started work. Two weeks later, Paul Hutchinson took his normal flight to Karachi, hand luggage only. On arrival, he disappeared straight into the toilets, coming out a different man: new clothes, new identity, new life. Finally, he took a flight to Lisbon, before connecting to Brazil. Where he kept his head down and just waited. Meanwhile, back in London, Stephanie had reported him missing, and unbeknown to her, or so she claimed, Sam Palmer had started to combine the images. Incidentally, he did some of the work at Effigy but most of it at home, where he had his own VFX suite.

Originally, the entire operation was supposed to take about two months but it overran badly. This was because it proved a little harder than they'd anticipated. Putting

Pervez Zaqqi, a known terrorist, into the shot proved to be the toughest part. Mind you, Rose Denton's late-night discovery, and her subsequent murder, probably didn't help matters either. That said, from my perspective, that lapse in time between the three videos only made the whole thing seem all the more plausible.

Finally, once the money was exchanged, courtesy of you know who, the 'execution' video appeared and then Stephanie finished it off by 'committing suicide.'

Why Gravesend? Because it's near the Thames *and*, more importantly, Ebbsfleet: Eurostar to Paris, Paris to Brazil, hook up with hubby. Game over. Except it wasn't.

There is one person I still haven't mentioned in all this, of course. Mr Asif Farooki, highly respected CEO of the Pakistan International Bank. That's because he was never charged with anything. Why would he be? All contact between the parties was word-of-mouth. No paper trails, electronic or otherwise. He refused to even fly over as a witness. Again, why would he?

But he was Mr Big, for sure. How do I know this? Well, without him, they wouldn't have been certain of getting the money, would they? If he was genuinely uninvolved, he may well have said no to the ransom. Then what would they have done? There'd be no way Hutchinson, Summers and Palmer would have gone to all that trouble without guarantees. But of course, that's not enough to charge a man, never mind convict him. In Farooki's own words: 'My bank was being blackmailed, for God's sake! What was I supposed to do?'

He did, however, pay the highest price of all. You see, you can muck around with the police and you can muck around with governments, but you can't muck around with God.

His headless body was found by the roadside earlier this month. The word 'retribution,' in Urdu script, was pinned to it. You see, in the eyes of genuine fanatics he'd made the greatest transgression of all. Avarice. He'd used God's name in pursuit of mammon *and* dragged real terrorist's names into it.

Conspiracy theories now abound, of course. CIA, MI5, Pakistani Government – all have been accused of killing him. Others go for the criminal fraternity; some for terrorists. Any or all of these theories could be true. After all, I'm sure there were others, at airports and hotels, etc., on his payroll. But I'd like to think he was indeed murdered by religious fanatics. It would be poetic justice. And if his missing head were to turn up, superimposed, on some hoax video, I suppose it could be termed artistic justice too.

You know, watching Paul Hutchinson, a dead man, talking in the witness box, has changed my perception of what's real and what's not. Now, when I see something on a screen, *anything* on a screen, I question it. And that point was epitomised perfectly by something that happened about a month after the court case had finished.

During that trial, Anna and I had got to know a couple of guys from another post production house in Soho. They had been called in by The Crown as expert witnesses and the purpose of their presence, apart from adding expertise to the proceedings, was to explain the pictures that had been salvaged from Sam's hard drive.

The reason why this was important was because it gave the jury visual, time-coded evidence of each stage in the process. This proved *what* each section was for, *when* it was done, and *why* Sam and Poppy were doing it. It also, obviously, proved intent.

The guys who gave this evidence were absolutely top notch, and had just finished working on a film called *Gravity*.

After the case finally finished, they invited Anna and me along to the film's premiere at Leicester Square. A sort of end of case celebration, I suppose. If it all sounds rather showbizzy and glamorous, it was. But, with the red carpet drenched, and the sponsors umbrellas unfurled, it was all rather wet, too. A soggy day in London Town.

The movie was amazing, of course, but more to the point it proved to me (if, given my recent experiences, it even needed proving) that the camera *does* lie. You see, none of that film was shot in space, and all of it had been created just around the corner from the theatre in which we were sitting.

Underlining this was something one of the guys said to us as we were standing in the auditorium after the film. He told me that Buzz Aldrin, one of the astronauts who'd made the first moon landing, had said that from a visual standpoint the film looked totally real. And the irony of that? Well, to this day many people think his moon landing *doesn't* look real. That it was all mocked up on a Hollywood backlot.

So in the topsy-turvy world in which we now live, fake looks real and real looks fake. Nowadays, every picture tells a lie. And this was a point that came up time and again during the trial.

And talking of fakes, and talking of lies, what about Stephanie? Just how fake had she been? With me, I mean? After all, we'd shared everything. Not just flights and hotels and taxis, but hope and sorrow, laughter and tears. How had she done all that so convincingly? Well, as I said, I believe she started genuinely enough, and, like all the best actresses, grew into the role.

I did try to catch her eye. When she was in the witness box, I mean. She knew I was there, I'm sure. But it was never going to happen. She was never going to look my way.

Why did she do it? Not really for money, but for love. For Paul. A man. How stupid is that?

Love? Men and stupidity? Pictures telling lies? Guess who that brings us to?

Bernard had been trying to get in contact with me almost since the day I ended it. Texts, emails, phone calls. Frankly, I just couldn't be bothered. He got through in the end though, using a different number.

'Hello,' I said.

'I'm really missing you,' he said.

My finger went straight for the red button.

'I need you,' he said.

'Need?' I said.

'Want, whatever. I miss you. I really do. And I've …'

He paused.

Was I supposed to ask what he'd done? Did I even care?

'And I've … I've told Cynthia all about it all.'

'That must have made her happy.'

'It's you I want, Pamela. Only you can make me happy.'

'Obviously. That's why you put my picture on the wall.'

'Yes,' he said. 'You're right. That *was* why I put your picture on the wall. Is that so bad?'

'And took it down again. And put it up again. And …'

'I was confused.'

'I bet you bloody were. Hardly knew which fucking day it was!'

'I don't mean that. I, I didn't know what to do. I was buying time. But now I know what I want. I want you.'

'You know, Bernard, I had loads of ideas. For revenge, I mean. I was going to turn up at Heathrow and hold up that picture, or trash your flat, even re-categorise your CDs. But, well, it just wasn't worth it. *You're* not worth it.'

I paused for a second. I didn't want it to end on a rant.

'Thinking about it, Bernard, correction. *We're* not worth it. So why don't we just leave it at that? You said you wanted to make me happy. Well, you did. It was great. I got what most women want: a bit of pampering, some average sex, companionship. Let's just move on.

'But why ...?'

'Why what?'

'Why can't we, well ...'

'Start again?

'Yes, no, we could ...'

'Could what, Bernard?'

'Well, if you wanted, we ... if you think it would work, I mean, you could move in.'

'Live together, you mean?'

'Yes.'

'Good idea, Bernard. I could help you with your picture hanging!'

'That's not fair.'

'Fair? Look, Bernard, life's not fair. Get over it. Goodbye, Bernard ... Goodbye.'

And with that, I did press the red button.

Did I feel cheated? Of course. Used? That, too. But remember, I used him just as much as he used me. That little flat was great while it lasted. And Soho was great – the lights, the nights – and all after a day of posh shopping!

No one can take those days, those memories away from me. And Bernard even cured me of a phobia or two – or nearly.

The truth is, it really *was* great. I'll probably never go through all that again. I'm fifty-six now, for God's sake. What I want, and what my body wants, are two different things. It was just one last hurrah. A very good hurrah, but a last hurrah.

I tell you this, though: I'll never trust a picture again. Or a man.